"Sorry about your bad luck, cowboy, but it looks like I get to choose our path from here." She looked in every direction, noting woods, fields, valleys, before pointing. "How about over there?"

Jonah was grinning.

"What's so funny?"

"That would've been my choice, too."

She arched a brow. "Why do I get the feeling you're teasing me?"

"Me?" He gave her a mock pained expression before laughing. "The truth is, you'll never know. Come on. Let's see if you made a good choice."

As they started off, Jonah studied the way she looked beside him, her hair windblown, her cheeks pink from the race. Just then, she looked over and he gave her a smile of pure male appreciation. He caught the slight flush that started at her throat and worked its way up.

She looked good enough to kiss.

"Smooth like good whiskey."

THE COWBOY NEXT DOOR

"Satisfying...This sweetly domestic story should win Ryan many new fans."

"*The Cowboy Next Door* is a work of art."

COWBOY ON MY MIND

"A strong, protective hero and an independent heroine fight for their future in this modern rough-and-tumble Western."

"This talented writer...invites you to join a little journey that has you biting at the bit for more."

REED

"4 stars! Ryan's latest book in her Malloys of Montana series contains a heartwarming plot filled with down-to-earth cowboys and warm, memorable characters. Reed and Ally are engaging and endearing, and their sweet, fiery chemistry heats up the pages, which will leave readers' hearts melting...A delightful read."

LUKE

"Ryan creates vivid characters against the lovingly rendered backdrop of sweeping Montana ranchlands. The passion between Ryan's protagonists, which they keep discreet, is tender and heartwarming. The plot is drawn in broad strokes, but Ryan expertly brings it to a satisfying conclusion."

—*Publishers Weekly*

MATT

"Ryan has created a gripping love story fraught with danger and lust, pain and sweet, sweet triumph."

—*Library Journal*, starred review

MEANT TO BE MY COWBOY

R.C. RYAN

FOREVER

New York Boston

Copyright © 2021 Ruth Ryan Langan
Excerpt from *My Kind of Cowboy* Copyright © 2020 by Ruth Ryan Langan
Cover photography © Rob Lang Images. Cover design by Daniela Medina. Cover copyright © 2021 by Hachette Book Group, Inc.

Forever
Hachette Book Group
1290 Avenue of the Americas, New York, NY 10104
read-forever.com
twitter.com/readforeverpub

First Edition: July 2021

Forever is an imprint of Grand Central Publishing. The Forever name and logo are trademarks of Hachette Book Group, Inc.

The publisher is not responsible for websites (or their content) that are not owned by the publisher.

The Hachette Speakers Bureau provides a wide range of authors for speaking events. To find out more, go to www.hachettespeakersbureau.com or call (866) 376-6591.

ISBNs: 978-1-5387-1690-8 (mass market), 978-1-5387-1691-5 (ebook)

Printed in the United States of America

CW

10 9 8 7 6 5 4 3 2 1

*For my family, who are the sun and the
stars of my life*

And for Tom, who hung the moon

*Many thanks to Julie Emery, Private Client
Banker with Chase, for her willingness to
share her valuable time and expertise.*

MEANT TO BE
MY COWBOY

PROLOGUE

Merrick Ranch, Wyoming—Twenty years previous

Six-year-old Jonah Merrick sat astride his spotted pony, eating the dust from his brothers' mounts as the three boys followed the lead of their father, grandfather, and great-grandfather across a high meadow. It wasn't unusual for the four generations of Merricks, who lived together on their sprawling ranch, to ride across their Wyoming ranchland on a pretty summer day. What was unusual was the absence of the Merrick women. After the death of their mother, Leigh, the three brothers were almost always accompanied by either their aunt Liz (their father's younger sister) or their gram Meg, who had assumed the mantle of both teacher and surrogate mother. But today was different, and Jonah's older brothers, nine-year-old Brand and eight-year-old Casey, had hinted that something monumental would be happening.

As they drew near the sprawling herd, Jonah's father, Bo, circled back to his sons to point up ahead.

"Now that the branding is over and the cattle are

settling into the summer rangeland, the wranglers have earned a weekend in town. We'll be spending the next two days and nights up here keeping an eye on the herd."

"Oh boy." Brand gave a whoop of delight and waved his wide-brimmed hat in the air, before digging his heels into the side of his horse and racing toward his grandfather up ahead.

Casey followed suit.

Bo wheeled his mount and started after them, but then he paused, pulled back on the reins, and turned to his youngest son, who was often caught daydreaming. "You coming, Jonah?"

"Yes, sir." The little boy nudged his pony forward. "Where will we sleep, Pa?"

"Under the stars, son." Bo looked up at the sky. "Unless it rains. There's a range shack nearby, but I'm hoping the weather cooperates so you boys can get a taste of what it's like to live the way your gramps Egan and great-grandfather Ham did when they were your age."

"They didn't have a house?"

Bo grinned. "They did. But they didn't have a team of wranglers to help them. Most nights they ate and slept with the herd from sunup to sundown, with hardly a break until they brought the herd back down for the winter."

Jonah watched as his father moved among the rough, bearded wranglers, handing out their pay.

Within the hour, the cowboys were gone, headed to town for baths, haircuts, and a chance to spend their money at Nonie's Wild Horses Saloon.

The Merrick men unsaddled their mounts and turned them into a corral. And though Jonah had to stand on an overturned bucket, no one offered to help him as he did the same.

That night, the three boys stayed awake listening to Ham's stories of his early adventures of him and his father taming this wilderness. And when at last his brothers fell asleep in their bedrolls, Jonah strained to hear as his father, grandfather, and great-grandfather spoke of more sinister things. Things that were never discussed in front of the boys.

"Give it up, Bo. Too many years have passed. The inspector couldn't prove the fire was deliberately started, and neither can you, son."

"I have all the proof I need right here in my heart, Pop." Bo Merrick's voice hardened. "I saw Des Dempsey's face when he found out the bank in Stockwell loaned me the money to buy the Butcher ranch. It was bad enough when Leigh gave him back the ring and told him she was marrying me. With the birth of each of our sons, his jealousy grew. But that day, when he heard about the loan, he was consumed with hatred. If looks could kill, I'd have been the one dead. Instead, his need for revenge killed the woman we both loved and left my boys without their mother. Believe me. One day he'll pay for what he did."

As the men fell asleep in their bedrolls, with the sound of cattle lowing and the fragrance of woodsmoke curling overhead, Jonah lay awake, wide-eyed, pondering all that he'd heard. It was almost more than his young mind could comprehend. The fire that killed their mother had been deliberately set? By Des Dempsey, the owner of the bank in town?

Whenever she read to him, Gram Meg always said Jonah had an overactive imagination. That night, as he drifted to sleep, his dreams became so real he awoke with his heart pounding, his pulse racing.

Jonah always knew he was destined to follow the lead of all the other Merrick men into ranching. But this night, with his father's ominous words playing in his head, he stumbled onto a new path. The germ of a story was already growing, with heroes and villains all living together in a small town, and all of them threatening revenge and disaster.

He couldn't wait to someday write the story and see how it would end.

CHAPTER ONE

Devil's Door, Wyoming—present day

Hey." Brand Merrick pushed his way through the crowd around the bar at Nonie's Wild Horses Saloon to slap his brother Jonah on the back. "Figured I'd find you here."

"It's Friday night, and this is the place to be, since the wranglers' pockets are stuffed with pay."

Their middle brother, Casey, walked up behind him. "And the ladies in town are eager to help them spend it, I see."

"Speaking of ladies..." Jonah looked from Brand to Casey. "Where are your wives?"

"Over at Julie Franklyn's place. Getting haircuts and color and whatever else women do there." Casey glanced around and nodded and smiled at Nonie's twin nieces, who were loading their trays at the waitress station. They waved back cheerfully, then turned away to begin serving another crowded table.

Jonah signaled Nonie behind the bar, and within a minute three longnecks appeared at his elbow. He passed them out to his brothers. "Are your wives meeting you here?"

Brand nodded. "They're in the mood for Nonie's chili. They told us to get a booth in the back if one empties."

"Good luck with that." Jonah took a long pull on his beer. "With the weekend just beginning, nobody's leaving until Nonie turns out the lights."

"That's what I told…"

Before Brand could finish, his wife, Avery, walked in, trailed by Casey's bride, Kirby. Heads swiveled as the two women made their way to the bar.

"Hello, beautiful." Brand wrapped Avery in a warm embrace. "Mmm. You smell good."

"Hello to you, too, babe." She accepted his offer of a sip of beer before glancing around. "No booth?"

"I warned you about Friday nights at Nonie's. You know how it is."

Avery shot a knowing look at her sister-in-law. "Come on, Kirby. Let's take a turn around the room and see if somebody's ready to leave."

Brand dug into his pocket and held out a bill. "Ten dollars says you'll never get a table tonight."

Avery shot a glance at Kirby before turning to her husband. "Make it twenty, babe."

"You may as well make it a hundred…"

"You're on."

"Wait a minute. But…" Brand's protest died on his lips.

The two women were already walking away, leaving only the sound of their sultry laughter mingling with Patsy's wail about being crazy coming over the sound system.

"Women," Brand said to his brothers.

Except for rolling their eyes, neither of them bothered to answer.

Brand's eyes crinkled with laughter. "I know I've been conned. But with a wife as pretty as Avery, I can't bring myself to care."

Jonah was about to tip up his bottle again when he caught sight of a beautiful stranger standing in the doorway. Instead of the usual jeans and sweater, a Friday-night uniform in these parts, this woman was dressed in business attire: a pencil-slim black dress and a red, hip-length jacket with jet buttons. On her feet were fancy high heels. Dark hair fell soft and loose around a face that movie stars would die for, with big eyes, a tiny, upturned nose, and full lips pursed in a mixture of puzzlement and concentration.

Brand and Casey turned to see what had caught his attention.

"You know her?" Brand shot a look at his brother, who was still staring at the figure in the doorway.

His smile came slow and easy. "Not yet. But I intend to."

He'd barely finished his sentence when he saw several cowboys hurrying toward the woman. Seeing them, Casey chuckled. "Better get in line, bro. Looks like a lot of other guys have the same idea."

Jonah shrugged casually. "I've got all the time in the world."

Just then, Kirby ambled over to say, "We have a booth in the back." She turned to smirk at Brand. "And Avery said to get out that hundred."

Casey's brows shot up. "I didn't see anybody leave."

Kirby merely smiled. "Avery and I persuaded a table of cowboys to...relocate to the bar so we could have their booth."

Casey and Brand shook their heads in disbelief as Kirby headed back toward their table.

"You realize you could have stopped at twenty," Casey muttered to Brand as they both turned to follow his wife.

"Twenty or a hundred. What were the odds?"

"When a pretty woman is involved, all bets are off, bro."

The two burst into chuckles and were slapping each other on the back when they noticed that Jonah wasn't getting up to join them.

Brand turned. "You coming?"

Jonah grinned and tipped up his beer. "I'd rather watch the action from here."

Brand glanced toward the doorway, where more than a dozen cowboys had gathered. "If you're hoping to meet that gorgeous stranger, I don't like your odds."

"Says the guy who just lost a hundred to his pretty little wife." Jonah's laughter followed them as they pushed their way through the crowd toward the back booth.

*   *   *

Annie stared at the sea of faces, feeling a little over-whelmed. None of this was what she'd been expecting. When she'd finished work and asked her uncle about a quick supper before heading home, he'd told her about Nonie's. He'd raved about the chili and the burgers. What he hadn't mentioned was the wave of sound that pulsed so loudly it throbbed in her temples. And he'd neglected to mention the mob of cowboys from the nearby ranches, who apparently congregated here by the hundreds to celebrate the weekend.

Pointedly ignoring their offers of a drink, she managed to push herself through the crowd and, seeing no empty tables, made her way to the grill, which was being worked by a pretty woman with soft curls around a sweet, sweaty face.

The woman looked up. "You want to eat here or order carryout?"

"Carryout, please. How about a burger with every-thing, and a bowl of chili?"

"You got it." Meat was slapped on the grill, sizzling over a bed of caramelized onions.

While it cooked, the woman managed to take more orders, all the while sliding bottles of beer along the counter and filling trays at the service bar.

"Good choice."

At the sound of the deep voice, Annie turned toward the cowboy seated next to her at the bar. Now, *there* was a heartbreaker. Dark shaggy hair curling over the collar of a denim jacket. Long, long legs encased in faded jeans. Western boots polished to a high shine. And a lazy smile guaranteed to make a girl's heart flutter.

Too handsome for his own good. Or hers.

She turned back to the woman, just in time to be handed a bag and given a bill.

"Thanks." She dug out her money. "That was really fast."

"That's the only way I know how to do it. I'm Nonie."

"Annie."

"Welcome, Annie. I hope you enjoy your supper. Come back anytime, you hear?"

Before Annie could respond, Nonie had turned away, filling yet another tray of drinks.

As she made her way to the door, Annie could feel the cowboy at the bar staring holes in her back. When she pushed open the door, she chanced a quick glance over her shoulder. Her eyes widened as she met his smoldering gaze.

He tipped his bottle in a salute and she gave a barely perceptible nod before stepping outside.

The door gave a loud creak of complaint before slamming shut. The silence after that wall of sound was deafening.

As she walked away, the thought of the cowboy's smile had her own smile blooming in the darkness.

Nothing could lift a girl's spirits like the admiring

glance of a stranger. Especially one as good-looking as that one.

Too bad nothing could come of it. She was here for one reason. After one of the stormiest times of her life, she intended to keep her head down, work hard, and avoid any entanglements. That meant allowing no strangers into her life. It was the only way she could feel safe. And right now, safety was her only concern.

CHAPTER TWO

You're up early, bro." Casey chose a pitchfork from a series of hooks along the wall of the barn and began mucking the stall next to where Jonah was already working.

"Got to bed early." He shot a sideways glance at his brother. "For a change."

Brand sauntered over to join them. "I guess that means you didn't score with the gorgeous stranger."

"Annie."

Casey paused to look over. "Annie? You met her?"

"Barely. She ordered carryout. Introduced herself to Nonie."

"But not to you." Brand chuckled. "Not that I blame her. With all those cowboys drooling over her, why would she bother with you?"

"You mean like old Bear Heller, who smells like one? Or maybe she'd be attracted to J. P. Hicks, who's missing his front teeth?"

"That's right. Toss out the names of the geezers."

Brand shared a grin with Casey. "How about all the young stallions who were practically knocking over their chairs to get to her first?"

"I guess they stumbled." Jonah dumped a load of straw and dung into the honeywagon and moved to the next stall. "All I know is she left alone."

Brand paused in his work. "You think she's staying in Devil's Door, or just passing through?"

Jonah shrugged. "It was pretty late to be passing through town. I had the sense that she would have stayed if there'd been a table, but it was packed, so she decided to just take her supper home."

Casey nodded his agreement. "You could always ask Nonie. If the mysterious Annie is staying in town, I'm betting that Nonie has already learned everything there is to learn about her by now."

"I could ask. Or I could just wait. Good things come to those who—"

"Yeah. We know." Brand rolled his eyes, getting a laugh from Casey. "You've got a saying for everything, Mr. *New York Times* Best-Selling Author."

"Comes with the territory." Jonah set aside the pitchfork and grabbed the handles of the wagon, pushing it out the side door of the barn.

Minutes later, he returned and set it alongside the wall while Casey and Brand finished spreading fresh straw in the empty stalls.

As the three brothers headed toward the house, Casey tried for one more bit of information.

"So. What did the beautiful Annie order for supper?"

"Burgers and chili."

"So she not only looks good, but she has good taste in food as well."

"That would be a yes. And when I learn more, I'll be happy to share it with the two of you."

"What makes you think she'll be back?"

Jonah gave one of his famous lazy smiles. "Because I figure she's having this same conversation about me, bro."

The three were roaring with laughter as they washed up in the mudroom and made their way to the kitchen for breakfast.

The rest of the family was already there, sipping either coffee or Billy's freshly squeezed orange juice while they gathered around the fireplace, discussing the weather, always uppermost in the minds of ranchers.

Bo looked over at his sons. "They're saying it will be a long, hot summer."

Brand brushed a kiss on Avery's cheek before picking up a mug of steaming coffee. "After that last spring blizzard, I'm ready for all the heat I can get."

"Amen to that." Gramps Egan smiled at his wife. "Meggie and I were just saying the summers keep growing shorter while the winters get longer every year."

"Bull burps." Ham, who would soon turn ninety-one, had learned to edit his cuss words when the women were around. "Winters today aren't anything like the ones in the old days. Why, when I was—"

"...just ten years old," his three great-grandsons said in one voice, causing everyone to burst into laughter.

Ham shot them the hairy eyeball before turning to Avery and Kirby, who were new enough to the family to still hang on his every word. "When I was no bigger'n a pup, I was already hiking the Tetons alone, in search of game, while my pa was tending the herd. It was nothing for me to be gone for a week or more. But I never came home empty-handed, or we'd have starved."

"You could've always killed one of the cows," Casey said reasonably.

"We needed every one of those cows for money. It wasn't like now, with a thousand head of cattle. We were lucky to make enough at the end of a season just to—"

"...keep body and soul together," his three great-grandsons finished in unison, bringing another round of laughter.

Gram Meg put an arm around her father-in-law's shoulders and kissed his cheek. "You know they love you, Hammond. This is their way of having fun at your expense."

He gave her a piercing look. "Don't defend them, Margaret Mary Finnegan. They're being smart alecks, and you know it."

"Breakfast is ready," Billy called.

Gram Meg winked at Brand, Casey, and Jonah as she led the way to the table, hoping to steer the conversation in a new direction.

*   *   *

"Great breakfast, Billy," Casey said as he caught Kirby's hand. "Ready to head into town, babe?"

She nodded.

"While you're there..." Gram Meg jotted down several items and handed the list to Kirby.

The young woman paused. "Want to come with us?"

At the invitation, Gramps Egan spoke for both of them. "We promised Buster and Trudy we'd stop by today."

As Jonah started toward the door, Brand called, "Want anything in town?"

Jonah shook his head.

"You headed to your cabin?"

"That's the plan."

Outside, he followed the path to the barn, then veered off and crossed a meadow before starting into the woods.

The air was cooler here, the sunlight filtered through the canopy of fresh spring leaves overhead.

Jonah loved this stretch of woods. As a boy, he'd claimed it for his own private retreat, where he'd fashioned a tree house that could only be entered by hauling himself up by a series of ropes and pulleys. Though Brand and Casey had often teased him by hiding the rope or even cutting it, they'd finally given up, leaving him to his own devices.

Even when he'd outgrown the tree house, he'd continued feeling a need to come here, simply to restore his soul. It was far enough from the ranch to afford the privacy he craved, yet near enough that he could hike home in time for supper. After the publication of his first novel, he'd built a rough cabin and equipped it with a bed and bathroom, a desk, and a tiny kitchen. That first novel had broken records, hitting the best-seller list and remaining at the top for more than six months.

Since then, he'd added more comforts to the cabin, building a stone fireplace and hewing a mantel from a fallen log. He'd discovered that he loved working with his hands, especially while mulling plot twists. He'd fashioned a glass-topped coffee table over a base made from a petrified tree trunk. A glacial boulder with bits of copper and silver veins served as a pedestal for one of his many awards.

Lately, caught up in his current work in progress, he often remained locked away in his woods over-night, emerging only when he felt the need to join his loud, raucous family and lend a hand with the ranch chores. Though his brothers teased him endlessly, he knew they understood his need for solitude and took as much pride in his success as he did.

He opened the door and walked around, cranking open the windows until the entire inside of the cabin was as fresh as a spring breeze and smelled of pine forest.

Turning on his laptop, he settled at his desk and felt a wave of annoyance when his cell phone rang.

He looked at the caller ID and brightened. "Hey, Max."

His agent, Max Friend, had a calm, relaxed manner

that had endeared him to Jonah from their first meeting. "Jonah. Good news. *Secrets and Lies* is still number one."

"That's great news, Max. Thanks for letting me know."

"There's more where that came from." Max paused for dramatic effect. "I just heard from the producer of *Hello, World*. They're hungry for an interview."

"You know what I—"

"I told them you've already refused to fly to New York, London, Paris, or Rome. So the mountain will come to you. Or rather to J. R. Merrick's remote cabin in Wyoming."

"No, Max."

"Wait. Listen. They're willing to fly their entire crew, at great expense, I might add, to your neck of the woods and set up shop wherever, whenever you say."

"I'm flattered. But it's still no."

"Jonah, do you know how many writers would kill for this opportunity?"

"I don't want to sound ungrateful but—"

"They love you, Jonah. They love your book. And the speculation that the fictional town in *Secrets and Lies* could actually be Devil's Door has them clamoring for details. Especially since there are rumors that the mysterious fire that killed the hero's wife could be"—he paused, choosing his words carefully—"deeply personal."

There was a moment of silence before Jonah spoke. His tone held a thread of steel that hadn't been there seconds earlier. "That deadly fire may have had its genesis in one fact, but everything else is pure fiction."

"Great. Then you can tell that to Duchess, and she'll have her audience drooling for more."

"No."

"Jonah, Duchess has the most popular show in the world. She's the only one to ever hold an international audience in the palm of her hand. The whole world knows her by name. A simple interview with Duchess and your sales will skyrocket."

"I'm sorry, Max."

There was a long, deep sigh. "I'm not going to give up. There has to be a way to get you to see how important this is to your career."

Jonah's smile returned. "It's my career, Max. Not my life. Here in Devil's Door, my life consists of wearing last year's jeans, mucking stalls and doing a hundred other ranch chores, and having a beer at the local bar. And I'm not about to change that for a TV interview. Now, if you don't mind, I need to get to work."

"You do that. But if you don't mind, I'll call you tomorrow. Maybe you'll have a fresh attitude."

"Bye, Max." Jonah tucked his cell phone in his shirt pocket and bent to his computer.

CHAPTER THREE

Jonah backed up his work for the day before shoving away from his desk. Pressing a hand to his back, he crossed the room and poured himself a cup of luke-warm coffee.

It had been a good writing day, even though it had taken a while to clear his mind after Max's phone call. He really liked Max, had since their first meeting in New York. They'd introduced themselves via a series of emails when Jonah was completing his first manuscript and beginning the search for an agent. After reading a couple of chapters, Max could hardly contain his excitement. He'd asked for the rest, insisting this was something he knew he could place with a publisher. A congratulatory phone call had followed, and when the two finally met in New York City, Jonah was pleased to learn that Max Friend was someone he could work with for a lifetime. The connection was instantaneous, and Jonah considered Max a friend as well as his agent.

He knew Max would continue to push for more

publicity. And though he was just as willing to push back, he couldn't fault Max for trying. He understood the game. Publicity sold books. Max was in the business of making his clients as much money as possible, thereby making more for himself. The only trouble with that was Jonah's insistence to continue living his life as he always had. He had more than enough money to live comfortably. He really didn't want to change his life in significant ways. He had drawn a line between his private life and his public one, and he was determined that no one and nothing would cross it.

J. R. Merrick the writer was successful and famous.

Jonah Merrick the rancher was a citizen of Devil's Door, Wyoming, who shared ranch chores with his family and lived as he always had.

Max would just have to get used to it.

Jonah finished his coffee and rinsed his cup in the sink before pausing in front of the window. The wildlife in the woods offered a never-ending show for his enjoyment.

Standing in front of the cabin was a deer nibbling the wildflowers Jonah had admired on his way in this morning. Now they'd become lunch for a hungry animal. A chipmunk climbed onto the plank resting on two sawhorses that Jonah used as a table when he felt the urge to work outside. He'd left a handful of peanuts there, and the chipmunk's cheeks were soon puffed out as it stood stuffing even more into its mouth.

Suddenly the deer's head came up sharply, and it froze before starting away.

The chipmunk made a dash down the sawhorse and disappeared under a layer of leaves.

Frowning, Jonah looked around to see what had spooked the animals. A hiker came into view. As he watched, the figure drew closer and he found himself smiling at the sway of a dark ponytail tucked beneath a baseball cap.

Annie. The stranger at Nonie's.

It was evident, by the way she kept looking down, that she hadn't yet spotted his cabin. No surprise. It blended so perfectly into the woods around it an unsuspecting stranger could nearly bump into it before realizing it was there.

As he watched, she stepped over a fallen log and lifted her head. He could see the surprise on her face as she halted midstride.

He opened the door and stepped outside. "Hi, there."

Her eyes widened. "Hello. Sorry, am I trespassing? I was told that this was public land."

"A natural mistake if you aren't familiar with the area. The public land is just beyond these woods, leading to the foothills of the Tetons."

She started to turn away. "I'm sorry for intruding."

"No apology needed." He stepped closer. "You're new to the area."

She nodded. "The weather is so perfect I thought I'd spend my day off hiking. I couldn't bear the thought of being indoors on a day like this."

He nodded toward the cabin. "I've been inside for hours and I'm ready to breathe fresh air. Mind if I join you?"

She was silent for a long moment, and Jonah was preparing himself for a rejection. Then her lips curved up in a guarded smile. "I guess since you live here, I won't have to worry about getting lost or trespassing on someone else's private land."

He offered a handshake. "Jonah."

"Hi, Jonah. I'm Annie. Didn't I see you at the saloon last night?"

"That's where everybody in Devil's Door congregates on Friday night. Nonie's Wild Horses Saloon. You didn't stay."

"I'm not good with crowds."

"How was the chili and burger?"

She chuckled. "You were paying attention."

"I couldn't help overhearing."

"They were perfect." She nodded toward a path in the woods. "Want to head that way?"

"Sure thing." He fell into step beside her as they navigated through dense woods until they reached a high meadow.

"Oh." That single word conveyed Annie's delight as she paused to look around. The range grass was knee-high and dotted with colorful wildflowers. A fresh breeze caused the grass to ripple, giving the effect of a giant ocean wave.

She lifted the sweaty baseball cap off her head and

tore the band from her ponytail, allowing the breeze to lift her hair, completely unaware of the way Jonah's eyes narrowed on her.

On the far side of the meadow, a herd of mustangs foraged while their leader, a black stallion, stood watch from a rise.

Spotting humans, he reared up and whinnied a warning. The mares drifted into a stand of trees until, within minutes, they were invisible.

Annie put a hand to shade the sun from her eyes as she watched their progress. "Were those wild horses?"

Jonah nodded. "There are a dozen or more herds of mustangs in the area."

"They're so beautiful."

He smiled. "I couldn't agree more. I like the fact that they live the way they always have. Free to roam wherever they please."

"I'd been told I might be lucky enough to spot a herd of wild horses one day. I can't believe I saw them on my first time out."

"You're one of the lucky ones. Lots of people hike these hills and never spot them. As you noticed, they're not exactly fond of humans."

"I wish I'd thought to grab a couple of photos." She touched her pocket. "I was too caught up in the moment."

"There's always next time."

"Oh, I hope there's a next time."

They hiked in silence for a while, until Jonah touched

a hand to her arm. Startled, she drew back until she realized he was signaling her to look to her left.

"Oh." The word came out in a sigh as she stared at the same mustang herd.

This time the stallion hadn't yet spotted them, giving Annie time to remove her cell phone and snap several pictures.

By the time the herd moved on, her smile was radiant. "Thank you. I was so determined to avoid stumbling over that tumble of rocks I'd have completely missed the mustangs if you hadn't given me a warning."

"I guess the lesson is, when you're out here in the middle of nowhere, don't spend all your time looking down." He was studying her with a steady look that had her blushing. "Sometimes you just have to pause and take in the amazing view."

Something in his tone, and that piercing look he was giving her, told her he wasn't just talking about nature now.

She felt the heat rush to her cheeks and had to swallow before she managed a smile. "Well, I suppose we should be turning back. How far do you think we've come?"

"Far enough to get your pictures. Close enough that you'll get home in plenty of time for any plans you've made for a Saturday night."

"No plans. I'm still settling in. I haven't even unpacked most of my boxes yet. I just arrived a few days ago."

"Where are you staying?"

"I'm renting an apartment over Julie Franklyn's salon in Devil's Door. Do you know of it?"

"Yeah." He smiled. "Where are you from?"

She took a great deal of time before answering. "California."

"That's a big state. Any place in particular?"

She shrugged. "The Bay Area."

"San Francisco? Pretty place. Though I have to say, I've never found any part of the country prettier than right here."

"You think maybe you're just a little bit biased?"

His smile was quick and sexy. "Maybe a little."

"Have you traveled a lot?"

"Enough to know this is where I want to be."

"You're lucky." When he glanced over, she found herself babbling to cover the heat that rushed to her cheeks. "I mean, some people never find that special place where they feel they belong for a lifetime."

"I'm sorry for them." He nodded toward a barely perceptible trail in the woods. "That way leads back to my cabin. If you keep heading this way, you'll find yourself down by the lookout. From there it's an easy walk to town if you don't have a vehicle."

"I left my car at the lookout."

"Then you can't get lost if you follow this path."

"Thank you." She turned to him and held out her hand. "And thank you for taking time from your day to hike with me. I know I'd have never seen those mustangs without you."

He accepted her handshake. "My pleasure, Annie. When do you get another day off?"

"Well, I don't have to go in to work until noon on Wednesday."

"Do you ride?"

She arched a brow. "Horses?"

At his nod, she said, "I've been riding since I was a girl. It's one of my guilty pleasures."

"Why the guilt?"

"Where I grew up, it was an expensive hobby."

"Around here it's considered an acceptable mode of travel, right up there with trucks and all-terrain vehicles. If you'd like to ride these hills on Wednesday before heading to work, I'll provide the horses."

"I'd like that. I'll meet you at your cabin."

"Sure you can find the way?"

She nodded before turning away.

Jonah remained there, watching as she followed the path until she dipped below a rise.

His first impression of her at Nonie's hadn't been nearly accurate enough. She wasn't just a pretty woman. She was gorgeous. The sunlight had revealed strands of mahogany and even ebony in that mass of dark hair. And her eyes up close had been more green than blue, like the Devil's Door creek as it tumbled down the high peaks of the Grand Tetons after a spring rain. She had a deep, throaty laugh. And her voice, when she grew excited by the sight of the mustangs, had trickled over him like warm honey.

The thought brought a rumble of laughter. There it was again. The writer in him was already searching for glowing words to describe her.

And then there was that hint of mystery about her. She'd actually trembled when he'd touched her arm, as though alarmed by the simple touch. And she certainly hadn't been forthcoming about where she'd lived before coming here.

Didn't he love a good mystery?

He flexed his fingers. His hand was still warm from their brief contact. And he knew, with absolute certainty, that he was eager to see her again. There was just something about the mysterious Annie that tugged at him.

Wednesday couldn't come soon enough to suit him.

CHAPTER FOUR

As she drove back to town, Annie was a jumble of emotions. She could hardly believe how, in the past few days, her life had taken such a turn. She'd left her job, her friends, her comfortable lifestyle to travel to a tiny dot on the map that was the exact opposite of everything she'd ever known.

When her life had first begun unraveling, she'd thought about hiding in plain sight. Changing her appearance, her habits, and possibly joining the throngs of professional people in New York or Chicago. But her uncle had persuaded her to come here, where she would have a guaranteed job, a quiet life, and a chance to gather herself while the mess she'd left behind resolved itself.

But how could it possibly be resolved without devastating consequences?

Even though she'd been warned not to, her uncle was adamant that she contact the authorities and let them get to the bottom of whatever trouble had sent her running in fear. At the same time, he was just as adamant that his name be kept out of any publicity. An impossible task, which was why she was in this limbo, unwilling to move until she had a chance to weigh the consequences of any action she took.

She needed to act wisely and with conviction. Otherwise, the ends of the earth wouldn't be far enough to save her.

She shivered and forced herself to think about other things.

Her day had started like all the others lately, with her pacing the length of her tiny apartment and back, turning over every little thing in her mind until they became so magnified she'd been filled with a sense of terror about her lack of control over her own life.

To keep from going mad, she'd forced herself to leave the pretty rooms she'd leased above the hair salon and drive out of town. Once at the lookout, the wilderness called to her. Putting one foot in front of the other, she began a hike into the unknown. It seemed a metaphor for her life, these days. But with each step, she could feel her fears dissipating and her heartbeat growing strong and steady.

Then the hike had taken quite a turn when she'd intruded on the cowboy's cabin.

The thought of Jonah had her smiling. Who'd have believed that the guy watching her at the town saloon would turn out to be such a pleasant companion?

At the time, she'd written him off as just another handsome cowboy in a town filled with them.

What was it about him that had caused her to violate her own rule about holding herself aloof from strangers until she had time to get her life sorted out? Granted, he was handsome and charming, but those were the very things that had caused her to let down her guard once before. And look where that got her.

Jonah was different, though she couldn't quite figure out why she believed that. He wasn't just easy on the eyes. He was easy to be with, easy to talk to. Except for that moment when he'd touched her arm. That had caught her by surprise, and it had taken all her will-power to keep from striking out in fear. As it was, she'd felt a tremor so palpable she wondered if he'd noticed it. If he had, he'd let it pass without comment, the mark of a gentleman.

She'd felt no pressure to talk about herself, despite his simple questions. Though it was impossible to not be aware of a guy with that much charm, she'd felt free to simply enjoy the beauty of the hills and its wonderful wildlife.

Mustangs. It was amazing to think that she'd actually seen them roaming wild and free, and that she'd snapped some pictures of them. Of all the things that could have distracted her from her troubles, wild horses were at the very top of her list.

She found herself looking forward to Wednesday morning. She missed riding. It was another of the simple joys that she'd had to forgo since drastically changing her life. But way out here in the middle of nowhere, there was no reason to feel any fear.

Was there?

She pushed aside the thought. Wednesday, she would be able to appreciate the beauty of the countryside while enjoying a horseback ride and Jonah's very pleasant company.

Not a bad way to begin a new life.

"Hey, bro." Casey spotted Jonah as he made his way inside the barn. "You're just in time to give me a hand with these supplies."

Jonah ambled over and began working alongside Casey, pulling sacks of grain from the back of the truck and stacking them neatly on the wooden shelves along one wall.

The two brothers worked efficiently until the truck was empty, then headed toward the ranch's back porch.

"Looks like you had a busy day in town, Casey."

"Yeah. Checked off everybody's list. And Kirby and I enjoyed a romantic lunch for two at Nonie's."

"Romantic? At Nonie's? With half the town watching?"

"The whole world could watch. When I'm with my bride, she's all I see." Hearing Jonah's snort of derision, Casey turned. "Go ahead and laugh. Someday it'll happen to you, and then you'll understand."

"What'll happen to Jonah?" Brand was standing at the top of the steps.

"Love." Casey walked into the mudroom and started washing up.

"Not our little brother." Brand gave a shake of his head. "He's too busy writing those blockbuster books." He turned to Jonah. "A good day at your cabin?"

Jonah merely smiled. "Yeah. A good day."

"For writing, maybe." Brand nudged Casey. "But that's no way to broaden your horizons, bro. You're never going to meet any interesting women if you keep on locking yourself away out there in the middle of nowhere, living in your head."

"Thanks. I'll keep that in mind." Jonah stepped into the kitchen and crossed the room to help himself to an ice-cold longneck. He opened the bottle, took a long drink, and glanced around the room to greet the family members gathered there.

"Egan and I had a lovely visit with Buster and Trudy Mandel." Seated beside her husband in front of the fireplace, Meg sipped her tea. "Avery, Trudy wanted me to tell you she's completely pain-free, thanks to all those hours of physical therapy you put in."

"Thanks, Gram Meg, but Trudy put in the hard work. I was just there to direct her."

"Buster says Trudy is so grateful she tells everybody you're an angel of mercy."

At the compliment to his wife, Brand beamed. "I could've told her that."

"You're biased, babe." Avery brushed a kiss to his cheek. "Though, if you recall our first meeting, I'm not sure that's what you would have called me."

The family burst into laughter, remembering how angry Brand had been when he learned his grandmother had hired a physical therapist to work with him without first consulting him.

"All in the past." He wrapped a big arm around his wife. "You made a believer out of me."

Meg looked over at Casey, who was standing beside his wife, Kirby. "What's new in town today?"

Casey shared a smile with Kirby. "The big news is that Nonie's girls have finished college."

"You don't say?" Meg caught Egan's hand. "I remember when those sweet little girls lost their parents and Nonie brought them home to live with her. There was so much turmoil, and everybody wondered how she'd manage to run her business and be a single mother to twin girls. And now they've become lovely young women and they've graduated from college. Where did the years go?"

"They do fly by, don't they?" Ham looked around at his family. "My father used to say to me, 'Don't blink, boy.' And he was right. In the blink of an eye, ninety years have flown by. But look at us. Still standing."

Across the room, Billy announced that dinner was ready.

As the family took their places around the table, the

talk turned to the weather, the herds, and more town gossip. Through it all, Jonah couldn't help smiling.

"How was your day, boy?" Ham's question broke through Jonah's reverie.

"It was a good day, Ham."

Bo arched a brow. "How many chapters did you write, son?"

"Not chapters, Pop. A few pages. But they were good ones."

"That's it?" Ham looked around at the others. "If all I had to show for a day's work were a couple of measly pages, I'd have to head to the barn and work off my frustration by mucking stalls until midnight."

That brought another round of laughter from the others.

Jonah joined in. Though his day had taken an unexpected turn, he wasn't ready to share it with the others. As the youngest of three, he'd had a lifetime of keeping things to himself. Maybe that was why writing suited him. While others did the talking, he could lose himself inside his own head.

"That was a lovely dinner, Billy." Meg smiled at the cook. "Why don't we take our dessert and coffee out on the porch? I'm in the mood for one of our spectacular sunsets."

"Yes, ma'am." Billy began loading his special four-layer chocolate torte, along with plates, forks, and a coffee service, on a wheeled trolley.

The family gathered on the porch, relaxing in sturdy

cushioned log settees and gliders and swings. Through the years, it had become one of their favorite gathering spots.

While they watched the sun set over the Tetons, Jonah enjoyed the teasing, the laughter, the easy flow of conversation that was such an endearing part of his family. But even though he joined in, a lovely distraction hovered at the edges of his mind.

Annie, her eyes filled with wonder at the sight of the mustangs. Annie, the sound of her husky voice wrapping itself around his heart.

Anticipating Wednesday, he held the secret close, feeling like a kid at Christmas.

CHAPTER FIVE

Jonah pulled himself into the saddle on his gelding, Thunder, and caught the reins of the mare he'd saddled for Annie.

He was more than happy to forgo a day of writing, since the past few days had been productive. One of the joys of being a writer was that he could lose himself in his story and put everything else out of his mind. A very good thing, since whenever he wasn't writing, he found his mind drifting to Annie. The way she'd looked when the breeze took her hair. The pure joy she'd experienced at the sight of the mustangs. That sudden jolt of fear when he'd touched her arm.

That singular moment stood out because, until then, she'd seemed so happy to be hiking with him. He didn't want to make too much of it, but it was such a strange contrast to the rest of the day. She hadn't been merely startled. She'd had, for one brief moment, a look of pure terror in her eyes.

It was true that everyone came with baggage, but he

couldn't help wondering what he'd uncover in Annie's past that would leave her feeling so vulnerable that a simple touch terrified her.

As Jonah rode past the equipment barn, Casey stepped out and shot him a questioning look. "Heading up to your cabin?"

"Yeah."

"What's with the spare horse?"

Jonah decided to ignore the question. Any answer he chose to give would lead to more questions, and he didn't want to be late. Besides, he liked having a few secrets from his brothers.

He nudged Thunder into a trot, with the mare keeping up beside him.

Casey's voice carried across the distance. "What else can you do with two horses except trick riding? Is that what you're really doing up in that cabin of yours?"

"It's a great plan B, in case the writing thing doesn't work out." Jonah was grinning as he disappeared into the woods.

With the horses tethered nearby, Jonah sat on the makeshift table outside the cabin, drinking coffee and watching the antics of a squirrel that had discovered the chipmunk's peanut stash. For every peanut the squirrel ate, he would bury two more at the base of a tree.

Jonah chuckled. "Come next winter, you're going to be the most popular squirrel in these woods."

"Are you talking to yourself?"

At the sound of Annie's voice, he swiveled his head. "Hey. You're right on time. Coffee?"

"Thanks. I'd love some."

"How do you like it?"

"Cream. No sugar."

"I'll be right back."

He stepped into the cabin, returning a minute later with a steaming cup.

"Thank you." She set aside her backpack and sat beside him on the plank before pointing to the squirrel. "Why isn't he afraid of humans?"

"Probably because I've been feeding him, and the rest of the wildlife, for years. Now they think of themselves as family."

"When you talk to them, do they talk back?"

He grinned. "Only the chipmunk. He chatters. But he's not here today. He's been in competition with the squirrel for the nuts I leave for them."

"Which one is winning?"

"The chipmunk manages to eat the most. Some days his cheeks are so full they're ready to explode. But this guy is storing up the most for a cold winter's night right over there."

"I'll bet your squirrel took one of those online classes on building a better future."

Jonah laughed. "Every time I see him burying another peanut I'll be reminded of that."

Annie nodded toward the saddled horses. "You're as good as your word."

"Did you think I'd forget?"

She shook her head. "I'd have been awfully disappointed if you did. I've been looking forward to this since Saturday."

"Me too."

She drained her cup and set it on the plank before shrugging on her backpack.

Jonah led the way toward the horses. "This is Thunder. He and I go way back." Then he ran a hand along the mare's neck. "And this is Honey. Don't let that sweet name fool you. She's got a lot of spirit. But she's respectful of a good rider."

"Hi, Honey." Annie combed her fingers through the mare's forelock before rubbing the silky-soft muzzle. "I hope by the end of the day we're friends."

As if in response, the mare bobbed her head.

Jonah held the reins while Annie pulled herself into the saddle.

"Comfortable?"

She nodded and he handed her the reins before mounting Thunder.

Within minutes they were moving out single file along a path that led toward the high meadows.

It was the perfect day for a ride. Mild, sunny, with enough breeze to keep them from overheating.

As soon as the trail widened enough, they rode side by side, enjoying the day and the view.

"Oh, Jonah." Annie gave him a heart-stopping smile.

"How I've missed this." She flushed. "You probably do this every day."

"Not even close. I sometimes go days without saddling Thunder."

"If I lived out here, I'd be in the saddle every minute of every day."

Jonah pointed to the top of the hill. "Let's head up there and take a look around. I'll let you decide which way to go."

"I have a better idea. Let's race. The winner gets to choose."

Before he could answer, she nudged Honey into a gallop.

Jonah allowed Thunder to take off, slowly gaining ground as they raced across the meadow.

They ran neck and neck until they reached the top of the hill, with Honey mere seconds ahead.

"I won." Annie bent down to press her face to Honey's mane. "I should say, we won. Good going, Honey."

Jonah was shaking his head. "You two make a good team."

"Yes, we do. Sorry about your bad luck, cowboy, but it looks like I get to choose our path from here." She looked in every direction, noting woods, fields, valleys, before pointing. "How about over there?"

Jonah was grinning.

"What's so funny?"

"That would've been my choice, too."

She arched a brow. "Why do I get the feeling you're teasing me?"

"Me?" He gave her a mock pained expression before laughing. "The truth is, you'll never know. Come on. Let's see if you made a good choice."

As they started off, Jonah studied the way she looked beside him, her hair windblown, her cheeks pink from the race. Just then, she looked over and he gave her a smile of pure male appreciation. He caught the slight flush that started at her throat and worked its way up.

She looked good enough to kiss.

His hand tightened on the reins, and he pulled back, allowing her to lead the way.

"Look."

At his hushed command, she paused and turned.

A herd of mustangs was melting into the trees, disappearing without a trace.

She held Honey still until Jonah's mount came up alongside. "I was hoping I'd see more horses today." Her smile was radiant. "Thanks. I'd have missed them if it weren't for you."

He nodded. "They're easy to miss. They've learned to slip away at the first sign of humans."

She shook her head. "I don't know why I'm so excited at the sight of them. I mean, I've grown up around horses. But mustangs are another matter."

"I know what you mean. They've always been special to me, too."

They rode on, enjoying the perfect day and the

picture-perfect countryside all around. The hills covered in green and sprinkled with colorful wildflowers. An eagle soaring overhead. The glorious mountains forming a magnificent backdrop to it all.

As they topped a rise, Annie pointed to a stand of trees up ahead. "How about taking a break there?"

Jonah nodded, and they slowed to a walk before coming to a halt and dismounting.

Jonah pointed to a nearby stream. "Thirsty?"

"I am. But I brought my own." She slipped off her backpack and pulled out two bottles of water before handing one to him. "I also brought us lunch."

Jonah saw the wrapped packets. "You made these?"

Her laugh was clear as a bell. "Sorry. I'm not that domesticated. I bought lunch at Katie's Kitchen, the little bakeshop in town. Katie told me she recently added a deli."

She revealed a plastic bag of red, yellow, and orange pepper strips to munch.

"No chips?" Jonah frowned.

"I'm into healthy." She laughed. "But I thought a rugged cowboy like you might like something more substantial, so I also got some chicken club sandwiches."

"Ah." His frown turned into a smile. "Good thinking."

"And...ta-da." She unwrapped a third package to reveal two big chocolate brownies.

"You get extra points for the dessert." With a laugh, he settled beside her on a fallen log and bit into his sandwich. "So. Have you unpacked yet?"

At her arched brow, he explained. "The other day you said you'd moved into the apartment above Julie's but hadn't unpacked."

She gave a negligent shrug. "I keep putting it off."

"Does that mean you're not sure you're staying in Devil's Door?"

"I am for now." She uncapped her bottle of water and took a long drink. "What is that called?" She motioned toward a towering peak in the distance.

Her attempt to change the subject had Jonah smiling. "Locals call it the Chimney."

She nodded. "I can see why. Have you climbed it?"

"When I was younger, it was a favorite challenge. When I was twelve, I decided I had to reach the top. So I set off all alone and started climbing. I was almost at the top when I slipped. Next thing I knew, I was falling and landed in a heap at the bottom."

"Oh." Her hand went to her throat. "Did you break a leg?"

He shook his head. "My collarbone. Hurt like hell. I had to drag myself onto Thunder's back. I was in such a haze of pain all I could do was hold on and hope he got me home."

"That sounds like a painful lesson to learn."

He gave a short laugh. "I guess I've got a really thick head. As soon as the doctor declared I was healed, I went back and tried again." He shook his head remembering. "And fell again."

"No." She looked pained. "Not your collarbone."

"My left arm. In two places." He looked over at the mountain peak, gleaming in the sunlight. "As soon as the cast was off, I was back climbing. I know it was pretty stupid, but I couldn't resist the challenge. And that time I made it to the top." He was grinning. "I remember standing there, feeling like the king of the world. I looked at how far I'd climbed, and then I jumped up and down, feeling this tremendous rush, shouting at the top of my lungs, hearing my voice bounce off the cliffs."

She laughed and nodded. "For a stupid kid trick, I have to admit I'd have done the same. I guess it proves one thing."

He turned to her.

"You're either right about having a thick head, or you're a guy who just can't quit until you succeed."

He winked. "Right on both counts."

She was studying him a little too carefully. "And now what? On to bigger and better challenges?"

He shrugged. "Why not? How about you? What kind of crazy things did you do as a kid?"

She polished off the last of her sandwich. "My best friend, Lori, and I were always getting into trouble. But nothing as awesome as climbing a mountain. We were more into bringing home wounded pelicans and patching them up, or sailing her dad's boat around the bay and throwing food to the sea lions sunning on the docks. The only dangerous thing we ever did was get tossed about during an unexpected storm and being rescued by the Coast Guard, after they were contacted by our frantic parents. Needless to say, we were grounded for the rest of the summer."

"How old were you?"

"Fifteen. And according to my father, lucky to live to see my sixteenth birthday."

They shared a laugh.

"Are you and Lori still best friends?"

"Yes. She's . . ." Annie seemed to catch herself before glancing at her watch and then pointing. "I need to get back. Is that the way to your cabin?"

"It is."

"Think we'll see another herd of mustangs on our way?"

"If we're lucky."

Seeing that he'd finished his brownie, she handed him half of hers. "Here. I'll trade you for those pepper strips."

He grinned. "I think I'm getting the best of this deal."

"All you're getting is chocolate and sugar."

"Two of my favorite food groups." He swallowed the confection in one bite.

A short time later, renewed and refreshed, they were riding down the hill toward Jonah's cabin.

At the fork in the trail, they dismounted. Annie gave Honey a final pat. "I wish I didn't have to run, but I really need to get to work. Thank you for this morning, Jonah. It was really special."

As she began to turn away, he dropped a hand on her shoulder, causing her to abruptly turn to face him.

Though she froze and her eyes went wide, to her credit she didn't back away.

"It was special for me, too." He kept his tone easy. "Thanks for lunch. And the extra dessert."

"You're welcome." Her breathless tone hinted that she'd been expecting something more.

He was about to let it go but then thought better of it and brushed a quick kiss over her mouth.

He'd meant it to be nothing more than a friendly good-bye. But the minute his lips touched hers, heat flared.

A little sigh escaped her throat, and she was smiling as she turned away. "I guess if I have to be late for work, that's a better reason than most."

He stood very still as she made a dash down the trail. Finding his voice, he called, "If you're not working Saturday, we could go hiking again."

"I'd like that."

He watched until she was out of sight.

The taste of her still lingered on his lips.

The knowledge that he would see her again had a smile lighting all his features.

CHAPTER SIX

On her day off, when she could have slept until noon, Annie was up early and twitching with energy. She couldn't deny the fact that it was the thought of meeting Jonah at his cabin and spending the day hiking that had brought on this burst of energy.

She was sensible enough to know that this day should be all about the hiking, and not the man. She'd learned the hard way that she should never put her trust in a man. Especially a good-looking one with all that easy charm. And it wasn't about Jonah, she told herself, though to be honest, he wasn't like the guys she'd known in the city. He wasn't one of those pretty boys, working out with a trainer to sculpt the perfect body, spending a fortune on designer suits, all for the purpose of having a pretty woman on his arm.

Everything about the cowboy, living in a remote cabin in the wilderness, put her at ease. From what she'd seen so far, he was down to earth, true to his word, and just what he seemed to be—a man who enjoyed the simple life.

With all the tensions seething in her crazy world lately, this was what she needed. No pretense. No drama. Just a nice, easy friendship.

Still, she couldn't put that kiss out of her mind.

True, it had been nothing more than a simple goodbye-thanks-for-the-lunch kind of kiss. She was sure that's what he'd meant by it. But in the dark of the night, when sleep eluded her, she'd had to admit that, for her, it had been something more. While it had been short and sweet, another second and it would have turned into something else. But even in that instant, Jonah's kiss had packed a punch.

At some other time in her life, she'd have been willing to give it another try, to see where it led. But right now, in her turbulent life, that wasn't an option.

Today they would hike, and talk and laugh, and hopefully see more herds of mustangs.

That would have to be enough. More than enough. No kiss goodbye, no flirtation, no matter how the day went.

That was her story, and she was going to stick to it.

Time to shower and dress for a day of hiking.

A sudden thought had her grinning.

She would be hiking with her handsome cowboy. A cowboy she would not kiss, no matter how appealing it may seem.

She brushed aside the thought and reminded herself why she was in Devil's Door, Wyoming.

It had the effect of dashing cold water on whatever fantasies she'd been about to indulge in.

*   *   *

When Annie walked into the clearing, Jonah was just pulling on his shirt. Noting the pile of freshly split logs, it occurred to her that if she'd arrived a few minutes earlier, she'd have caught him shirtless and chopping wood.

Maybe it was just as well that she'd missed it. This cowboy was tempting enough fully clothed.

She paused to watch him carry an armload of logs that would stagger most men. He stacked them neatly alongside the cabin before turning for more.

When he saw her, he buttoned his shirt before starting toward her. "'Morning, Annie."

"Good morning. You've been busy. Want some help?"

"No, but thanks for offering. I'll finish up another day." He gave her a smile. "Ready for that hike?"

"I am. I woke up thinking about mustangs. I hope we see some today."

"If you'd like, we could head a little higher into the hills. That's where they usually spend the warm months."

"Great." She followed his lead along a nearly in-visible trail until they'd left the shelter of the woods and stepped out into a lush meadow.

Jonah frowned as he looked up. "Clouds are gather-ing. We may get some rain. Do you want to risk it?"

Annie shrugged. "It's worth a try. A little rain never hurt anything."

"Okay. Your call."

They hiked across the meadow, moving upward as they went, until they reached the summit. From there they could see for miles as the hills folded one into another, and they were all so lush and green it looked like an artist's rendering.

Annie gave a sigh of pleasure. "It's almost too pretty to be real."

Jonah nodded. "This is one of my favorite spots." He pointed to the dark outline of the Tetons in the distance, rising up like a fortress in a medieval novel. "When I was a kid, I pretended I was a superhero who defended this paradise against invaders."

"You had quite the imagination."

"Yeah. Still do." He turned to her, and the steady look he gave her had the heat rising to her cheeks.

She felt the need to say something. Anything, to deflect from the wolfish look in his eyes. "Which way should we go?"

He smiled. "Let's try that way."

Before they had a chance to move on, there was a crack of thunder, and the sky began to turn ominously dark.

Jonah pointed. "We need to turn back. I'm not sure we can outrun those storm clouds rolling in, but we can try."

Annie followed him as he started back the way they'd come. They were halfway across the meadow when the storm broke, and the sky opened up with a torrent of rain.

Jonah caught her hand and the two of them ran

the rest of the distance. Once in the woods, they were partially sheltered by the thick foliage, though they could hear the sound of the rain pelting the leaves overhead.

By the time they reached his cabin, they were soaked.

Jonah pushed open the door and led her inside. While he made his way to the fireplace to strike a match to kindling, Annie stood in the doorway and looked around.

She'd been expecting a rough cabin, and it was. There was a serviceable sink. Modern appliances. A wooden table and two chairs with an intricate design. Through a doorway she could see a bed, covered in a dark green comforter, and an upholstered chair alongside a table stacked with books. But the interior of the cabin was also much more than it appeared to be from the outside. There were shelves along one entire wall, filled with books. There was an amazing glass table on a base that appeared to be some sort of petrified wood, polished to a high shine. Across the room was a desk and, atop it, a computer.

"Here." Jonah crossed the room and wrapped her in an afghan. "Come sit by the fire while I find something dry for you to put on."

Annie settled into a chair and welcomed the heat.

He walked into the bedroom and returned minutes later wearing a dry shirt and carrying a second one.

"This will be too big, but at least it's not wet. We can hang yours here by the fire until it dries."

"Thanks." She accepted the shirt and walked to his bedroom, closing the door.

After slipping out of her shirt and pulling on his, she began rolling the sleeves. As she did, she moved around the small room, getting a glimpse of the man who slept here.

There was a second fireplace in here, and she thought how cozy it would be on chilly nights. The smell of wood smoke reminded her of her childhood home, where her father often had a log burning in the hearth.

She stepped out of the room and draped her damp shirt over the back of a chair, set near the fireplace.

Jonah had made a pot of coffee, and the smell, mingling with the smoke from the fireplace, filled the little cabin with even more warm memories.

"I like your cabin."

"Thanks."

He handed her a cup of coffee. "One cream."

She arched a brow. "You remembered."

He merely smiled.

"Did you build this place yourself?"

"Most of it. And some of the furniture."

She seemed surprised.

He waved a hand. "This table and the chairs, for instance." He pointed across the room. "And that table."

She crossed the room to study it. "What a fabulous base."

"It's a petrified stump I unearthed while digging the

foundation. I loved the shape of it, and the grain of the wood, and decided to polish it up."

"It's beautiful." She looked over at him. "So you earn your living making furniture?"

He laughed. "Afraid not. It's just a hobby." He drained his coffee and turned toward the door. "I think the storm's blowing over. I'm going to haul in another log. I'll just be a minute."

When the door closed behind him, she continued sipping her coffee as she slowly walked around the room.

Intrigued by the shelves of books, she paused to read the titles. There were biographies, fiction, and nonfiction. Several books on woodworking and several more on soil conservation and climate.

She noted several copies of the same hardcover and bent to read the title.

Secrets and Lies by J. R. Merrick.

She recognized it as a recent best seller she'd seen in bookstore windows in San Francisco and found herself wondering why he'd bought so many copies of the same book.

Gifts for family or friends?

She was about to move on when she noticed one of the books opened to the inside back cover.

She nearly bobbled her coffee. Alarmed, she set aside her cup and bent to study the photo and blurb about the author.

Just then, Jonah stepped inside and hauled a log to the fireplace. After setting it in place, he stood and wiped his hands down his jeans before turning with a smile.

Annie was looking at him as if she'd just seen a ghost.

He started toward her. "What's wrong?"

"You're...him." She held out the book. "Why didn't you tell me that you're J. R. Merrick?"

Without waiting for his answer, she dashed across the room and yanked her damp shirt from the back of the chair, then hurried into the bedroom. A minute later she returned, wearing her shirt and heading for the door.

"Annie. Wait." Jonah crossed to her in quick strides and caught her arm.

"Don't touch me." She shot him a look that had him lifting his hand and backing away.

"Okay. I understand why you're angry." He couldn't hide his frustration. "But this is exactly why I didn't tell you. You're reacting the way so many people do when they find out I'm a published author instead of just another cowboy. But I'm the same guy you hiked with and rode horses with. Annie, I'm just a guy..."

Her voice was pure ice. "You're a Merrick."

"Yes. I'm..." Her obvious anger had him pausing. "Jonah Merrick. What's wrong?"

"This cabin isn't your home. You just...play here, or pretend to live here, or whatever you do here."

"I write here. This is my office."

"I see. Of course."

"Of course? What does that mean?"

"My uncle told me the Merrick family lives on a big, sprawling ranch set on a thousand or so acres and that I was to steer clear of them. So, of course, I never connected a cowboy living in a cabin in the wilderness with the infamous Merrick family."

"Infamous?" There was a pause before he found his voice. "What does any of that have to do with why you're so angry?"

"I've heard all about your family, and the fact that all of you have shunned my uncle and his family—my family—for years."

"Your family?" He couldn't seem to wrap his mind around this sudden change in the conversation. "I don't know what you're talking about. Would you mind explaining what I'm missing?"

"I should have introduced myself properly the first time we met. But then, you should have done the same." She took in a breath. "My name is Annie Dempsey. I'm here working for my uncle, Des Dempsey, at the bank in town."

"Dempsey." After the initial shock of hearing her name, he slowly nodded. "I see." In a purely knee-jerk reaction, he opened the door to the cabin and stepped aside. "You're right. We should have formally introduced ourselves right away. Now that we both know the truth, I think it's best that you leave."

She lifted her chin like a prizefighter as she walked stiffly past him and out the door.

*   *   *

Jonah stood in the open doorway and watched until Annie was out of sight.

When he finally closed the door, he could feel a definite chill in the cabin, despite the fire.

The day, which had started out with so much promise, was now as dreary as the sky, threatening more storms to come.

CHAPTER SEVEN

Casey and Brand were laughing together as they walked into the barn.

Seeing the stalls already clean, the two exchanged puzzled looks.

"This is the third day in a row that Jonah was up before dawn to do our chores." Casey turned to his brother. "You think he's having trouble with the new book?"

Brand gave a shrug. "Must be. What else could be bothering Jonah? Writing takes up his whole life."

"Yeah." Casey turned toward the door. "We need to find our little brother a hobby."

"Or a woman."

"Hey, we're talking about the loner in the family. There have been plenty of interested women but you know after a couple of dates, he always moves on. My money's on a hobby."

"The same could've been said about us a couple of years ago." Brand punched Casey's shoulder and the two shared a chuckle as they made their way back to the house.

Once in the kitchen, they strolled across the room to join the family.

Casey picked up a steaming mug of coffee and leaned over to kiss his bride's cheek. "Morning, sleepyhead."

Kirby returned his kiss. "How did you finish your chores so early?"

"They were already done." He looked around before asking, "Where's Jonah?"

Billy looked up from the stove. "Gone to his cabin. He didn't want any breakfast. Just took a coffee and headed out."

Casey turned to Brand. "Told you." To the rest of the family he said, "We figure Jonah's having a problem with this book he's writing. That's the only explanation for the way he's been acting. Up at dawn. Chores finished before we can help. And off to his cabin to brood."

Ham set aside his empty mug. "What you're describing usually means trouble with a woman."

"Except we're talking about Jonah." Brand nudged his brother. "Casey and I think it's time to drag him out of that wilderness and back to the land of the living. He's been spending way too much time alone up there."

Liz, who often locked herself away in her studio in the barn for days on end, was quick to defend her nephew. "When a gifted writer like Jonah is distracted, it doesn't always mean he's troubled. It could simply mean he's working out some kinks in his story."

Meg nodded her agreement. "Jonah has always had a good head on his shoulders. I'm sure if we leave him alone, he'll figure things out."

Egan laid a hand over his wife's. "Right you are, Meggie girl."

The two shared a smile as Billy announced that breakfast was ready.

Jonah stepped into his cabin and started a fresh pot of coffee before walking to his desk.

As he booted up his computer and stared at the screen, he struggled to focus.

His dark thoughts, as they'd been these past few days, weren't on his work, but on the woman who'd breezed into and out of his life like a summer storm.

How could he have misread her so completely?

The stranger he'd met had been fun to be with. Filled with a kind of innocent wonder about the beauty of this place and its wildlife. She liked hiking and riding, the two things that he'd always enjoyed doing alone because, until now, none of the women he'd dated were willing to accept a life half spent in the wilderness. He'd convinced himself that he would probably never find a woman he cared about who would share this part of his life.

So here he was. Alone.

The word that had always defined him now seemed to mock him. Why? What had caused this change in a matter of days?

Annie Dempsey.

Everything he enjoyed had been even more enjoyable because it had been shared with Annie.

But she was the niece of Des Dempsey, his father's enemy.

All his life, Jonah had grown up hearing the story of the fire that had burned their ancient ranch house to the ground, killing their mother, Leigh, and leaving their father devastated. To this day, Bo lived alone rather than try to build a life with another woman. He'd buried himself in work and in his family. This land, this legacy, were what helped Bo face a life without the woman he'd loved and lost.

And though Bo Merrick couldn't prove his theory, he fully believed that Des Dempsey had started that fire to avenge losing Leigh, jealous of the life she'd built with his rival, Bo. And that just further ignited the feud between the Merricks and the Dempseys, which started when Leigh chose Bo over Des.

The Merrick family, including Bo's sons, had carried on the family feud without question.

They drove more than fifty miles to the town of Stockwell to do their banking, rather than trust their finances to the Dempsey family, the owners of the only bank in nearby Devil's Door. Though Des and Bo had once been boyhood friends, the Merrick family hadn't spoken to the Dempsey family since even before that fire.

When the coffee was ready, Jonah poured himself a fresh cup and turned to stare out the window.

A herd of deer drifted past, foraging as they went. For the first time in his memory, the beauty of those creatures didn't stir him. The chipmunk was back, stuffing his cheeks with peanuts. Even his silly antics couldn't snag Jonah's interest.

He stared morosely at the rays of sunlight sifting through the dense foliage and felt no warmth.

Why did he have to spend so much time thinking about the one woman who could never have a place in his life?

Too frustrated to even think about his work, he dumped the coffee down the drain and stalked out the door. He would hike the hills until exhaustion forced him to stop. Maybe that would help him exorcise Annie Dempsey from his mind.

The sun had made its arc across the sky, bathing the clouds that hovered around the peaks of the Tetons in shimmering shades of gold.

Jonah's long day of hiking hadn't helped him clear his mind. After hours of mulling over the situation, he'd had more questions than answers. But one thing was clear. He'd decided to let Annie know that, despite the fierce loyalty he felt to his family, he didn't consider her a part of their family feud.

He walked past his cabin without stopping and made his way home. Once there, he headed to his room for a long, hot shower. When he was dressed, he stepped into the kitchen to greet his family.

"Another long day, bro." Casey handed him a chilled longneck. "I hope you got a lot of work done on that award-winning novel."

"It's got a long way to go before it can win anything."

Brand shared a grin with his wife. "Cut the humble act. Knowing you, it'll be another blockbuster."

"From your lips." Jonah took a long drink before setting aside the half-full bottle.

Turning to Billy, he said, "I won't be staying for supper. I'll see you all later."

When he was gone, the family shared puzzled looks.

Brand turned to his great-grandfather. "You think he's heading back to the cabin to work?"

Ham smiled. "In case you didn't notice, boy, Jonah's hair was damp from the shower. And he was wearing a clean shirt. That doesn't say work to me. I still say his trouble these days may be with a female."

As they gathered around the table, Ham's words were greeted with scoffs and jeers from his great-grandsons.

Brand nudged Casey. "Jonah's always been all work, little play. Why should this be any different?"

CHAPTER EIGHT

As Jonah drove to town, he kept going over what he would say when Annie opened the door.

Hey. I just happened to be in town and…

Hi, Annie. Sorry to bother you but…

Good evening. Can we talk…?

Nothing rang true. Maybe he ought to try a little honesty.

Ever since you left, I've been miserable…

I wonder if we could start over…

Don't slam the door until you hear what I have to say…

He pulled up behind Julie Franklyn's hair salon and parked. Thankfully there was a back stairway to the second-story apartment, so at least he wouldn't have to go through the salon, where he'd have to face Julie and her customers. Anything and everything that happened in public in Devil's Door became fodder for gossip enjoyed by the entire town.

Jonah wasn't in the mood to be this week's featured player.

The outer stairway led to a large, open balcony and double sliding glass doors for easy access to and from the apartment. The outdoor lights hadn't been turned on, leaving the exterior in darkness. Drawn draperies hid the view inside the lighted apartment.

Jonah lifted a hand to knock on the door. His fist paused in midair when he heard a man's voice inside, raised in anger.

Hearing it, Jonah stepped back into the shadows of the balcony, intending to leave. He certainly hadn't come here to poke his nose into Annie's business.

Before he could make his getaway, the door opened and a stranger stalked out, unaware of anything but the stairs, which he took two at a time before slamming a car door and driving off with a squeal of tires.

Jonah turned back to the apartment to see that the draperies were drawn aside. Annie was outlined in the doorway seconds before she flipped a switch, bathing Jonah in light.

For a moment she stiffened, and the fearful look on her face spoke volumes.

When she realized it was Jonah and not the stranger, she slid open the door and threw herself against him, pressing her face to his chest for the space of a moment before practically dragging him inside.

"Jonah." His name came out on a breathy sigh before she seemed to realize what she'd done.

Just as quickly, she stepped back and avoided look-ing at him.

"Hi. I wasn't eavesdropping. I just stopped by to..." He caught her by the upper arms and studied her. "You all right?"

"No." She looked around wildly. "Yes. I'm..."

"Your first answer sounded more sincere. You're not all right. You're shaking."

She released another deep sigh before she turned away. "I'm so glad you're here." She crossed to the small galley kitchen, as though hoping to put some space between them while her nerves settled. "Would you like a drink?"

"If you're having one."

She opened a cupboard and selected a bottle of red wine. "Is this all right?" She rummaged in the cabinets for a corkscrew and a couple of glasses.

"It's fine. Want me to open it?" Without waiting for a response, he went over to her, took the bottle and the corkscrew, opened the bottle, and poured the wine into two glasses.

He waited until she'd taken a sip before saying, "Want to talk about it?"

Instead of responding, she gestured toward two bar stools at the small counter.

As they sat, he saw the way her hands shook. He put his hand over hers. "You're cold."

"It'll pass."

"Who was the guy?"

"He said his name is Park. He said he was sent by...a man I knew in California. He had a message from...him. He was to let me know I couldn't hide from him."

"This guy in California have a name?"

"Arlen."

"Arlen...?"

At his prompt, she said, "Arlen Lender."

"Why would you hide from him?"

"Because I'm in trouble."

"What kind of trouble?"

"I don't know."

He set aside his wine. "If you don't know what kind of trouble you're in, how do you know you're in trouble?"

She took a deep breath and turned to face him. "It's a long story. How much time do you have?"

"As much as you need."

She perched on the edge of the seat, as though poised to run. Nerves had her practically twitching.

Watching her, Jonah thought she seemed so different from the relaxed, easy-to-be-with woman who'd hiked and rode the hills with so much joy.

She was silent for a long minute before saying, "Because of my family's connections in banking, I grew up learning the trade. I was working in the financial sector in San Francisco, and through my work I met Arlen. He was handsome and charming, and he made me feel special. In no time at all he was talking about a future together, though I wasn't nearly ready." Her tone hardened. "Now I realize it was all a con. He never cared for me. He was only using me for whatever scheme he was involved in."

"And that was...?"

"I don't know what the scheme was, only that I'd been marked to take the fall."

"How do you know that?"

"When I uncovered a bank account in my name with one million dollars—"

"Wait." He lifted a hand to stop her. "A million dollars?"

She nodded. "I told Arlen about it, saying that I planned on going to the authorities. You can imagine my shock when he calmly told me that if I contacted the authorities, I would go to prison for years for accepting stolen money. That the bank account was set up for that purpose alone."

"So you ran."

Another nod. "That night. Without any plan, other than to get as far away as I could from San Francisco, from Arlen, and whatever scheme he was involved in."

"Does your uncle know why you're here?"

"Not all of it. I told him I was in trouble and needed a job and a place to hide." She closed her eyes as the horror of it all washed over her. "And now I've brought whatever trouble I'm in to my uncle's door." She looked at Jonah. "I know your family hates mine, but you have to believe that my uncle Des is a good man. He has spent a lifetime building a reputable banking business. He doesn't deserve to be involved in this."

"Neither do you."

Her eyes widened. "How can you say that? You don't know anything about me. How do you know I haven't made this whole thing up to cover some criminal activity?"

"The woman I met at my cabin is a good person."

She looked at him with gratitude. "Thank you." She spoke the words in a whisper as she twisted her hands in her lap. "When Arlen realized that I'd run, he sent me a text message, warning that I'd be sorry and that he has enough damning evidence to send me to prison for years."

"If this guy is as dangerous as he sounds, prison may be the least of your worries. Now that he's found you, what's to prevent him from eliminating you altogether?"

Seeing the shiver that passed through her, he touched a hand to hers. "You know, now that this guy has found you, you can't stay here."

"I know. But it won't take me long to run, since I've barely unpacked."

"Run? Where?"

She shrugged. "Somewhere even more remote than Devil's Door. I should have known that someone would find the connection between Uncle Des and me. This time, I'll go where I don't know a soul, and hopefully I can start over with a new identity."

"I have a place where you can be safe while you work with the authorities to clear this up."

"You heard what I said. Arlen warned me not to go to the authorities."

"Criminals always say that. But the authorities are your only hope of clearing your name."

"Even though he didn't know what trouble I was in, that's what my uncle said. When there's trouble, call the authorities."

"Your uncle's right. In the meantime, let me keep you safe."

"Jonah, I know your cabin is remote, but if this guy has been trailing me without my knowledge, he probably knows every place I've been."

"Not necessarily. He found you here because you signed a rental agreement. You probably didn't even bother to use a phony name."

"This is so far from San Francisco it never occurred to me to hide my identity on the lease." She closed her eyes. "I need to leave. Tonight."

"My ranch is big, and so is my family. Big enough that you never have to be alone or afraid."

"Your family?" She was already shaking her head. "You'd ask me to stay with the very people who have a grudge against my family?"

"It's not personal."

She gave a huff of disapproval. "It is to me. If they hate my uncle, they hate me, too."

"*Hate* is a strong word. And that's actually why I'm

here tonight. After giving it a lot of thought, I came here to say that the family feud shouldn't involve us. Whatever history my father has with your uncle, it's between them."

"Those are nice words, Jonah. But I'm sorry. I have enough trouble in my life without adding to it."

"All right. Then consider this. You need a place to hide right now. Tonight. The guy who raced out of here has no doubt already contacted Arlen Lender and is getting his marching orders."

She put a hand to her mouth to stifle her gasp.

"Annie, let me take you home to my family, at least for tonight. If, by morning, you still feel the need to escape, I'll take you wherever you want to go."

She was shaking her head as she bit her lip. "I suppose you plan on introducing me under a phony name."

It was his turn to shake his head. "I have no intention of lying to them. I'll tell them your name, and that you're my friend, and that I expect them to respect the fact that you need a safe shelter."

"And just like that, you think they'll take me in."

"I'm sure of it." He nodded. "Just like that."

She stood and hugged her arms as she began to pace. "I know I can't stay here. Even with the door locked and all the lights on, I'd never feel safe from that awful man. And I can't take this to my uncle. I've already burdened him with too much. So why would you want to bring this trouble to your door?"

"Once you meet my family, you'll understand. We're

big and rough and loud, and at times we fight among ourselves. But in times of trouble, we stand together. And if someone needs a safe haven, trust me, there's no safer place to be than with the Merrick family."

For just a moment she looked as though she might cry. Then she took in a breath and gave a slight nod. "All right, you've sold me. Just for the night. Because I'm desperate." She turned toward the bedroom before saying over her shoulder, "Now, I hope you can sell your family on welcoming a Dempsey into their midst."

CHAPTER NINE

While Annie packed, Jonah switched off the outdoor lights, leaving the upper balcony in darkness.

Inside the apartment, he went about turning on lights, along with the television.

When Annie stepped out of the bedroom with a giant suitcase, she glanced around. "What's all this?"

"I think it's wise to leave this place looking like someone's home."

Before she could ask him to explain, he merely smiled. "I write mysteries. Humor me."

She nodded. "I'm glad one of us has a brain. Right now, I'm just running on adrenaline."

He walked over and took the handle of her suitcase. "I'll take this down to my truck. While I'm there, I'll look around. If your visitor is gone, I'll come back up for you."

"And if he's come back to watch in the dark?"

Jonah gave a chilling smile. "Then I'll politely ask him to leave."

As he walked out into the darkness, Annie crossed her arms and tapped her foot as she waited, imagining a dozen different scenarios, all of them bloody and violent. There had been a thread of steel in Jonah's voice that she hadn't noticed before. But if he decided to fight the stranger and came up against a gun...

By the time Jonah returned, her nerves were reaching the breaking point. When the door opened, she flew across the room and clutched at his arms until her nails dug into his flesh. "Are you all right?"

He shot her a sexy grin. "Nice to know you missed me."

"That's not funny." She stepped back.

"No. It isn't." He drew her close and ran a hand down her back. "I'm sorry. But we may as well laugh. It beats cursing our bad luck."

She took in a breath. "I'm not so sure about that."

"If you feel like swearing a blue streak or breaking something, go right ahead."

She stood very still for a moment, then nodded. "Okay. You're right. Those things won't help my situation. Let's go."

He caught her hand and they stepped out onto the darkened balcony. Together they descended the stairs, and once they approached his truck, he held open the passenger door.

She held back. "What about my car?"

"I think it's best to leave it here, to add to the illusion that you're still upstairs."

She nodded and he helped her into the truck before circling around to the driver's side.

Minutes later, as they drove through town, she closed her eyes and let her head fall back against the headrest. "Want to know the craziest thing about all this?"

"What?" Jonah glanced over.

"If I hadn't uncovered that million dollars in my bank account, I'd still be blissfully ignorant, gallivanting all around San Francisco with a man who was planning on destroying me."

Jonah reached over and covered her hand with his. "Don't think about that now. Think about this. Arlen Lender didn't know who he was dealing with when he targeted you. You're a strong woman, Annie. Strong enough that you didn't cave. Instead, you did the right thing and decided to fight back."

"Some fighter. I ran like a scared rabbit."

"Well now you're ready to fight back."

She sighed in the darkness, but this time she didn't draw away. Instead she absorbed the warmth of Jonah's hand on hers and let his words wash over her, strengthening her resolve.

"We've been driving for a while now. Just when do we reach this ranch of yours?"

Jonah smiled. "We've been on Merrick land for the last half hour. The house is up ahead."

Annie looked around, trying to get her bearings. Instead of the secluded forest where she'd met Jonah, she saw fields and meadows, black with cattle. Then a three-story house came into view as they rounded a bend. And looming up behind it, the darkened outline of the Tetons, and above their peaks, the end of a glorious red sunset.

Jonah parked behind a line of vehicles, then hopped out and circled around to open her door.

As he took her hand, he said in a low voice, "Brace yourself. You're about to meet my family. And there are a lot of them."

"Out here?"

He led her up the steps to the porch, and she realized he wasn't kidding. Porch lights illuminated the scene before her. There were people sitting in rockers and on gliders and porch swings. Some were eating cake. Others were drinking from steaming mugs of coffee.

Then, suddenly, a circle of faces was staring at her as if she'd dropped from the sky.

Jonah's voice broke the silence. "I'd like you all to meet a friend of mine. Annie Dempsey, this is my father, Bo Merrick."

"Annie." Bo set aside his coffee and got to his feet, offering a firm handshake.

"My aunt Liz."

A pretty blond woman half hidden in shadow gave a timid smile and a nod in acknowledgment.

"Our ranch foreman, Chet Doyle."

He offered his hand. "Ma'am."

"My brother Brand and his wife, Avery."

As she nodded toward the couple snuggled together on a porch swing, Jonah added, "My brother Casey and his wife, Kirby."

Annie turned to acknowledge them, sitting close together on a comfortable-looking settee.

"My grandparents Meg and Egan."

"How lovely to meet you, Annie." Instead of a handshake, Meg moved in to give her a warm hug, and Egan followed suit. Both of them smelled of cinnamon and coffee.

"Our cook, Billy Caldwell."

"Welcome, Annie. We're having cinnamon coffee cake. Will you have a piece?"

"No, thank you, but it smells heavenly."

Jonah led Annie across the porch to a figure in the shadows, seated on a glider. "And this is my great-grandfather, Hammond Merrick. Everyone calls him Ham."

"Ham." Annie was smiling as she extended her hand.

The old man gave his great-grandson a piercing look. "Did I hear you say Annie Dempsey?"

Jonah nodded. "You did."

He turned to Annie. "You related to Des Dempsey?" He spat the name like an insult.

She stiffened, prepared to defend her name. "He's my uncle." She started to lower her hand.

Seeing it, Jonah said, "Ham…"

The old man shot him a stern look, silencing his words. He stuck out his hand, forcing Annie to accept his handshake. He looked her squarely in the eye while saying, "Any friend of Jonah's is a friend of ours. It's a pleasure to meet you, Annie Dempsey." He put the emphasis firmly on her last name.

He patted the empty spot beside him. "Sit here."

It was not an invitation, but rather a stern command.

As she sat, she arched a brow at Jonah, who was hovering beside her like an avenging angel.

"Why don't you head to the kitchen and get yourself and your guest a couple of drinks, boy."

"I'll get them, Jo—" Billy started, but was immediately silenced by a look from Ham.

"Jonah can fetch for himself."

"Beer, wine, or coffee, Annie?" Jonah asked his guest.

She gave him a tremulous smile. "I'll have whatever you're having."

With a last look at Annie, Jonah walked to the door and let himself into the house. By the time he returned with two chilled beers, Ham and Annie were chatting like long-lost relatives.

"California? What part?"

"San Francisco." She smiled as she accepted the drink from Jonah, who pulled up a chair alongside the glider.

"A pretty part of the country."

"You've been there?" Jonah arched a brow.

"Been plenty of places I haven't told you about, boy." Ham pointed to the sky awash with color. "Bet they don't have sunsets that can compete with that."

"It's glorious. And with those mountain peaks turning that same amazing shade of red, it's breathtaking. It looks like something an artist would paint."

"That's who did it. A heavenly artist." Ham gave a nod of satisfaction. "It never gets old. This is my favorite time of day. Just sitting out here, watching the sun setting over my land, whatever worries I have just fade away." He turned to Annie. "Don't you agree?"

She gave a sigh. "You're right, Ham. It's like a drug. Just experiencing this, I can feel my heartbeat slowing and my whole day beginning to slip away."

"That's a good thing, girl." He looked over her head to where Jonah sat watching the two of them. "You brought this friend of yours to the right place, boy, and at the right time."

"I was just thinking that, Ham."

The two shared a secret smile.

Jonah took a long drink of beer and felt his own world begin to settle as well. He'd been right to bring Annie here. Whatever feud his family had with hers, they'd already silently agreed to a truce.

At least for tonight she was safe. And while she slept, he would have to come up with a plan.

Though he didn't want to probe his feelings too deeply just yet, he knew he was already in over his head.

This mysterious woman had begun to matter to him. And he intended to do as much as he could to keep her safe from whatever trouble was closing in.

CHAPTER TEN

As the various family members began drifting off to their rooms, Jonah turned to his grandmother. "I would have phoned ahead, but there wasn't time. I hope you don't mind but I invited Annie to stay the night."

Meg gave a nod. "You'll show her to the guest suite." To Annie she said, "I hope you enjoy your stay with us. If there's anything at all you need, be sure to let Jonah know. If it isn't in the room upstairs, we're certain to have it somewhere."

"I'm sure I'll be fine. Thank you."

Jonah put a hand on Annie's arm. "I'll get your suitcase from my truck."

Hammond waited until the others were gone before getting to his feet. "It was good meeting you, Annie Dempsey."

"Thank you. It was good meeting you, too."

"You in some kind of trouble, girl?"

Seeing the look of surprise on her face, he leaned down. "Didn't mean to pry. But I couldn't help noticing the way my great-grandson was hovering. Like a body-guard in charge of the crown jewels in a room full of thieves."

That coaxed a smile to her lips. "Maybe he was worried about my reception because of my name."

"Maybe. But I'm thinking it's something more. Like trouble."

"Am I that obvious?"

Seeing Jonah toting a suitcase up the porch steps, he stepped back. "Good night, Annie." He looked over. "'Night, Jonah."

"'Night, Ham." Jonah held the door and waited for Annie to precede him.

Once inside, she looked around, noting the luxurious great room they passed while heading toward the stairway.

Upstairs, they moved along a hallway until Jonah paused to open a door.

He went in and set her suitcase by the nightstand before waving a hand. "I think you'll find whatever you need here, but if you don't, let me know. My room is just across the hall."

She stood clasping and unclasping her hands. "You weren't kidding about your family. There are a lot of them."

"We can be a little overwhelming."

She shook her head. "No. Even when your great-grandfather challenged my name, his reaction wasn't at all what I was expecting."

"Yeah. For a minute there I thought we might have to fight our way off the porch."

She smiled. "He actually referred to you as my bodyguard."

"Was I that obvious?"

Now she managed a laugh. "I said the same thing. He said you looked like you were guarding the crown jewels."

"Ham may be ninety now, but he's still sharp. Nothing gets by him."

"Is he really that old?"

Jonah nodded.

"He's amazing. And as you said, very perceptive. While you were getting my suitcase, he asked if I was in trouble."

Jonah gave her a long look. "I know you need some time to process what happened to you, but I hope by morning you'll agree to meet with Noble Crain, the police chief in Devil's Door."

Annie took in a quick breath. "I know I should, but I can't forget that ominous threat about what will happen to me if I go to the authorities."

"Promise me you'll at least think about it. Noble is a good man. And, Annie, this isn't something you can handle on your own. You need to bring in the authorities."

She gave a slight nod. "I can't promise anything, but I'll think about it."

"Good. Here—put Noble Crain's number in your phone contacts."

He waited until she picked up her phone before inputting Noble Crain's number on it. "His day starts early and ends late, so don't be afraid to call him first thing in the morning if you're so inclined. It will give him an excuse to come out and enjoy Billy's breakfast. And there's another reason to meet with him here instead of in town. In case your visitor from last night is still watching, he won't see the two of you together."

With that, he started toward the door. As he passed her, he paused and put a hand on her arm. "Try to sleep. You're in a safe place, with a lot of people who look out for one another. Nobody and nothing is going to hurt you here."

"Thank you, Jonah. It's strange, but I do feel safe here."

"I'm glad."

His gaze lingered on her mouth, and his eyes narrowed slightly before he took a step back. "Good night, Annie."

"Good night."

When he stepped into the hall and pulled the door shut, she stood still for a moment, staring at the closed door and wondering at the electric current that had snaked along her arm the moment he'd touched her.

For the space of a heartbeat, seeing the way he'd looked at her, she'd thought he might kiss her.

She'd wanted him to. She'd like to think it was because of the strong, steady feel of him. But it was more than that. More than she wanted to think about at the moment. But if she were honest, she'd simply admit that she was attracted. And had been from the moment they'd met.

She sank down on the edge of the bed and sighed as she looked around, noting the desk and chair and a wall of shelves holding an assortment of books, CDs, and a TV.

She crossed to the floor-to-ceiling windows that offered an amazing view of the majestic mountains looming in the distance. The sun had set, leaving the sky dark and brooding.

Then she walked into the adjoining bathroom that seemed to be a sea of marble. The floor, shower, and jetted tub were all in white, as well as the sink and countertops. A white dressing table held an assortment of lotions in anticipation of anyone who stayed here.

This wasn't what she'd expected to find on a ranch in Wyoming. She'd envisioned something rustic. Or at least utilitarian. But this was so much more.

She opened her suitcase and removed a pair of tailored pajamas, which she carried into the bathroom. Turning on the taps, she filled the tub, settled into the warm water, and lifted an oval of scented soap.

After such a terrifying visit from that stranger, and the threatening message he'd delivered, she ought to be too wired to even give a thought to trying to sleep.

But half an hour later, pleasantly relaxed from her bath, she climbed beneath the covers of the big bed and was asleep within minutes.

*   *   *

As was his custom, Jonah was awake and dressed before dawn. In the kitchen he snagged a mug of coffee and headed for the barn. Once there, he set aside the empty cup and began the rounds of endless ranch chores, beginning with turning the horses out into a fenced meadow before mucking stalls.

Brand and Casey strolled in a few minutes later, followed by Bo, Egan, and Hammond.

Jonah paused in his work and gave a shake of his head. "Why am I not surprised? Since it doesn't take all of you to clean stalls, I'm guessing you're here to grill me."

"Good call, bro." Brand leaned an arm on the top rail of the stall. "You just had to go back to Nonie's and find that pretty stranger, didn't you?"

"As a matter of fact, I didn't. The pretty stranger found me."

Brand shared a look with Casey. "What's that supposed to mean?"

"I never went back to look for her. We met at my cabin. She was out hiking and thought she was on public land."

Brand chuckled. "Only our little brother could have such luck. So she intruded on your private space. But when you found out she was a Dempsey, why didn't you send her packing?"

"I didn't know her name then. The two of us hiked

and formed an instant friendship. A few days later we went riding together and—"

"The two horses," Casey interrupted, snapping his fingers and pointing at Jonah. "And you didn't bother to tell us that you were seeing someone?"

"It was none of your business. Besides, it was too soon. We just spent the morning riding, and then she went to work. Again, we hadn't exchanged last names yet. It wasn't until she came another day..."

Casey turned to the others. "They've been seeing each other for who knows how long, and he keeps it all a big, dark secret."

Jonah ignored the interruption as though it never happened. "...and we were hiking the hills when a storm blew in. We headed back to my cabin, and while I was getting firewood, she came across one of my books and saw my name and picture and put it all together. She told me her uncle had warned her not to go near the Merrick ranch, and she had no idea that I was one of 'them.'"

He made air quotes to emphasize his words.

Bo had remained silent throughout Jonah's narrative. Now his voice was low with emotion. "Once you realized who she was, you had to know this new 'friendship'"— he made the same air quotes—"couldn't continue."

Jonah nodded. "We both agreed about that. She knew there was some sort of feud between her uncle Des and our family. She left my cabin and that was the end of things until I realized I wanted to see her again. I went to her place in town last night to tell her that I could accept her friendship if she could accept mine."

Bo's eyes narrowed. "Despite knowing how I'd feel?"

Jonah put a hand on his father's arm. "Even knowing how you'd feel, Pop. Annie's a good person. We enjoyed each other's company those few days we spent together, and I'm not willing to walk away because of her name."

"And so you brought her to our home and put us in the awkward position of either accepting her or asking her to leave."

"It wasn't that simple. She's in trouble."

The attention of every Merrick sharpened at that word.

"I knew it. What kind of trouble?" Ham demanded.

"I'm not at liberty to say until Annie has had a chance to speak with Noble Crain."

Egan shared a look with the others. "This woman is in trouble with the law?"

"I didn't say that. But she needs to be the one to say what her trouble is, and it may take some time for her to trust us enough to share something so private. For now, I want you to know that I was worried about her safety last night, which is why I brought her here without warning."

Ham glanced at the others before saying, "You haven't been yourself lately, boy, and your brothers thought you were having trouble with the book. But I figured it might be something—someone—else."

"You called it, Ham." Casey shot his great-grandfather

an admiring smile. "You said it sounded like trouble with a woman."

"Most of the really important things in this world are about a man and a woman, boy."

"Right now," Jonah said firmly, "Annie is a *friend*"— he emphasized the word—"of mine who's in trouble, and I intend to be here for her. All I want is for her to be safe."

Bo dropped an arm around his son's shoulders. "Any friend of yours is a friend of ours as well. And since Annie matters to you, son, she matters to us, too."

"Even though she's Des Dempsey's niece?"

"I guess I'll just have to overlook that for the time being."

"Thanks, Pop."

The conversation clearly over, the three older men turned and headed toward the door of the barn.

Brand was grinning. "And here I figured with all these extra hands we'd have the chores done in half the time."

He and Casey chose pitchforks from an assortment of tools hanging along the wall and joined Jonah in cleaning the stalls.

"Let's get going," Casey urged. "Billy's making steak and cheese omelets for breakfast this morning, and I'm already starving."

CHAPTER ELEVEN

Annie heard the chorus of voices long before she entered the kitchen.

Once there, she found herself smiling in spite of her nerves. The room was perfumed with the most wonderful fragrances, from gooey cinnamon rolls fresh out of the oven to freshly ground coffee beans, to sizzling steak under the broiler. "Good morning."

"Annie dear." Meg, seated between Egan and Hammond, hurried over to take her hand. "How did you sleep?"

"Like a baby. Thank you for that sumptuous guest suite."

"I'm glad you were comfortable."

As they talked, the others began slowly drifting into the room.

Brand and Avery were all smiles. Casey, hair still damp from showering after his morning chores, had his arm around Kirby's waist. The two were laughing together at something he'd told her. Their aunt

Liz, wearing faded jeans and a denim shirt, smiled shyly before helping herself to coffee. Chet, his sleeves rolled to the elbows, his face and arms still slick from the mudroom sink, strolled in and greeted everyone before picking up a mug of coffee and speaking softly to Liz.

Jonah walked up beside Annie. "We have orange juice, milk, coffee, and tea. What's your pleasure?"

She glanced at the tray of drinks on the counter. "I'll have some orange juice."

Jonah handed her a frosty glass.

After her first sip, she looked up in surprise. "Is this freshly squeezed?"

Jonah was smiling. "According to Billy, anything other than freshly squeezed isn't worth the time or money."

The cook nodded. "And that's the truth."

Annie took another sip before saying, "I haven't tasted orange juice this good in years."

Billy was beaming as Annie turned to Jonah. "I took your advice and phoned the police chief."

Jonah saw the way his family had come to attention. "What time do you need to get to town?"

"I told him what you said about meeting here this morning." She looked around at his family. "I hope that's all right with all of you."

Meg was quick to say, "Noble is always welcome here. And this is the perfect excuse for him to enjoy Billy's fine breakfast."

The cook was smiling his approval.

"What about work?" Jonah asked.

"I called my uncle to say I'd be delayed. He told me to take the day off. But I think, after I meet with Chief Crain, I should talk with Uncle Des and let him know as much as I can about...all of this."

Jonah nodded. "I think that's wise."

Billy glanced out the window. "The chief is just pulling in."

"I'm betting he broke every speeding record between Devil's Door and here," Brand muttered.

"That's not a problem for him." Casey was chuckling. "Who's going to ticket the chief of police for speeding?"

At a loud rap on the back door, Jonah stepped away from the family. Moments later he returned with the police chief trailing behind him.

Noble Crain was tall and muscled, and his uniform, as always, was spotlessly clean and pressed. His dark hair showed a dusting of gray at the temples and was cut military short.

"'Morning, folks." He whipped off his hat and smiled at everyone, saving his warmest smile for Meg. "Miss Meg, you're looking fine this morning."

"Thank you, Noble. I'm so glad you're able to join us for breakfast."

"I wouldn't miss the chance." He smiled his thanks as Billy handed him a steaming mug of coffee. "Two creams, two sugars. Just the way I like it," he muttered after taking a big sip. "You never forget."

He turned to the pretty woman standing beside Jonah. "Miss Dempsey?"

"Please call me Annie. It's lovely to meet you, Chief Crain."

"I heard you were working at the bank." He shot a glance at the Merrick men before saying, "You're Des Dempsey's niece?"

"That's right. Before coming here, my home was California. The San Francisco area."

"Devil's Door is a long way from there."

Just then, Billy announced that breakfast was ready, and they gathered around the big table. As soon as they were seated, they began passing platters of grilled steaks, thick slices of fried potatoes with grilled onions, and cheesy omelets, as well as a basket of sourdough toast and another of warm cinnamon buns.

As they ate, the conversation centered on the weather, which had been mild, with rain falling nearly every evening for the past week or more, turning the country-side a deep, emerald green.

Noble cut into his steak and nearly sighed in pleasure as he tasted it. "The folks in town are saying they've seen more wildflowers sprouting on the hills this year than they've seen in years."

Chet nodded. "The range grass is higher than it's been in years, too." He glanced at the others. "If the weather continues like this, we'll have the healthiest herd ever."

"And the healthiest profits," Bo said with a contented smile.

Hammond, seated at the head of the table, arched a brow. "I thought I taught you better, boy. You never count your money until it's in your own hand."

Bo nodded. "That's what you taught me, Ham." He glanced around. "What you taught all of us."

Ham sat back. "So we'll forget our profit-and-loss sheets for now and just hope the weather continues the way it's started."

Billy circled the table filling cups with coffee. When he paused beside Annie's chair, he said softly, "You didn't like the omelet?"

"It's the best I've ever tasted." She looked at her half-finished meal. "But I just couldn't eat all this."

Billy grinned at the others. "Ham has a saying for that."

Before Billy could recite it, Ham looked over. "Your eyes were bigger than your stomach, girl."

That had everyone grinning, including Annie.

"I'll remember that in the future, Ham." She sent him a smile as she noted those around her not only cleaning their plates, but also taking seconds.

Of course, she reminded herself, these ranchers had already done more chores in a morning than most men would do in a week.

But it wasn't a lack of hunger that had her unable to enjoy all this wonderful food. Nerves were churning inside her at the thought of what she would have to reveal to the police chief as soon as this meal ended. As a man of the law, she couldn't expect Noble Crain to accept her word as easily as Jonah had. And there was Jonah's family. She was struggling with whether or not to invite them to hear what she had to say. She had the right to ask for privacy, of course. But she had already accepted this family's hospitality. How much easier it would be to let them sit in on her interview with Noble Crain, so neither she nor Jonah would have to recite this horror a second time.

Or was she courting disaster by inviting all of them into her private hell?

Noble drained his third cup of coffee and sat back. "Billy, it's a good thing I don't get here very often. If I had the chance to eat like this every day, I'd need to order my uniforms three sizes bigger."

While the others shared a laugh, he looked around. "I don't know how you all manage to stay so fit."

Brand patted his flat stomach. "Try mucking stalls and hauling a hundred-pound manure cart outside before breakfast and you'll get an idea of why we require so much fuel."

Noble nodded. "The one thing I've learned is that ranching's not for the fainthearted."

Billy was smiling as he circled the table with a wheeled trolley, loading dishes and handing around extra plates of cinnamon rolls.

Seeing that the family intended to linger awhile, Chief Crain turned to Annie. "Maybe you and I could go in another room and have that talk."

She felt Jonah's hand close over hers beneath the table and welcomed that small act of comfort. Whatever doubt she had dissolved.

"Since Jonah already knows my story, maybe it would be easier if you and I talked here, in front of the others." She looked around until her gaze settled on Meg. "After your kind hospitality, I don't want any of you to think I'm keeping secrets."

"If that's what you'd like." Chief Crain took a small notebook and pen from his pocket before giving her his complete attention.

"Yesterday I was at the little apartment above the hair salon that I rent from Julie Franklyn, when I heard a knock on my door. I thought it was Julie or one of her sons, but it was a man—a stranger. Before I could close the door, he pushed his way inside and told me he was delivering a message from Arlen Lender. He said that Arlen wanted me to know that I couldn't hide from him."

"Who is Arlen Lender and why would you hide from him?"

"Like my uncle Des, I work in banking, in the financial sector in San Francisco. Arlen was a man I had been seeing for some time, until I discovered a huge sum of money that had been deposited in a bank account opened in my name without my knowledge."

Noble held up a hand. "How much money are we talking about?"

"A million dollars."

Annie heard several sounds of surprise issued from the family around the table.

She kept her gaze averted, unwilling to meet their eyes. "When I told Arlen what I'd discovered and that I intended to report this to the bank and the authorities, he told me that would be a mistake."

"Did he say why?"

"He said that I would be arrested for accepting stolen money and would spend the better part of my life in prison."

"Did he reveal where the money came from? Did he identify anyone who was actually involved in the theft?"

"He didn't. But I have to believe that he was involved in some way and deliberately chose me to take the fall."

"Why would he set you up?"

"He didn't say, but I believe it's because I'm an insider in banking. Like Uncle Des, my parents made their money in banking and encouraged me to follow their lead. I suspect this was all part of some grand plan."

Noble pursed his lips. "Does your uncle know about this?"

"Not all of it. But now that you know, my next stop will be the bank in Devil's Door. I'm hoping you'll go there with me."

The chief nodded. "Now, about Arlen Lender. How did you meet him?"

"I was introduced to him at a dinner for the president of the bank where I worked as a private investment banker. After meeting me, he requested that I handle his finances. The bank president was thrilled. He said word was that Arlen would be bringing not only a great deal of money to us, but other wealthy investors as well."

"Did you have any reason to suspect Arlen of anything illegal?"

"Not a hint."

"What about the bank president? Do you think he and Arlen were connected in some way?"

"I have no idea. But I seriously doubt that. He seems to be an honest, honorable man. But then, so did Arlen, before all this came to light."

"You said you believe you were targeted. Do you think it was deliberate, because of your family's connections, or do you think you just happened to be a convenient mark?"

She shook her head. "Again, I don't know." She took a deep breath. "Just telling you all this, I realize how much I don't know. But I do know this. The man who came to my apartment last night left me terrified."

"Did he threaten you?"

"Only with insinuation. I didn't see a weapon. He didn't raise his fists. But I was absolutely terrified, not only by how he'd forced his way into my place, but also by the impression I got that he would absolutely do whatever Arlen told him to do."

"Were you afraid of Arlen Lender?"

"Not at first. He was handsome, charming, and seemingly well connected. But once he warned me not to go to the authorities, I was terrified."

"Of him?"

"Yes. As he was threatening me with prison time, I had a growing sense that he was evil. I'm ashamed to admit that I ran. I left town that night, even though I had no idea what I would do or where I would go. But I knew I couldn't stay there another day. Not while he was setting me up for something sinister."

Throughout her entire narrative, the Merrick family had been silent and watchful. Even Billy, who had been collecting dishes for the dishwasher, had paused behind the kitchen counter, keeping a respectful silence.

Noble Crain closed his notebook. "I'll need to report all of this to the state police. They have the resources to do a thorough investigation of this Arlen Lender and learn who his associates might be. They'll also be able to find out if there is a bank theft of a million dollars that hasn't been resolved."

He stood, and Annie got to her feet to face him.

"I suggest you phone your uncle and arrange a meeting at his bank today. Let me know the time and I'll be there."

"Thank you, Chief Crain."

He offered a handshake. "I wish I could tell you we'll have this sorted out in no time, but that will be up to the state police. And if this turns out to be something more, we could be including federal authorities in this as well."

Annie nodded. "Thank you for whatever help you can give me. It's nice to know I'm not alone."

"Speaking of alone..." Noble turned to the Merrick family. "Of all the places to spend the night, how did you happen to end up here?"

"I know what you're thinking." Annie managed a tight smile. "Jonah and I met by accident and formed a friendship before learning each other's last name. But once we introduced ourselves, we realized any friendship would be difficult, if not impossible."

Chief Crain turned to Jonah. "And yet, here you are, together."

Jonah nodded. "I'd already concluded that our families' feud needn't be carried into another generation. But just as I arrived at Annie's place last night to tell her this, the stranger stormed out of her apartment. When I heard that he'd threatened her, I invited her to spend the night here."

Annie turned to include the others. "Where I've been warmly welcomed and felt completely safe. I'll never be able to thank you all enough, especially since you had no idea that I was involved in something so unsavory."

Meg circled the table and put an arm around Annie's

shoulders. "Now that I've heard your story, I'm so glad Jonah had the sense to bring you here."

"Thank you, Miss Meg. I'm so thankful to be here."

"Well." Chief Crain nodded to Annie. "I'll get back to town and get the state police started on this. You call me whenever you and your uncle have decided on a time for that meeting."

He turned to the others. "Thanks again for that fine meal."

When he was gone, the others paused beside Annie to touch a hand to her arm or to say a few words of comfort before heading off to their work for the day.

Ham paused beside her and fixed her with a look she couldn't discern. Though his eyes were slightly narrowed and his tone was firm, his words were measured. "Trust Noble and the state boys to get to the bottom of this. In the meantime, I'm wondering how your uncle will take the news."

"When I told him I was in trouble and needed a job and a place to stay, he was very supportive."

"That's good. But he doesn't know the extent of your trouble?"

She shook her head. "That's why I need to meet with him today. When he hears everything, he may regret inviting me here. After all, his bank is his great pride and joy. If he believes that I've done anything to tarnish his reputation, he may turn on me."

Ham started to say something, then seemed to think better about it and walked away.

Annie turned to Jonah. "Before I call my uncle, I need to know if you're free to drive me to town."

He nodded. "Whenever you say."

"Thank you." She took a deep breath. "I'll call now and see when Uncle Des is available."

CHAPTER TWELVE

Jonah drove the truck along the curving ribbon of asphalt that led to the highway. In the back of the truck was Annie's luggage. She'd insisted on packing her belongings and leaving a note of thanks for the night she'd spent with his family.

Seeing her hands twisting in her lap, he reached over and put a big hand over hers. "How're you doing?"

She tried for a smile. "I'm a mess."

"It's going to be okay, Annie."

"I wish I could believe that." She sighed. "Just telling it all to the police chief made me realize what I'm facing. This isn't some little misunderstanding. I've been set up by someone who must have known I would panic when I discovered a million dollars in my name. Maybe Arlen thought I could be controlled by threats, or maybe he thought I would simply trust him to take care of me. When the chief said the state police might be calling in federal authorities, it hit me like a building had fallen on me. Whoever Arlen is associated with, I'm guessing they have to be professionals who have probably considered every angle before any of this started. They probably went over every scenario, to plan what they would do if I went to the authorities or if I fled California. They've probably been watching me right from the beginning. I never had a chance to hide from them. For all I know, my office, my apartment, could be bugged. Maybe they have a camera watching me right now…"

"Hey. Don't do this to yourself, Annie. You have to confide in your uncle and trust in the police…"

"And what if they can't help? What if I did exactly what Arlen and the others expected? Devil's Door isn't exactly a teeming metropolis. That stranger found me in a matter of days."

"Don't sell our chief and our state police short. They're professionals, too. And if they invite federal authorities into the investigation, they'll bring in even more smart guys."

"Oh, I hope so, Jonah." She turned to stare at the passing countryside. "But even if the authorities are up to it, this meeting with my uncle has me tied in knots. What if he doesn't believe me? What if he does but believes that I've brought shame on his good name?"

"Don't get ahead of yourself, Annie. When you told him you were in trouble, he invited you to come here and even offered you a job. That doesn't sound like someone who would toss you to the wolves."

"That was before he knew the full extent of my troubles."

As they drove slowly along Main Street, Jonah pulled into the newly paved parking lot of the Devil's Door bank. Des Dempsey had added a new glass-and-chrome façade to the hundred-year-old brick building just a year ago, and the big windows gleamed in the late-morning sunlight.

Jonah brought the truck to a stop beside the entrance and circled around to open the passenger door for her.

Annie stepped down and paused.

They were so close their bodies were touching. He felt the heat of her through his shirt and had an almost overpowering desire to wrap her in his arms and tell her everything would be all right.

She looked up at him, and he absorbed the jolt through his system.

"Will you come in with me?"

He shook his head. "Nobody named Merrick has been inside this building since I was a toddler. There's no need to add to your uncle's discomfort today. But I have plenty to do while you meet with him. I have a list of supplies to pick up. Why don't you text me when your meeting is over and we'll have lunch at Nonie's."

She put a hand on his arm, adding another rush of heat through his system. "Thanks. I'd like that." She sucked in a breath. "Wish me luck."

His tone lowered. "All the luck in the world."

He watched as she lifted her head and marched determinedly into the bank, the expression on her face both resolute and resigned.

*   *   *

"Hi, Nonie." Jonah sauntered into Nonie's Wild Horses Saloon and headed toward a back booth.

She looked up from the grill. "Ready for a chilled longneck?"

"Make it two." He kept on going and settled where he could see the door.

Minutes later, Nonie set two bottles of beer in front of him. "You must be having some kind of a day."

At his questioning look, she chuckled. "Two beers before lunch?"

"Oh." He smiled. "The other one's for..." His smile grew as he caught sight of Annie stepping through the doorway.

Nonie followed the direction of his gaze and nodded. "Leave it to you to snag the prettiest new woman in town." She leaned close to whisper, "You realize she's a Dempsey."

"Yeah. That she is." He got to his feet as Annie threaded her way through the crowded tables. "And as you said, the prettiest woman in town. Except for you, of course, Nonie."

"Liar. But a sweet liar."

They were both laughing as Annie walked up to the booth. Jonah took her hand and waited until she was seated before taking the seat across from her, all the while staring intently at her face, hoping to read her mood.

"You two need a little time before ordering?"

Neither of them acknowledged Nonie or even looked at her.

"Yeah. Well...let me know when you're ready." With a knowing smile, she walked away.

Jonah searched Annie's face. "How are you?"

"I'm...okay."

"And your uncle?"

Annie shrugged. "To his credit, he listened without comment, though I could tell he was getting more upset with every detail. He agreed with Chief Crain that if bank fraud is involved, the state police will have to call in federal authorities."

"What about your job?"

She looked down at the scarred wooden tabletop, as though memorizing every initial carved there over the years. "He doesn't think I should be working in a bank while the investigation is ongoing. He said if word got out about my involvement in some kind of million-dollar theft, his regulars would leave in droves."

"How would they hear about it?"

"Uncle Des believes it will make the headlines sooner or later." She sighed. "I hope he's wrong, but if not, I hope it's much later. I don't think I'm ready to have my life laid bare for everyone to pick over."

"Did Des at least invite you to stay with him?"

"Aunt Bev is in poor health. He said she was 'delicate,' so he doesn't think it's a good idea. But he said he'd make arrangements for me to stay in a bed-and-breakfast just outside of town. He knows the owners and said they're good people who would be able to keep an eye out for any shady characters while keeping me safe."

Jonah made a sound of disgust. "He's right about one thing. Mandy and Jamie Ward are good people. They also have a big spread, four little kids, and they just opened their ranch as a bed-and-breakfast to help pay the bills. Jamie's in the fields all day and Mandy's cooking and cleaning for guests while raising her little ones. Those two are hardly equipped to do all that and watch out for strangers who may or may not be a threat to your safety."

She sat back, looking defeated. "The chief wants me to remain here in Devil's Door. I don't know what else I can do."

"You can stay out at my family's ranch."

"That isn't an option."

"I see it as your only option. We're off the beaten track. Anyone attempting to get to you would be spotted by one of the dozen or more wranglers working the herds, or one of us." Seeing the way she was about to protest, he added, "You may have noticed that there are a lot of us. Some might say too many. But that's all in your favor. If you found yourself in any sort of trouble, the odds are half a dozen of us would be there for you."

"You said yourself that no member of the Merrick

family has set foot in my uncle's bank since you were a toddler. What makes you think he'd sit still for his niece living with the Merrick family?"

"Unless he has a better offer, why should he have a say in the matter?"

"Jonah, he's not only worried about my safety. He's also worried about the reputation of his bank if even a hint of scandal should be leaked to the public."

"And his idea of keeping you safe is to put you up in a bed-and-breakfast that welcomes strangers?"

"He's a good man, Jonah. But I could see how torn he was between worrying about me, Aunt Bev, and his precious reputation."

"Which is why your wisest course of action is to stay at my place until all of this is resolved."

"This investigation could take weeks. Months, even."

He adopted a drawl. "Then it looks like we'll have time to make a real cowboy out of you, little missy."

"That's not funny."

"Listen to the man." At Nonie's voice, they both looked up. She was smiling. "I've been standing here for ages waiting to see what the two of you want for lunch. Right now, I'm thinking you're both ready to eat fire and brimstone."

Jonah managed a grin. "Chili. Hot."

"Two, please," Annie said.

"Done." Nonie walked away just as Noble Crain took her place beside their booth.

"Nonie wasn't the only one listening." He shot Annie an apologetic look. "Sorry," he said as he slid in next to her. His voice lowered. "But I came over here to let you know that the state police are on the case and have already involved the feds. It won't take them long to determine where the million dollars came from. That kind of theft doesn't happen every day. Once they have that information, they'll start to move on the people involved, starting with Arlen Lender. I'll let you know once I hear anything more."

He started to get up, then seemed to think better of it and sat back down. "And for the record, Annie, I agree with Jonah. The safest place for you to be while this is being resolved is at the Merrick ranch."

"I can't just—"

"Miss Meg is a pro at making folks feel welcome. Just ask Brand's wife, Avery, or Casey's wife, Kirby. Miss Meg will do the same for you, Annie. And I'll tell you this. I'll breathe a whole lot easier knowing you're there. There's no tougher family I know than the Merrick family. And even though I don't always agree with the way they rush in where angels wouldn't tread, I know this. If I'm ever in the fight of my life, I'd want them to have my back."

He did stand then, and tipped his hat. "I'll be contacting you whenever I have any news. You two have a good lunch now, you hear?"

As Noble strolled away, Jonah reached across the table and caught Annie's hand. "There you have it.

Straight from the horse's mouth. The Merrick family is one kick-ass bunch. You stick with us, and we'll see you through this, ma'am."

She couldn't stop the smile that tugged at the corners of her mouth. Or the feeling that he was right. If last night was any indication, his family, despite knowing her last name, had been able to put aside whatever feelings they had for her family to make her welcome. And the toughest of them all, old Hammond Merrick, who had seemed none too pleased at first, had even begun to soften, at least a little, when he realized she was in trouble.

When Nonie served their bowls of steaming chili along with a tray of chopped onions, shredded cheese, and thick slices of garlic toast, she crowded into the booth beside Jonah and studied Annie closely. "I can't say I'm surprised that this cowboy made a move to cut you out of the herd. After all, the Merrick men have an eye for pretty women. But how in the world did a Dempsey agree to eat lunch with a Merrick, when your families haven't spoken in years?"

Annie exchanged a grin with Jonah before turning to Nonie. "Maybe it's time the two of us decided to break the ice."

"Ice? Honey, it's been more like a wall of steel between Des and Bo Merrick."

Annie shrugged. "The truth is, I have no clue about their feud. I'm hoping someone will fill me in."

Nonie put a hand on Jonah's arm. "I'll leave that

to the man who makes his living using all those big, fancy words."

As they shared a smile, she got to her feet. "Next time you come to town, bring that handsome father of yours."

"I'll give it my best, Nonie."

Annie watched as Nonie walked away. " 'That handsome father of yours'?"

Jonah chuckled. "She's had a thing for him for years. It's the worst-kept secret in town."

"Does he share her feelings?"

"Pop plays his cards close to the vest." He winked. "But he stands a little taller whenever he walks in here."

The two were smiling as they bent to their lunch.

As Annie took a cooling sip of beer, she surprised Jonah by saying, "After lunch, I'd like to visit a florist shop."

At Jonah's arched brow, she grinned. "I want to bring Miss Meg the biggest bouquet of flowers I can find. Not that it will make up for the extra work my presence will cause, but maybe it might ease the burden a little when she learns that she's about to have a boarder who has no exit plan. I could end up being there so long you'll see moss growing on me."

Jonah merely smiled.

She gave him a long look. "What's that for?"

"I'm glad you agreed to stay with us. And I'm just thinking that even draped in moss, you'll be the prettiest girl around."

CHAPTER THIRTEEN

As Jonah and Annie walked out of Nonie's, he led her across the street to a little shop nestled between the bakery and the hair salon.

He pointed to the gorgeous display in the window. "Let's see if Melissa has some kind of lavish bouquet that will soften up Gram Meg—not that you need it."

Annie paused outside the shop, her brow furrowed. "The doubts are creeping in again. As much as I'd like to feel safe, I just can't imagine asking your family to put up with me for an unknown length of time. Jonah, I don't know if this is a good idea."

"Hey, you two."

At the feminine voice, Jonah and Annie turned to find Avery and Kirby walking toward them. Behind them strolled their husbands, their arms filled with handled bags.

"I told you it was them." Avery turned to Brand, who was shifting a heavy bag from one hand to the other. "We'd just stepped out of Stuff and thought we'd spotted you."

While the others gathered around, Kirby touched a hand to Annie's arm. "How did your meeting go with your uncle?"

"To say he was shocked would be putting it mildly. But he said he supports me and just wants the whole thing cleared up with as little publicity as possible."

Avery linked her arm through Brand's. "Will you be staying with him?"

Annie shook her head, avoiding looking at them. "My aunt isn't well, and he thinks I'd be more comfortable somewhere else."

Avery put a hand on Annie's. "Oh no. So where will you stay?"

"With us," Jonah said firmly.

"Perfect." Avery, Brand, Casey, and Kirby spoke in unison.

"It isn't that simple." Annie was shaking her head. "I was trying to explain to Jonah how complicated this could be. Until the investigation is complete, I could be in a kind of limbo for weeks, or even months."

"But you can't be alone. That stranger found out where you were staying. You said yourself when you tried to close the door in his face, he pushed his way inside." Avery looked at Kirby for confirmation. "Jonah's right. There's safety in numbers. Come stay with us. We'll see to your safety until this matter is settled."

Brand added, "I'd like to see that guy try to force

his way into our house. He'd be in for the fight of his life."

Annie looked at Jonah's brothers and their wives, then up into Jonah's face.

He was grinning as he lifted his palms in mock surrender. "Before you start accusing me, I give you my word that I didn't pay them to say all that."

After a moment of laughter, Avery felt the need to explain. "Annie, both Kirby and I lived through some really terrifying situations, and both of us are here today because of the Merrick family." She glanced at Kirby before saying, "Remind us to tell you about it one day."

Annie's smile spread slowly as she caught Jonah's sly grin. "You did warn me that there are a lot of you. And apparently you all stick together." She glanced around at the brothers and their wives. "You all can be very persuasive. I promise to think about what you've said."

"While you're giving it some thought, why don't you two join us?" Brand winked at his wife. "We were just heading to Katie's Kitchen." He pointed to the bakeshop.

Jonah and Annie exchanged a smile and a small nod before following the others into a pretty little shop, inhaling the wonderful fragrance of sugar and cinnamon that filled the air.

"Hi, Merrick family. Welcome." The young woman behind the counter held out a crystal plate. "These are my specials today. Peanut butter brownies. Feel free to sample one."

Amid oohs and aahs, they tasted while they studied the endless parade of fancy desserts in the glass display case.

Before they could make up their minds, Casey made a suggestion. "Let's each get something different so we can all have a taste of everything."

"Says the cowboy who never met a sweet he didn't love," Kirby said with a grin.

"And you ought to know, babe. You're my sweetest weakness of all."

Instead of Jonah's usual disdain for his brother's silly love talk, he held his silence. That had his brothers glancing over at him.

Brand studied the assortment of goodies. "I like the way you think, bro. I'm willing to try a little of everything. Just see that you don't take giant bites. Leave some for the rest of us."

With much laughter, they made their choices before settling at a round table in a corner of the room.

Jonah called out, "What does everyone want to drink?"

After taking their order, he remained at the counter to collect mugs of coffee and cups of Earl Grey, while the others began passing around coconut macaroons, lemon bars, fudge brownies, and one of Katie's assortment packages that offered mini cookies and handmade candies.

Casey leaned close to Annie. "Before Jonah gets here, we're all wondering what kind of magic you used to get him away from his latest work in progress."

"Magic?" She looked around and, seeing they were all listening, couldn't resist saying, "Maybe that's it. Have you ever thought that I could be a master of black magic?"

"So you used a love potion," Brand muttered. "That explains it. You do realize our brother has never let anything, or anyone, get in the way of his work. So you must be special."

That had them all grinning just as Jonah circled the table, handing out their drinks.

He glanced at Brand. "What's so funny?"

"You, bro. Do you realize you haven't once said that you need to get back to your cabin and work?"

"Maybe I'm doing research while I'm here."

"Only if you're researching how to satisfy a sweet tooth."

"Well, there you go." He settled himself beside Annie and casually put a hand over hers.

Around the table, the others took notice and shared meaningful looks.

While they began tasting, the door to the bakeshop opened to admit a bewhiskered Ben Harper.

"All three Merrick brothers." Ben ambled over to shake hands with Jonah, then Brand, and then Casey, before tipping his hat. "And their ladies. Hello to all."

Jonah nodded toward Annie. "Ben Harper, owner of the grain and feed, this is Annie Dempsey."

"You Des's niece?" The man doffed his wide-brimmed hat.

"I am."

Annie saw the way he glanced quickly at Jonah, then at his brothers, before looking away. Knowing the question on his mind brought a smile to Annie's lips.

"Nice meeting you, Annie. And good seeing all of you." He headed toward the counter, where another man who'd just entered approached.

"Hey, Doc."

At Casey's greeting, the man with the bowl haircut, dressed in a white lab coat, turned. Seeing them, he hurried over. "Good to see all of you. How's that great-grandfather of yours?"

"As tough as ever," Jonah said with a laugh. "Doc Peterson, I'd like you to meet Annie Dempsey."

"Annie." He offered a handshake. "Any relation to Des Dempsey?"

"My uncle."

He arched a brow. "Very nice meeting you, Annie." He turned away. "Sorry to rush off. I have to get back to the clinic, so I called my order in ahead to save time."

At the counter, Katie handed him a handled bag before he dashed out.

When Noble Crain walked in, Jonah nudged Annie,

and the two of them shared a laugh before Jonah called, "Are you following us, Chief?"

Noble strolled over to their table. "I see we all had the same idea. The best way to quench the fire of Nonie's chili is with some of Katie's sweet treats."

"That's what we're doing." Brand pointed to the plates scattered around their table. "We decided to try one of everything."

"It's a good thing you work as hard as you do. This little visit will cost me a hundred sit-ups."

Casey pointed to the chief's flat stomach. "You might want to go for two hundred if you try those peanut butter brownies."

Noble was chuckling as he made his way to the counter to place an order.

When the last crumb had been eaten and their cups emptied, the party made their way to the sidewalk, pausing every few steps to greet neighbors and old friends.

After she answered a dozen questions about the relationship of Annie to her uncle Des, Jonah turned to her. "Sorry. It's part of being a small town, where everyone knows everyone's business."

She couldn't hide her smile. "I was just thinking the same thing. It's not something I've ever experienced before, but, despite the questions, I like it."

"You do? You don't find the explanations tedious?"

"I think it's sweet that they know my uncle and wonder why I'm"—she fumbled for a word—"consorting with the enemy. And that they're all too polite to pursue the issue." She breathed a sigh. "They're just good, concerned people."

Jonah felt an odd burst of pride.

Brand, Casey, and their wives had their heads together briefly before walking up to surround Annie.

Brand spoke for all of them. "We have to head home. But we're all in agreement that we really hope you stay at the ranch until this…business is decided. Just remember, Annie, there's safety in numbers."

As they said their goodbyes and walked away, Annie turned to Jonah with a hint of a smile curving her lips.

She took in a breath before saying, "Okay. You win. The Merrick family is a mighty force. Let's visit the florist and see how many bushels of flowers I can buy to soften the blow when your grandmother gets the news of her latest boarder."

Melissa, owner of the flower shop, had fashioned a glorious mixture of hydrangeas, ivy, and the palest pink roses for Miss Meg, all wrapped in a cloud of silky white paper and streams of ribbons.

Outside the shop, Annie handed the bundle to Jonah. "If you wouldn't mind carrying these to your truck, I need to let Julie Franklyn know that I'm canceling my lease on her apartment. Since I paid her for the first month, plus a cleaning fee and a deposit, I don't owe her anything, but I want to let her know she's free to find a new tenant. And while I'm in town, I'd like to take a walk through the apartment to make sure I haven't left anything behind. Then I'll follow you to the ranch in my car."

Jonah considered a moment. "I think it's a mistake to take your car. It might be better to leave it parked behind Julie's."

"Why?"

"So that if Park is reporting back to Arlen Lender, he'll continue to believe you're still here. We can hope that he's gone, but if not, at least you're buying a little time by having him think you're upstairs."

She gave it a moment's thought before nodding. "All right. I guess I won't need my car. I'm willing to leave it here for now."

Jonah closed a hand over hers. "I'll drive the truck over here and wait for you in the back of the building. And, Annie..." He paused. "You may want to casually ask if anyone was around looking for you last night."

She gave a thoughtful nod.

Jonah watched her walk toward the hair salon before crossing the street to retrieve his truck.

Once there, he phoned his grandmother to explain that he'd invited Annie to stay with them while Chief Crain and the police handled their investigation.

He could hear the smile in her voice as she said, "I'm glad she's coming back. Should we expect the two of you for supper tonight?"

"Yes. She's going through her apartment now. We'll be at the ranch in an hour or so."

"I'm looking forward to her company."

"Thanks, Gram Meg." He paused. "This means a lot to me."

"I know it does. And you mean a lot to me, Jonah dear."

He sat there for a moment after disconnecting. There were so many things his grandmother could have asked. How the meeting went with Annie's uncle. Why she wasn't staying with her relatives. But Gram Meg had always been a remarkable woman. He'd never known her to be anything less than warm and welcoming. And that, he thought, was exactly what Annie needed right now while she made her way through this maze of troubles.

Annie hung the last of her things in the guest room closet and stowed her suitcase. Afterward, she walked to the wall of floor-to-ceiling windows and stared at the serene countryside. Just seeing the hills black with cattle and the sturdy mountains rising in the distance had a calming effect on her. How could anything dangerous or criminal be lurking in this pastoral setting?

She crossed her arms over her chest and watched the flight of a hawk, drifting almost lazily on a current of air. Suddenly the hawk took a nosedive, heading to the ground with such speed she was certain it would crash and shatter into a million pieces. Instead it caught something in its talons and lifted into the air before landing on a flat stretch of lawn below her window.

Through the closed pane of glass, she could hear the pitiful cry of a tiny creature before that sharp beak was lifted, filled with flesh and fur. Blood pooled around the predator and its victim.

She turned away and covered her face with her hands, horrified at the carnage.

She walked unsteadily toward a chair and dropped down, shoulders slumped.

There was her answer. Even here, in this picture-perfect setting, there were predators and prey. Victors and victims.

She made her way to the luxurious bathroom and splashed cold water on her face before looking in the mirror. Satisfied that her color had returned, she made her way downstairs to face Jonah's family.

She lifted her chin. No matter what Arlen Lender and his cronies thought, she intended to prove to her uncle and to herself that she was nobody's victim.

Despite the million questions that plagued her, and the fear that came over her in waves whenever she thought about the threats made since her discovery of that bank account, she was committed to seeing this through.

The family had gathered, as always, in the warm kitchen, close to the fireplace. The chorus of voices grew silent as she stepped inside.

Jonah walked over to take her hand and lead her toward the others.

"So." Hammond set aside his longneck. "You're back, girl."

Before she could say a word, Casey winked. "We were hoping you couldn't stand to leave us. In fact, we were counting on it. It happens all the time."

That had the desired effect, leaving her relaxed and smiling.

"What's your drink of choice tonight?" Jonah indicated the tray.

She walked over and helped herself to a glass of red wine.

Meg called, "I'll have one of those too, dear."

Annie handed her a glass and the older woman smiled and sipped before asking, "Are you all settled in?"

"I am. Thank you again."

Avery clinked her glass to Annie's. "I'm so glad you're here."

"Thank you."

"Me too." Kirby touched the rim of her beer to Annie's glass. "It's always nice to have another female in the house to counter all these guys."

At that, Liz looked up almost shyly before turning to her mother. "I never thought of it that way. There are still way more men than women here, but we're catching up."

Meg chuckled before saying to Annie, "Liz is right. We'll take all the woman power we can get."

"Amen to that." Casey lifted his beer in a salute, while the others laughed.

When Billy called them to dinner, they gathered around the big table adorned with Annie's exotic floral display and began the nightly ritual of passing platters and filling one another in on the details of their day as they enjoyed another of Billy's fabulous meals.

CHAPTER FOURTEEN

Meg touched a napkin to her lips. "Another perfect dinner, Billy." She looked at the others. "Shall we take our dessert and coffee on the porch?"

With nods of approval, they began making their way from the kitchen and settling on the comfortable furniture on the back porch. Billy pushed a trolley through the doorway and began filling cups with coffee before handing them around. He lifted the lid from a footed cake plate to reveal a pineapple upside-down cake.

Meg turned to her husband. "Oh, Egan. Your favorite."

The older man beamed as Billy handed him the first slice. After a taste, Egan looked around with a bright smile, then settled his gaze on Annie. "When you get a taste of this, you'll understand why it's been my favorite my whole life." He turned to Hammond. "Remember how Ma used to make this for me every year on my birthday?"

Ham nodded. "It was the only cake you asked for.

And every year I used to hope you'd change your mind and just for once ask for her Black Forest cake."

"That was for your birthday," Egan said between bites.

"Indeed it was." Ham fell silent, and the others knew that when he turned to look at the sunset over the mountains, he was really seeing his beloved Mandy's grave.

They lingered over their dessert, enjoying the cool evening, the red glow of the sun setting behind the Tetons, and second helpings of Billy's pineapple upside-down cake.

Later, as Ham, Egan, and Meg called their good nights before heading off to bed, Casey turned to his father and brothers. "I brought down one of the calves from the herd. He's in the barn."

Bo looked up. "What's the problem?"

"Some sort of infection in the eye. I want him isolated in a stall until I determine if it's no big deal or if it's contagious."

"Good thinking, son."

"Want to have a look?"

"Sure thing."

The men started toward the barn, while on the porch Billy loaded up the last of the dishes on the trolley and made his way to the kitchen.

Avery glanced at Kirby, Liz, and Annie. "Anybody tired?"

"I'm not," Kirby answered, setting the glider she was sitting on into motion before turning to Annie, who'd shared a porch swing with Jonah. "How about you? Is the day catching up with you?"

Annie shook her head. "I'm so wired I'm not sure I'll be able to settle down enough to sleep at all tonight." She patted the empty seat. "Would one of you care to join me?"

Liz left the chaise and settled herself beside Annie.

"I know what you mean about being wired. I still remember the feeling." Avery pulled her chair between the swing and the glider so that the four of them had formed a close, comfortable circle.

Annie looked over. "What had you wired, Avery?"

"The trouble I'd left in Michigan when I came here to offer my physical therapy services to Brand."

"Trouble?" The word had Annie leaning toward her.

In as few words as possible, Avery told her about the text threats she'd received and the decapitated mouse that had arrived in the mail in a padded envelope.

"I was sure the cause of all my troubles was a doctor I'd dated, because one of the nurses told me he'd only singled me out so he could win a spot on my father's surgical team."

"What a jerk," Annie muttered.

"Yeah. My thoughts exactly. That same nurse came here to warn me that he was out to harm me. It turned out, when Liz and I were alone with her up in the hills, she was the one planning on doing the harm."

"Oh, how horrible." Annie looked from Avery to Liz. "Thank heaven you had each other."

"We didn't." Avery shook her head. "She managed to separate us, and then she drugged me, hoping to get rid of me."

Liz picked up the thread of the story. "When I realized what she'd done, I ran to my family, who'd heard from Chief Crain that the nurse was dangerous and were fanning out to find her. I was so afraid that we would all be too late. But we rallied, and by the time the state police arrived, Avery was safe and the nurse had been subdued by her own drugs."

"And," Avery added, "just as I was about to fly back to Michigan with my father, Brand turned into my knight in shining armor by admitting that he loved me and didn't want me to go."

"Oh. How romantic." Annie placed a hand over her heart. "And so dramatic."

"That's just the beginning of our dramas." Liz smiled at Kirby. "Tell Annie how you and Casey met."

Annie was shaking her head. "It's going to be hard to top that story, Kirby."

That had Kirby laughing. "Casey and I met up in the hills. In a cave, where Casey had taken shelter from a snowstorm. My boss had texted me about an escaped convict in the area, and I was trying to leave the hills when I took a nasty tumble and broke my ankle. I was desperate for shelter for the night, and when I found Casey in the cave I'd stumbled upon, I aimed my rifle at him, thinking he was the convict."

Annie shook her head. "Wow. Talk about drama."

"Yeah. We wrestled for the gun, and he won by sheer brute strength. But seeing the tender way he treated an injured mustang in his care, I was convinced he was a veterinarian, just as he claimed. And he ended up bringing me to his ranch, after we managed to dig ourselves out of the cave that got buried in an avalanche. Then I discovered that my truck was stolen and my apartment had been ransacked, so I came back to stay at the Merrick ranch until I could buy my uncle's ranch, which had been deserted since his death. When I learned I couldn't buy it, I made a sentimental journey there to see it for the last time and was kidnapped by the escaped convict who had been using it for his hideout."

Annie put a hand to her mouth to stifle her little gasp. "How did you escape?"

"Casey arrived at the ranch, and when I tried to send him away to save his life, he figured out something was wrong. He and his family stormed the ranch house, and though he took a bullet, he fought like a madman for me."

"As I recall, you fought just as hard for him." Avery exchanged a grin with Liz, who nodded.

Annie turned to Liz. "Okay. Two out of three. Don't tell me you have a tale of danger to top theirs."

Liz was shaking her head when Avery said, "Hers is a real heartbreaker. The danger wasn't physical, but it was a terrible blow to her heart." Gently she asked, "Can you talk about it, Liz?"

For a moment the shy woman paused, as though

unsure how to respond. Then slowly, painfully, she told Annie about falling in love with Luke Miller, and how her best friend CC Farmer hated him and refused to be her maid of honor at their wedding. By the time she spoke about her wedding day, and learning that Luke and CC had run off together, her voice was little more than a whisper laced with pain.

"Oh, Liz." Caught up in the story, Annie reached over and gathered both of Liz's hands in hers. "How horrible. I can't imagine the pain and humiliation you must have suffered."

Liz looked up, blinking back tears. "For nearly fifteen years I avoided going to town and could barely speak to strangers. I'd locked myself away in my own private little prison." She took a breath. "And then one night, over wine..."

"An entire bottle of wine," Avery said with a laugh.

"That's right. After an entire bottle of wine, I told Avery the whole miserable story, and she said something that changed my life."

Annie glanced at Avery, who merely smiled.

Liz said solemnly, "Avery said this doesn't define who I am. The shame is on Luke and CC. And the loss is theirs, not mine. She told me to walk through town proudly, with my head held high."

Annie turned to Avery. "Good for you." She squeezed Liz's hand. "And good for you, too."

Liz managed a wry smile. "To be honest, I still avoid going to town as much as I can. But when I have to, I refuse to feel any shame. And ever since I've opened up about my painful past, I have a new sense of freedom. To ride. To be myself. To travel the hills taking my photographs."

"That's right, Jonah told me you're a photographer."

"Wait 'til you see her studio," Avery boasted. "Since Liz won't brag, I'll do it for her. You've probably seen her photos in all kinds of glossy magazines. Her work is amazing."

Liz blushed. "You're welcome to visit my studio anytime, Annie."

"Is it in town?"

Liz shook her head. "It's right here on the ranch. Out in the barn."

"Oh, I'd love to see it."

"I'd love to show it to you. If you're free tomorrow, let me know."

"Tomorrow I may join you." Kirby stifled a yawn. "But right now, I need my beauty sleep."

"Me too." Avery got to her feet, and Annie and Liz followed suit.

Inside, as they called good night and went their separate ways, Annie climbed the stairs and let herself into the guest room.

Her room, she thought. For the next few days or weeks, this would be her home.

She sank down onto the edge of the bed and thought about all she'd heard tonight.

What amazing women. And each of them with a story.

As she went over again in her mind all they'd revealed, she realized that sharing their stories with her was their way of letting her know that she wasn't alone. Each of them had faced a crisis and had survived. They were telling her that she would survive this, too. A soft sigh escaped her lips.

Oh, this was what she'd feared missing the most when she left San Francisco and her best friend, Lori. This connection with other women.

She closed her eyes on a wave of emotion. The kindness of those women, strangers just days ago, threatened to bring her to tears.

CHAPTER FIFTEEN

The following morning, while she showered and dressed, Annie heard doors opening and closing, voices lifted in greetings, in shouts, in sharp words, and in muted conversation. The difference between all this noise and the muted traffic sounds she'd become accustomed to had her shaking her head with a grin.

"You're not in San Francisco anymore, Annie my girl," she said to her reflection in the mirror.

When she stepped out the door of her room, she nearly bumped into Jonah. He was holding two lidded cups.

"'Morning, Annie." He held one out to her. "Coffee. One cream, no sugar."

"Thank you." She felt herself blushing at the way he was staring at her. That long, steady look that was so like his great-grandfather Ham. Cool. Assessing.

"If you're a lover of breakfast, Billy is fixing steak and eggs for the hungry mob. Or, if you'd like to join me on a hike to my cabin, he's fixing a to-go package of scrambled eggs on an English muffin."

"Is that his idea of a McBilly carryout?"

Jonah chuckled. "Careful. Any suggestion of fast food will insult him."

"We wouldn't want that." She paused. "Let me grab a jacket. I'd love a morning hike."

A minute later, she joined Jonah and they descended the stairs together. In the kitchen, they called a greeting to the others before picking up Billy's to-go bag.

Jonah stood by patiently while Annie made small talk, assuring everyone that she'd slept well, that her rooms were more than comfortable, and that she would survive without eating the man-sized breakfast Billy was preparing.

Liz walked over to take her hand. "I know I invited you to visit my studio today, but would you mind if we did it another day?"

"Oh, Liz, that's fine. I know what it's like to have my workday get out of control. I'll let you choose the day."

"Thanks for understanding."

Meg looked at the bag in Jonah's hand. "You two aren't staying for breakfast?"

He gave his grandmother a smile. "It's a great morning for a hike in the woods. We'll eat on the run, Gram Meg."

"All right, dear. If you say so. You two enjoy yourselves."

With smiles all around, Jonah and Annie headed outside.

The air was clean and crisp, and the sun was already climbing high enough to have them digging out their sunglasses.

"Oh." Annie looked around with a bright smile. "This is glorious. I'm so glad you decided to go on this walk."

Jonah led the way along a well-worn trail behind the barns. Soon they were leaving the open meadow and stepping into the damp, dim forest that smelled of earth and pine.

When they reached his cabin, she stood still, studying the way it looked.

Jonah paused. "Something wrong?"

She shook her head. "Just thinking how perfect it looks here. The woods, the cabin, the solitude."

"It might not work for most people, but it works for me." He unlocked the door and let her precede him.

He set their breakfast on the table and walked around opening the windows, letting the fresh breeze blow in.

He plugged in a coffee maker. "Mine isn't as good as Billy's. He grinds his own beans. But it's hot and strong, and I like to think it clears the clutter from my brain while I'm working."

She studied the books on the shelves. "I can't believe you actually wrote these. It must be so satisfying to see your book in stores and in someone's hand at the beach or the library."

"Yeah. It's a rush. But I do it mainly for myself. The story's in me, and I can't rest until I get it all out."

"And then you do it again. And again."

He laughed. "That's my hope."

He pointed to the plank set on two sawhorses outside the window. "Want to eat out there?"

She nodded and led the way.

They sat side by side, nibbling the egg sandwiches and sipping coffee and watching in silence as the wildlife stepped cautiously from the woods to entertain them.

A short time later, Jonah gathered up their coffee containers while tossing the crumbs on the ground. "I'd better get to work. Do you want to head back to the house?"

She shook her head. "Since I can't report to work, I think I'll hike into the hills."

"You know the way back?"

"I do. And if I get lost, I'll call you."

He laid a hand on her arm and she absorbed the tingle all the way to her toes. "Phone service in the hills is sketchy. Figure out some natural landmarks right now, so you can find your way back here." He pointed. "In that direction, the mountains will always be in front of you. When they're behind you, you'll see the herds and then the ranch house. My cabin lies somewhere in the middle."

She smiled. "Got it. No matter where I end up, I'll always make it back to you."

She set off at a brisk pace.

Jonah stayed where he was, watching as she left. The words that had slipped so easily from her lips played through his mind.

No matter where I end up, I'll always make it back to you.

Thoughtful, he turned away at last and forced himself to get to work.

It could have been an hour later, or several hours, when his phone rang. He barely glanced at it, intending to ignore it as he always did when working.

Noting the police chief's name, he picked it up on the third ring. "Hey, Noble. Do you have some news?"

The chief's voice lacked its usual warmth. "I've been trying to reach Annie Dempsey, with no luck."

"She's hiking the hills. You know what cell service is like up there. She should be back soon." He glanced at the time, noting that he'd already been working for three hours. "I'll have her call you."

"Tell her I want to meet with her."

"So, you have something?"

"Nothing good." Noble paused, as though considering whether or not to share. "The feds have uncovered the million-dollar theft."

"That was quick."

"That was the easy part. And since we know where the money ended up, the big question becomes who put it in Annie's account and why? Why not just divvy up the spoils and blow town?"

Jonah leaned back and propped his feet on his desk. "I'm sure you'll find your answers just as quickly, Chief."

"Right now the feds aren't convinced that Annie didn't have a hand in all this."

Jonah sat upright, his feet dropping heavily to the floor. "What's that supposed to mean?"

"Let me ask you something, Jonah. If you noticed a million dollars in a bank account you claim wasn't yours, wouldn't you immediately go to that bank and demand to know the identity of the person who opened it?"

"I would but..."

"I know you and your family have generously offered this young woman a safe haven. But I feel it's my duty to warn you and your family that you may be harboring a criminal."

"Noble..."

"Jonah, I don't have time to debate you on this issue. When Annie Dempsey finishes her hike, I'd appreciate it if you would bring her into town to answer a few questions."

"Of course."

"And, Jonah, I think it's best if you don't tell her about this conversation. I'd like to hear her answers to my questions without giving her time to prepare some sort of phony defense."

"Phony...Noble, that's not..."

The line went dead.

Jonah stared at the cell phone in his hand before tucking it slowly into his shirt pocket. Getting up, he paced to the window and back, letting the chief's words play through his mind.

It was true that though there had been an instant attraction between him and Annie, he really didn't know anything about her, except that he'd defied his family's lifelong mistrust of her uncle to pursue a relationship with her.

But what was their relationship?

Other than an attraction, there was nothing between them. They were two adults tiptoeing around one another. He didn't even know if the attraction he felt was shared by her.

When she'd learned his name, she'd been perfectly willing to walk away. In truth, he'd felt the same way. But something had propelled him to go after her. And then, witnessing that visit from a stranger, and the effect it had on Annie, all his protective instincts had kicked in.

Maybe that was it. Maybe the only thing between them was the fact that she was a woman in trouble, and he felt compelled to help.

Could the authorities be right in their suspicion that she'd had a hand in the theft and the subsequent bank account?

He paused. Wasn't he doing exactly what the authorities were doing? Assigning blame before all the facts were known?

He continued pacing until he convinced himself to withhold judgment until he heard everything Chief Crain had to say.

In the meantime, he would continue to trust his own

instincts. And he would stick to his belief that Annie Dempsey was a good person who had been set up by someone out to do her wrong.

He watched the approach of a deer and stood still. A slow smile came to his eyes. It didn't hurt that Annie was just about the prettiest woman he'd ever met. And that she shared his love of solitude and wildlife.

But a pretty face and a love of animals didn't mean a thing if she was just using her wiles to hide out on his family's ranch.

Even as the thought took root in his mind, he was dismissing it. As the youngest in the family, and a writer, he considered himself an observer of the human condition. He'd had a lifetime sorting through family dynamics and knowing his brothers and his elders better than they knew themselves. He'd used that knowledge to flesh out flawed, very human characters in his books. That's what made him a success. And right now, he had very definite thoughts about Annie Dempsey. No matter how it looked to others, until there was concrete evidence to the contrary, he would continue to believe that she was the innocent victim in this twisted scheme.

CHAPTER SIXTEEN

Jonah looked up from his computer to see Annie moving briskly along the trail leading to his cabin.

He walked to the window and watched the way the breeze took her hair, sending it sailing out behind her like a dark, silky cloud.

She paused, and even from this distance he could see the smile that seemed to light up all her features. A doe and her fawn ambled into his line of vision, and he couldn't help smiling as well.

The fawn, no more than a couple of days old by the way she picked her way through the vegetation, jumped back when a low-hanging branch of an evergreen brushed her head. Seeing the doe moving ahead, the fawn did a little leap in the air, trying to run to catch up.

When they'd drifted into the woods, Annie started toward the cabin and Jonah opened the door, smiling a greeting.

"Did you see them?" Annie's eyes were wide with pleasure.

"I did. Mamas and babies are always entertaining."

"Oh, Jonah, just seeing them took my breath away."

He held the door open and she brushed past him.

"Sounds like you had a good hike."

"A very good hike. I saw a herd of wild horses, or I should say I caught the quickest glimpse of them. They were there one minute, and the next they'd disappeared like ghosts."

"They're adept at making themselves invisible. It's a matter of survival."

She nodded. "What little I saw of them was almost mystical. A big red stallion watched me until the last of his herd was safely in the woods. Then, without a glance back in my direction, he was gone. The strange thing is, even though I watched him, within minutes I couldn't distinguish him from the trees around him. It was as though the forest swallowed him up."

She nearly danced in her eagerness to tell him everything she'd experienced. "And I think I saw a big cat."

"You think you did?"

She laughed. "Like the horses, this guy was there on a thick tree limb one minute, like a king surveying his kingdom, but when I blinked and looked again, he was gone."

"They're famous for climbing high and hiding among the vegetation. If you'd looked closely, you might have caught a glimpse of his eyes peering through a veil of leaves."

"To tell the truth, I was a little afraid to look too closely. I had the feeling that if I lingered in his territory too long, he might decide I was a tasty meal."

Instead of the laugh she was expecting, Jonah touched his palm to her cheek and pinned her with that stern look he'd perfected.

"Don't tell me you agree."

"To what?"

"That I'd be a big cat's lunch."

"Tasty. I believe that's how you described yourself." His smile came then. "I'm afraid I do agree."

Aware of what he'd revealed, he lowered his hand and turned away before moving to his desk to carefully back up his work before shutting down his computer.

"You're finished for the day?"

He nodded. "I heard from Chief Crain. He'd like to meet with you in town this afternoon to fill you in on what the authorities have learned so far."

"Oh." She brought a hand to her throat in a gesture of excitement. "Already? That's quick. Did he tell you anything?"

Jonah busied himself at his desk, stacking his notes, setting aside his pens. "I guess we'll learn soon enough." He looked up. "How about some lunch at Nonie's before we meet with Noble?"

She was fairly twitching with anticipation. "Honestly, I couldn't eat a thing until I hear what Chief Crain has to say."

"Okay. Your choice." He lifted his cell phone off the

desk, all the while watching her expression. "Let's see what time he's free to meet."

Noble Crain stood as his wife ushered Annie and Jonah into his office.

Annie was smiling broadly. "Good afternoon, Chief Crain. Jonah told me you have some news to share. He wanted to wait in the outer office so that we could meet alone, but since he already knows what I know, and since I'm staying with his family, I'm willing to share whatever information you have with them."

"That's fine." Noble indicated the chairs facing his desk and waited until Annie was seated before settling back down.

Jonah sat beside her, his face carefully devoid of emotion.

"To begin with"—Noble folded his hands on his desktop—"the feds have identified the victim of the million-dollar theft. His name is Richard Thornton."

"Richard?" Annie reacted as though she'd been slapped.

"I believe you know him."

She nodded, swallowing several times. "He was one of my private banking clients. Just a sweet, charming man who retired some years ago and is living comfortably on his ample savings." As soon as the words were out of her mouth, she lifted a hand to stifle her cry. "But a million dollars? That would wipe him out."

"Indeed." Noble was watching her closely. "I'm told the bank had to make good on the theft."

"Oh." She made a sound of relief. "That's such good news."

"For Richard Thornton. Not such good news for the bank or rather, their insurers. But because their investigators have determined that it was an inside job, they had no choice but to reimburse him the full amount that had been taken from his account."

"An inside job?" She leaned forward. "They know who did this?"

"The feds, after extensive interviews with the bank investigators, have determined that it was Mr. Thornton's private banker."

She sat back as though a hand had shoved her hard against the chair. "But I just told you that Richard was one of my private banking clients."

"Exactly."

Her eyes went wide. "You're accusing me of stealing from one of my own clients?"

"He was the bank's client. You were assigned by the bank to help him handle his finances. Isn't that so? Don't you have knowledge of all your clients' bank statements?"

"Of course I do. But I take great pride in my work and I'm not a criminal. I would never steal from my clients, especially not Richard. If you knew him, you would understand. He's the sweetest man you'd ever meet. How could anyone want to harm him?"

Chief Crain typed something into his computer before turning it around so that Annie and Jonah could see the screen.

"The feds sent me this." At Annie's arched brow, he explained patiently, "I believe you're familiar with East Bay Bank?"

She shrugged. "Of course I know of it. This is the bank that sent me a statement showing a million dollars in an account in my name, even though I never opened such an account."

"Then how do you explain this?" He touched a finger to the prompt, which initiated a video. "This is a copy of East Bay Bank's security tape from a month ago."

Annie and Jonah stared at the screen where a woman dressed in a bright red coat was shown meeting with a bank representative.

Noble stopped the tape. "Is that your coat?"

Annie was shaking her head. "I own a coat just like that. But that woman isn't me."

"Let's go on." He pushed the button, and the woman, wearing a scarf on her head that covered her hair, her forehead, and much of her neck, and big sunglasses that nearly obscured her entire face, presented the banker with documents. The camera zoomed in on Annie's name and her personal identification, including her Social Security number.

She sat forward in her chair, shaking her head at the computer screen. "I know what this looks like, Chief Crain, but that woman isn't me."

He turned the computer around. "Just a week after this was recorded on the bank's security camera, a million dollars was wired to that new account in your name."

"Not only do I deny setting up that account, but I've never been inside that bank. Why would I, when I was employed at a competing bank?"

"Your employer would certainly notice if a million dollars was deposited in one of their employee's accounts. According to East Bay Bank, that very thing happened with the account in your name. A million dollars just happened to be deposited into an account in the name of Annie Dempsey."

With every word out of the police chief's mouth, Annie's shoulders slumped a little more until she was hunched over, as though holding herself together by a thread.

"According to your former employer, Mr. Thornton wasn't even aware of the theft until he'd been told by the bank investigators. Of course, it was kept quiet and never made the news, in order to spare the bank's reputation. They have quietly restored his money to his account, and a new, trusted private banker is now handling Mr. Thornton's account while the investigation continues."

Jonah had remained silent throughout this narrative. Now he asked, "So, Noble, you're saying that the investigation is still ongoing?"

The chief nodded.

"Why, if they believe Annie is the thief?"

"They're convinced that she had accomplices."

"Arlen Lender?"

At Jonah's question, Chief Crain shook his head. "They've searched all their data banks. So far, there is nobody by that name in the San Francisco area. Either he's using an alias or he has a record so clean he's never had so much as a speeding ticket. Or"—he turned to stare at Annie—"Arlen Lender is a figment of the imagination."

"But," Jonah said, "don't forget that Annie was introduced to this man by the president of the bank."

"Actually, he was introduced to me by another bank employee. But it was at a company party at which the bank president was the guest of honor." Annie lowered her head, as though feeling the weight of evidence piling up against her.

Jonah kept his tone even. "Noble, are the investigators going to continue looking at every angle?"

"They're trained investigators, Jonah. But once they saw that security video, they became convinced that they'd found their thief. As Agent Mavis Johnson, in charge of the federal investigation told me, a million dollars is a mighty big temptation for even the most honest person." He turned his piercing gaze on Annie. "They figure you were unable to resist the lure of a million dollars, until your conscience got the best of you and you ran. But that visit by Park spooked you, and now you want protection from Arlen by throwing him under the bus."

Annie looked at him in disbelief and her voice betrayed her shock. "Am I under arrest?"

Chief Crain shook his head. "Not yet. But you are a person of interest. And if the evidence continues..." He laid his palms flat on the desktop and shoved his chair back. "You're free to go, Annie. For now. But I would advise you to remain in town."

"You can find her at my family's ranch, Noble."

The chief seemed about to say something before he caught himself and merely nodded.

Jonah took Annie's hand and helped her from the chair before leading her from the office.

As they passed the chief's wife, she was frowning, her lips pursed as though she'd tasted something vile.

CHAPTER SEVENTEEN

Outside the chief's office, Jonah turned to Annie. "You've hardly eaten a thing today. You must be hungry."

She pressed a hand to her stomach. "I just want to"— she looked around—"get away."

Once in his truck, they began the long drive back to the ranch, and Jonah decided to find a way to get her to talk. "Annie, I know it looks bad. Seeing that video had to be a shock."

She turned to stare out the side window, avoiding his eyes. "The authorities have already declared me guilty and are now looking for 'my' accomplices."

"Videos can be faked. We all know that."

"Do we?" Her voice lowered. "They've stopped looking, Jonah. They're already convinced they have their criminal. I can deny all I want, but I know what they're thinking. I could see it in the chief's eyes. Hear it in his tone of voice. And his wife made her feelings obvious."

"MaryAnn Crain is a puppet who will repeat whatever her husband tells her."

"To everyone in town."

Jonah had no argument for that.

He waited, choosing his words carefully. "I hope you realize that we have to tell my family what the authorities have found so far."

She nodded. "They'll ask me to leave, and I don't blame them."

Jonah reached over and caught her hand. "My family is far from perfect. We have all the flaws of families everywhere. But we're also fair. I believe, once they hear all this, they'll insist that you stay on where you'll be safe from the gossip and innuendo."

"If they do, they'll have to be on guard with their valuables, since they have a thief in their midst."

"A person of interest."

"Jonah, we both know that's a mere technicality. The authorities, according to Chief Crain, have all the proof they need. Now they just want to tie up the loose ends before arresting me."

Though she turned her head away, he continued to hold her hand. It was trembling, he noted, and though she was struggling to be stoic, he could see that she was close to tears.

Over supper, both Jonah and Annie were subdued, allowing his family to carry the conversation. Jonah had decided not to spoil their appetites with unpleasant news.

When Meg suggested taking their dessert and coffee on the porch, Jonah saw it as the perfect opportunity to bring them up to date on the investigation. With twilight fast approaching, Annie could hide in the shadows and avoid feeling like she was under a spotlight. Though he knew it would be painful, he hoped he could ease her through the worst of it.

Billy pushed the trolley onto the porch and began passing around cups of coffee and plates of his apple pie with vanilla ice cream mounded on top.

"Ham, you get the first slice." Billy handed it to the patriarch of the family and the others observed the smile of pure delight that crossed Ham's features.

"Um-humm." Ham took a bite, then a second and a third, before letting out a deep sigh. "I do believe I could eat this every day of my life."

Meg, always the practical one, remarked, "If you did, it wouldn't be a special treat, now, would it?"

"Margaret Mary Finnegan, stop trying to be logical. This isn't the time for logic."

Jonah cleared his throat. "Maybe this is the time to let you know that Annie and I met with Chief Crain today."

Everyone turned to him, including Annie.

He accepted a plate from Billy and set it aside for the moment. "The authorities found a security video of a bank in San Francisco showing a woman in a scarf and sunglasses obscuring much of her face and hair, wearing a bright red coat, opening a bank account in Annie's name. She had all of Annie's information, including her Social Security number."

His family, he noted, had gone completely silent.

"They've also located the victim of the million-dollar theft. He was a private banking client of Annie's. The bank has already reimbursed him the money and is quietly linking their investigation with that of the authorities, in the hope of keeping this quiet, since it will bring unwanted notoriety. Within days of the theft, a million dollars was wired into the new bank account in Annie's name."

Egan was the first to speak. He directed his question to Annie.

"What did you say to the chief when you were told all this?"

"I told him I know it looks bad, but I know, too, that the woman in the video isn't me."

"Of course it isn't." Meg looked around at the others, daring them to disagree.

"Thank you, Miss Meg. But Chief Crain doesn't believe me. And neither do the authorities. They've already moved beyond me to try to find out who else is involved in this scheme."

Meg's voice rose in disbelief. "He told you that?"

"Not in so many words, but he made it clear that if I look guilty, I must be guilty."

"Rubbish." At Ham's outburst, the others turned to him.

He pointed a finger at Jonah. "If you were writing a

scene in one of those books of yours, and your character was doing something secretive, would you dress her in a bright red coat?"

A smile tugged at Jonah's lips. "Of course not, Ham. I'd dress her in something plain and drab."

"That's right, boy. And you know why?"

"People don't forget a bright red coat."

"Exactly." He turned to Annie. "I imagine you own a coat like that red one?"

"It's identical to one I own."

"Uh-huh." He looked around at the others. "And I bet you own half a dozen more that are less...colorful."

Jonah interrupted. "But the authorities are fixated on this coat and the woman on that security tape. And once they've decided they have their perpetrator, it's hard to get them to think beyond that."

"Then we need to nudge them, boy."

While the others began debating ways to turn the investigation around, Jonah suddenly turned to his grandfather. "Gramps, what about your old friend Newton Calder?"

Avery, who had been listening without comment, nodded. "Wasn't he the retired investigator who was the first to discover that Nurse Renee Wilmot had both motive and opportunity to harm me?"

"It was indeed." Egan got to his feet and began to pace before stopping in front of Annie. "My friend Newt is retired now, but years ago he was the lead investigator for the state police. That makes him uniquely qualified to do some private investigations from time to time. Not only is he well trained, but he is welcomed by the law-enforcement community as one of their own. As long as he's willing to share his information with them, they're willing to do the same."

He turned to the others. "I believe I'll call Newt and see if he's willing to lend a hand."

While the family sat quietly, he stepped indoors. Minutes later he returned to the porch, his face wreathed in smiles. "Newt admitted that he's intrigued and would love to offer his services."

Annie was shaking her head. "I don't know if I can afford..."

Egan held up a hand. "What you can't afford is having the investigation stalled. We'll talk about Newt's fee later. Right now, there's no time to waste. I've given Newt permission to contact the authorities and let them know he's working for you. He pointed out that this is important for two reasons. First, it's a signal to them that you now have someone on your side who isn't going to settle for easy answers. They can't coast simply because they think you're guilty. Second, you're giving them notice that you want the truth as much as they do, and you're willing to let the chips fall where they may as the bulk of evidence plays out."

"Oh, Egan, that's brilliant." Meg rushed over to wrap her arms around his neck and kiss him full on the mouth.

When she stepped back, the old man wore a satisfied

smile. "Thank you, Meggie girl. But none of this was mine. That all came from Newt."

"Nevertheless, you were the one who called him."

"And Jonah was the one who suggested it." Egan clapped a hand on his grandson's shoulder. "Good work."

As the others began heading indoors, murmuring among themselves, Bo sat quietly, staring at the mountains in the distance.

When all but he and Jonah and Annie remained, Jonah broke the silence.

"What's bothering you, Pop?"

Bo looked over. "This has been a lot to digest." He aimed his words at Annie. "You know your uncle and I haven't spoken in twenty years or more."

"I know. And I'm sorry that I—"

"There was a time when we were good friends. We'd meet at Nonie's for a beer while we talked about our work. We were young and ambitious, and while I was busy with ranch chores, he was struggling to build up his little family-owned bank to compete with some pretty big players." Bo shook his head. "That all ended after I met Leigh. I was unaware that she was engaged to Des." His eyes narrowed. "Both of us had kept our private lives private. And though I didn't plan it, once Leigh broke their engagement and began seeing me, there was this yawning chasm between us that neither of us was willing to cross. We were no longer friends and he refused me a loan to buy the old Butcher ranch. And then when it burned..."

"You can't believe my uncle had anything to do with that."

Bo frowned. "He was a man scorned who'd made no secret of his fury."

"That's a far cry from deliberately setting a fire. I'm sorry but I can't listen to this. I think it's best if I leave..."

Bo stood and held up a hand to silence her. "You've a right to defend your uncle. And I've realized that this shouldn't be about him and me. I had some misgivings when Jonah told us who you are. And even tonight, when he started telling us about all the compelling evidence against you, I began questioning myself. Why was I allowing the niece of my old enemy to live under my roof?"

Annie scrambled to her feet. "I'll go now..."

He reached out a hand as though to grab her, then suddenly lowered it to his side. "I can't force you, of course, but what I'm trying to say is that I hope you'll stay."

"I'm not going to sever my relationship with my uncle. And I refuse to listen to more false accusations about him. That ought to be reason enough for you to ask me to leave."

"There's a stronger motivation for you to stay. You're safe here. Somebody went to a lot of trouble to set you up. If Newton Calder is as good as we think he is, those same people will become desperate when they find out someone is on their trail."

"Then you believe me? And you think I'm in danger?"

"I do. And I'm not inclined to allow someone in my home to face danger alone."

Bo walked to the back door and opened it. Over his shoulder he called, "Good night, Annie. Son."

When they were alone, Jonah took Annie's hand. It was cold as ice. She was shaking.

"Hey." He wrapped his arms around her, drawing her close.

And in that moment, she realized she'd been holding her emotions together by a mere thread.

With a little moan, she went limp in his arms, sobbing against his chest as though her heart would break.

CHAPTER EIGHTEEN

Jonah felt a wave of such tenderness he could hardly keep from crushing her in his arms. Instead, he forced himself to be gentle as he held her. When her tears finally subsided, he handed her his handkerchief.

"Thanks." She blew her nose and wiped her eyes before stuffing the handkerchief into her pocket.

She kept her gaze averted. "Sorry."

"Annie." He put a finger under her chin, forcing her to look up.

She closed her eyes to hide her shame. "I don't usually go all weak and weepy."

"You have a right. You're in the fight of your life against some very clever cons."

Her eyes opened. She shook her head. "That isn't what brought this on, though I have to admit I'm terrified that I'm being drawn into something so big, so well organized, I may have no defense. I'm almost afraid to let myself think about what's happening. But these tears are about your family."

Seeing his puzzled look, she searched for the right words. "You said they might surprise me. And I may have hoped they wouldn't come right out and condemn me. But I never dreamed they would actually stand together to not only hire a detective to defend me, but also insist that I stay on here." She shook her head in wonder. "What an amazing family you have."

"Yeah. They continue to amaze me, too."

"I'll never be able to repay them for this kindness."

"Yes, you will."

At the tone of his voice, she blinked.

His eyes were as steely as his words. "Seeing you vindicated will be all the payment they want. I know it's the only thing I want for you."

"Oh, Jonah, I hope you're right. Sometimes I just feel so overwhelmed by what's happening..."

He lifted both hands to smooth the tear-dampened hair from her face. Though he'd intended it as a soothing gesture, the minute his fingers were plunged into the tangles, he paused for the merest second before lowering his head and covering her mouth in a kiss so hot, so hungry, he was consumed by it.

The fire raging through his veins caught him by surprise. He backed her up until she was pressed against the door, and still the kiss went on and on.

He felt her arms close around his waist as she clung to him like a lifeline. That was all he needed to change the angle of the kiss and take it deeper.

He heard her little murmur of approval and dragged

her against him until he could feel the erratic tattoo of her heartbeat, keeping time with his. His fingers tangled with her hair and he kissed her until they were both breathless.

And still, holding her, kissing her, wasn't nearly enough.

All his thoughts scrambled except one. He wanted her. Desperately. Right here. Right now. This minute.

They were practically crawling inside one another's skin, and still it wasn't enough. He wanted, needed all.

"Jonah."

Over the buzzing in his ears, he thought he heard his name as his mouth moved over hers with a fierce hunger.

"Jonah. Wait."

Through a haze of desperate hunger, he lifted his head and struggled to get his bearings.

Annie lifted a hand to his cheek. "We need to…"

"All we need is this. Here. Now."

"I know. I want that, too. But not here. Not now. Not like this. Oh, Jonah…"

He realized that her breathing was ragged, and her words were halting. He'd almost crossed a line, thinking of taking her right here on the porch like a madman.

"Yeah. Give me a minute." He put his hands on either side of her head, pressing his forehead to hers, before taking a half step back. "We need to…"

"Breathe," she said with a short laugh. "At least I need to."

"Yeah. Right."

As his world began to settle, he took another step back, even though what he really wanted was to get back to that place where he'd completely lost himself in her.

"It's late. And you've put in a rough day." He reached around her and held the door open. "I guess we should head upstairs."

She brushed past him, careful not to touch him with any part of her body, as though aware that they were both dangerously close to the edge.

He did the same, following slowly, taking his cue from her. He was so hot, if she just touched him he would surely explode with a need stronger than ever.

Upstairs, he paused outside the guest room.

She opened the door before turning to him. "Earlier today I thought I'd be leaving here."

"I'm glad you're staying." He was staring at her mouth until he realized what he was doing and lifted his gaze to her eyes.

"I'm glad, too." Her eyes were wide with emotion, looking too big for her face.

It should have been easier for him to walk away, knowing she was sharing the same feelings. But somehow, it made it more difficult. One more touch, one more kiss, and the spark would ignite into another blaze of white-hot passion. Since he was still vibrating with need, it could be the same for her. It was so tempting.

It took all his willpower to step back. "Good night, Annie."

"'Night, Jonah."

He waited until she closed the door before heading to his room across the hall.

Once inside, he tugged off his shirt and balled it up before tossing it with a muttered curse against the wall. He kicked off his boots and left them lying where they fell, stepping over them to cross to the windows. Barefoot and shirtless, he leaned a hip against the sill and stared at the darkened hills outside.

He'd always loved this view of the land. It was where he drew his inspiration. But tonight he looked without seeing. With his passion still so raw, all he could see, all he could taste was Annie.

He wanted her. God, how he wanted her.

He hadn't meant for this to happen, but there it was. There was no sense trying to deny what his heart already knew. He wasn't willing to give this feeling a name yet, but the attraction he'd felt the first time he'd seen her at Nonie's hadn't dimmed. In fact, it had grown and bloomed inside him until now here it was, nameless and fully formed and about to drive him mad.

Annie paced to the window and back, her arms crossed over her chest, her thoughts in turmoil.

What was happening to her?

She'd kissed plenty of men in her life, but she'd never had a simple kiss affect her like this. Maybe, she thought, it was because nothing about that kiss had been simple. With that first taste of Jonah, she'd been lost. He had taken her higher, faster, than she'd believed possible. She'd wanted, in those few moments, to beg him to take her.

Crazy, but there it was.

She considered herself a smart woman. Right now, she was in the fight of her life. She was caught up in some vile scheme that was threatening her future, her good name, her very freedom. She was staying at the ranch of a family that had long regarded her family as their enemy.

And yet tonight, with a single kiss, everything had been wiped from her mind except for that hard, driving need for Jonah.

While she undressed and prepared for bed, she forced her mind to go over the day and the things Chief Crain had revealed. But once she crawled between the covers, her thoughts returned to Jonah and that kiss.

That kiss.

It had rocked her world, and she'd wanted the same thing he'd wanted.

Oh, he'd made it very plain what he wanted.

It had all happened so suddenly. One minute she thought he was simply consoling her. The next, he was setting her on fire with a kiss that was unlike any she'd ever shared with a man. With a single kiss, he'd had her not only willing to let him do whatever he wanted, but also ready to beg him to.

She still didn't know quite where she'd found the courage to stop him. The voice that had come out of her mouth sounded too weak and breathless to be her own.

Right now, she didn't know whether to laugh at her stupidity or weep over the fact that she'd stopped him. If she had the chance to do it over, she wasn't at all certain whether she'd end it as she had or let the whole scenario follow along to its natural conclusion.

As she lay there, letting the scene play through her mind, she felt again the quick, sensual jolt and that amazing rush of fire and ice through her veins the moment his lips were on hers.

Who would have thought that beneath that cool façade he showed the world, Jonah Merrick was a man of such passion? It had been exciting to watch the transformation in him. One moment he'd been the tender bodyguard, shielding her from the unknown danger. The next a fierce savage about to take her right there on the back porch of his family home.

A man like Jonah Merrick would be an amazing lover.

The thought of freeing herself to ride that wave of unbridled passion with him was oh so tempting. It would be wonderful to forget, for a little while, the dark, mysterious scheme that had somehow wrapped itself around her, drawing her into a web of lies and deceit. But one of them had to be sensible. After all, his family had offered her sanctuary here in their home. How could she dare to do anything to dishonor them?

She gave a deep sigh of frustration. Until this mystery was resolved, she would be forced to spend a lot of time in Jonah's company. Just the thought of him had her sighing. How was she going to ignore the passion he stirred in her, when her poor heart was already lost?

As she mulled her dilemma, she tossed and turned.

It was going to be a long, sleepless night.

CHAPTER NINETEEN

Annie followed the sound of feminine voices to the kitchen, where Liz, Avery, and Kirby were enjoying coffee, while Billy was flipping pancakes at the stove.

She paused to help herself to a cup. "Good morning."

"'Morning, Annie." Liz separated herself from the others. "The guys are out in the barn, doing manly things. If you have time, I thought you might want to visit my studio."

Annie nodded. "I'd like that."

"Good. As soon as we stuff ourselves on Billy's pancakes, we'll head over there."

The four women took their places at the table, while Billy set the first platter in front of them and started another batch.

"Oh." Annie couldn't stop the sigh of pleasure at her first taste. "Billy, these are wonderful."

"Thanks, Annie. They're Miss Meg's favorites." He shot her a smile before returning his attention to the griddle.

"I can see why." She passed the syrup to Avery. "Will you be joining us in Liz's studio?"

"Not today." Avery crossed to the counter to retrieve a carafe of coffee before topping off her cup. "My first client of the day is half an hour from here. Nell Compton."

Liz nodded at the name. "I hear she broke a hip."

"Actually, it started with what Dr. Peterson thought was a simple ankle sprain. She took a fall on her ranch, and then a second tumble down the stairs while she was recovering from the ankle. That fall caused the broken hip. Now that she's mobile, he wants to get her as much therapy as possible before something else happens."

Annie turned. "How about you, Kirby?"

Kirby smiled. "I offered to go with Casey as he makes his rounds."

Annie chuckled. "Seeing him working alongside the others in the barn, I forget that he's a veterinarian."

"Our neighbors never let him forget. They keep him busy. After he looks at Buster Mandel's bull, the last patient on his list, we'll probably have lunch or an early supper at Nonie's."

"That sounds like fun." After finishing a stack of pancakes, with a side of crisp country bacon, Annie turned to Liz. "I can't wait to see your studio. Avery and Kirby have been telling me about the number of magazines that routinely use your photos, not only in their articles, but also on the covers. What an honor to have one of your pictures on the cover of a magazine read by thousands of people."

Liz managed a shy smile. "That's a lot of hype to live up to." She pushed away from the table. "If you're ready, let's head over there now."

Annie turned to Billy. "Thanks for that wonderful breakfast. I can see why your pancakes are Miss Meg's favorites. They're on the top of my list now, too. Although I have to admit," she said with a laugh, "anything I don't have to cook becomes an instant favorite."

The others were laughing as she followed Liz from the kitchen.

Liz switched on the lights in the equipment barn, revealing rows of vehicles of every shape and size.

"Oh my gosh." Seeing the tractors and excavators and machines she couldn't even name had Annie gaping. But when she spotted the giant combine standing several stories tall, her eyes went even wider. "Does somebody actually climb way up there and drive that thing?"

Liz was laughing. "All three of my nephews can drive it, as well as Chet. I've been in it a time or two with Chet. The cab is heated and air-conditioned and has its own GPS to guide the driver."

"The driver must feel like a minnow trying to steer a whale."

Liz nodded. "That's about right. You feel really

small up there." She continued walking past the rows of machines before opening a door and flipping a few switches. Overhead lights came on, bathing the room in light.

"Welcome to my studio." Liz stepped aside to allow Annie to walk past her.

"Oh." The word came out like a sigh as Annie studied the light-filled room.

The walls were lined with shelves filled with photographs, some in color, others black and white. They seemed evenly divided between wildlife, portraits, and views of the fabulous Tetons.

In silence, Annie slowly circled the room, her interest caught by the photos of mustangs in every season. Mares with their foals in springtime, with patches of snow still visible beside rocks and beneath low-hanging evergreens. Herds grazing in a meadow with lush grass to their bellies. A small herd surrounded by trees wearing fiery autumn foliage. A stallion, his black coat in sharp contrast to the snow-covered hills as he watched over his mares during a blizzard.

"I see that you're partial to my horses."

At Liz's voice directly behind her, Annie turned. "Oh, Liz. These are stunning."

"Thank you. I'm glad you like them." Liz was beaming. All trace of shyness was gone, now that she was in her element. "That particular shot of the black stallion was chosen for the cover of *Wildlife Magazine* last year."

"I can see why. You've captured exactly what I saw on my hike into the hills the other day."

"I'm so glad you had a chance to see some of our mustangs."

"So am I. Jonah said some people hike here for ages without spotting any."

"Wild creatures like to keep to themselves. And they're adept at slipping away the minute they spot humans."

"I noticed. I told Jonah they're like ghosts."

"It sounds as though the two of you have spent some time in the hills."

Annie's smile was radiant. "That's how we met. I was hiking on what I thought was public land until I came across his cabin. He stepped out, startling me, and I apologized for trespassing on his land. That's when he decided to join me on my hike. And since then, we seem to spend as much time as possible hiking the hills around his cabin."

"You like my nephew." It was a simple statement, and Annie found that she couldn't lie to this sweet woman.

"I do. But I'm aware of the...issues between our families and realize that nothing can come of it."

"Says who?"

At the challenge, Annie felt herself color. "It wouldn't be wise..."

"If I've learned anything in my crazy life it's this. Love isn't wise. It can't be planned. Or faked. Love is inconvenient. It has no rhyme or reason. It happens when you least expect it, or want it. Love..." She shrugged. "Love just is."

"I wasn't talking about love."

"Weren't you?"

Despite her shyness, or maybe because of it, Liz had a surprisingly direct manner. When she challenged Annie with that piercing look, it was exactly like the look her grandfather, Ham, and her nephew Jonah, gave people.

Annie lowered her head to avoid eye contact. "Liz, just so you understand, I can't afford the luxury of falling in love. I'm very grateful to your family for allowing me to remain here. They had every right, once they heard my story, to order me to leave and never darken their door again. Right now I'm reeling from the blow of not even being certain just what I'm involved in, but I seem to be the target for something cruel, and very dangerous. And even with the help of your father's friend Newton Calder, there's no guarantee that I won't be found guilty of grand theft, resulting in time in prison and my family's name being ruined. I think those are very good reasons for...not getting involved with Jonah. Right about now, I'd like to crawl into bed and pull the covers over my head and hope when I wake this was all a bad dream."

Liz put a hand over Annie's. "I know that my humiliation over being left at the altar by Luke Miller, my old love, doesn't compare with the trouble you're facing. But I'm going to share with you what I learned from my experience. It shames me to admit that I crawled into my own private cave of despair, where I hid for years, afraid to face people. Then Avery came into our family and when she heard what I'd endured, she reminded me that we can't let life's setbacks define us."

She put her hands on either side of Annie's face, forcing her to meet her direct gaze. "Forget about crawling into bed and hiding from that dark cloud hanging over your head. You're better than that, Annie. And stronger. You know someone targeted you and is trying to destroy you. You can't back down. You need to stand up and fight back with everything you have. And trust me, when you do, my family and I will be right there beside you, fighting with everything we have."

"Even knowing that by fighting alongside me, they might get dragged down into the mud, too?"

"Just watch. We Merricks love a good fight. Especially when the cause is just."

Annie felt her eyes fill and blinked furiously.

She lifted a hand to Liz's and swallowed hard. "Thanks. I needed that lecture."

"Not a lecture. A reminder."

Annie managed a weak smile. "Whatever you call it, I'm grateful." She sniffed and lifted her chin. "Thanks, too, for letting me visit your studio. I'd love to come back another time, when I'm not feeling so overwhelmed. I'd love to see more of your amazing photographs."

"You're welcome here anytime." Liz stepped back. "Where to now?"

Annie turned toward the door. "To find Jonah and ask him to drive me to town. I want to know everything Chief Crain has learned." She paused with her hand on the doorknob and gave Liz a knowing look. "After all, if I'm going to follow your advice to put up the fight of my life, I need to be armed with as many facts as possible."

"Good for you." Liz was positively glowing as Annie walked away.

CHAPTER TWENTY

Jonah paused to back up his work on the computer. Not that he'd accomplished much. All morning he'd been distracted by thoughts of Annie.

She'd been so emotional last night, after his family had vowed to help in any way they could. He accepted the fact that she was feeling overwhelmed. But was it, as she'd said, because of his family's kindness? Or was she only now beginning to realize just how deeply she was caught up in this mysterious scheme that had completely taken over her life?

The scene afterward hadn't been planned. He'd simply wanted to comfort her. But then comfort had morphed into something very different.

Different.

He was a man who loved playing with words. *Different* couldn't possibly describe what had transpired between them.

Transformational.

Now, there was a word that came closer to describing that kiss.

That solitary kiss had been a tiny match dropped into dry tinder, causing an inferno of epic proportions in his world.

He stood and began to pace.

He'd fallen asleep wanting her. He woke this morning wanting her. Right this minute, with his thoughts in disarray and his focus everywhere but on his work, he wanted her.

Not just physically, though that was a powerful urge. But he wanted her body, her mind, her very soul. He'd quite simply become obsessed with her.

When he saw her moving along the overgrown path lined by foliage, he thought for a moment he'd simply conjured her because he wanted her so badly. Then he blinked and the image drew closer.

He hurried to open the cabin door.

"Hi." He stood there, drinking her in, all pink-cheeked and windblown from her hike.

"Hi." She brushed a strand of hair from her eye. "I know I shouldn't bother you while you're working…"

"I'm finished for the day." He stepped back and held open the door.

She brushed past him, careful not to touch him with any part of her body.

He was reminded of the night before, when her reaction had been the same.

Had she built that wall of reserve because he'd

overstepped his bounds? Or could it be that she was trying to cover feelings that matched his? He had to know. Was desperate to know.

"Coffee?"

"No thanks." She glanced toward his desk and seemed relieved to see his computer closed. "You're really through for the day?"

He nodded, watching her in that careful, steady way. "I missed you this morning."

"Liz invited me to see her studio."

"What did you think?"

"I could have spent hours looking at her photos. What incredible talent she has."

"Yeah. That's my aunt Liz. She may be shy, but she speaks volumes about Wyoming and its people and wildlife through her work."

Annie nodded. "I saw the pictures of our mustangs."

He smiled, wondering if she was aware that she'd called them "ours."

"Why that smile?"

"No reason except I'm happy you're here."

"The walk through the woods helped me clear my mind. I've been feeling so confused this morning since…"

His smile faded as he closed the distance between them to put a hand on her arm. "I'm sorry if that kiss last night upset…"

Seeing her bewildered look, he paused. "I didn't mean to interrupt. Go ahead. You were saying…?"

Annie seemed to gather herself. "Liz is very insightful. I suppose that comes from being an artist."

"My aunt has a way of seeing past all the fluff and getting to the heart of things. What did she have to say?"

"She told me things about myself that I'd thought I was hiding pretty well."

"What sort of things?"

Annie felt heat rush to her cheeks as she thought of what Liz had said about the love she'd glimpsed between her and Jonah. That was way too personal to repeat.

She turned away to hide the blush she knew he would see. "One of the things she noticed about me is a feeling of helplessness because I don't know who is targeting me, or why."

"That's natural enough. Anyone would feel the same."

"Liz wanted me to know that she believes in me and thinks it's time to stop letting fear win. She told me it's time to stand tall and fight back."

"Isn't that exactly what my family told you?"

Annie nodded and turned back to him, keeping her emotions under control. "They did. But maybe it meant more coming from Liz, now that I know her story."

He couldn't hide his surprise. "She told you about Luke and CC and her heartbreak and humiliation at their hands?"

Annie nodded.

"Wow. That's good news."

"Why in the world would that be considered good news?"

"Not the backstory. That will always be painful for her. But it's good because the more she's willing to share, the more she's willing to move beyond that painful time in her life." He lifted his hands to her arms, and this time she didn't draw away. "I want that for you, too, Annie. I want you to overcome whatever hell is threatening your happiness, so you can move beyond it." He ran his hands lightly down her arms before taking her hands in his. "So what's the plan? How would you like to begin fighting back?"

"I'd like to meet with Chief Crain and see what else he's learned. I want to know what your grandfather's friend Newton Calder has uncovered so far. And I want to let both of them, as well as the state and federal authorities, know that even though I'm their prime suspect, I'm also the victim of a scheme and have the right to be kept in the loop while they work their way through this investigation."

"Now that's what I've been hoping to hear you say." His smile warmed her. "Let them think whatever they want. But once they've put all the threads together, we know that your name and your family's reputation will be restored."

Her smile matched his. "That's the plan. I'm so glad you agree. Can you spare the time to drive me to town?"

He nodded. "My time is yours."

*   *   *

"Annie. Jonah. Good to see you." Noble Crain, fresh from lunch with the town council at Nonie's Wild Horses Saloon, stood and gestured to the chairs across his desk.

He sat back, his arms crossed over his chest. "What can I do for you?"

Jonah kept his tone conversational. "You're aware that my grandfather invited Newton Calder to join the investigation."

Noble nodded. "I am. And I welcome any and all help. Of course, I'm more or less at the bottom of this investigative food chain. Once it was labeled a federal crime, the feds took the lead on this, while working as little as necessary with the state police. Being a small-town cop, I'm just allowed to remain in the loop."

"At least they're sharing their information with you, Chief." Annie leaned forward. "I know that I'm a suspect, but I'm also, whether you and the others care to admit it, a victim of this scheme. It's my good name that is being smeared. My family's reputation is on the line. I realize, since the victim of the million-dollar theft was one of my clients, that it's easy to assume that I'm involved. But you have to acknowledge, at least somewhere in the back of your mind, that I would have had to be the dumbest thief in the world to steal that much money from one of my own clients and then deposit the loot in an account in my own name in a competitor's bank."

"I've run into a lot of stupid criminals in my day." Realizing what he'd implied, Noble uncrossed his arms and straightened in his chair. "Not that I'm calling you a stupid criminal, Annie. But all that glaring evidence is pretty hard to ignore."

"That's what the real criminal is hoping. As long as the authorities believe they already have their thief, he hopes that they'll get lazy and refuse to spend time looking elsewhere."

"That's where Newt comes in," Jonah added. "Gramps Egan knows that Newt won't be lulled into a false sense that the first and most obvious trail is the only trail. He'll keep on digging until he finds what the others may have overlooked."

The chief leaned close, tapping a pen on his desktop. "That's my hope, too." He let his gaze settle on Annie. "Let me be candid. I liked you, Annie, from the first time I met you. I'd like to believe that you're innocent and that this whole thing is an elaborate setup. But a good cop can't ignore evidence that's right under his nose."

"I understand, Chief." Annie took a breath. "But I've decided to stop running and hiding and denying. Since I intend to remain here in Devil's Door until this is resolved, I'd appreciate it if you would share whatever information you can."

Noble seemed to think about it for a moment before giving a nod. "I can tell you this. I learned today that there are more than half a dozen Arlen Lenders around the country, but none of them show up on any police files."

Jonah shared a look with Annie. "An alias?"

Noble shrugged. "Or a man with a clean record. The feds have run every Arlen, Allen, and Alden Lender in their data bank." He turned to Annie. "None of them have been in the San Francisco area. None of them fit the profile of the man you described. It would help if you had a picture of him."

Annie shook her head. "I don't." She gave it more thought before saying, "I remember being in formal dress for a charity affair and asking Arlen to pose with me. Instead, he insisted on taking my phone and clicking off a couple pictures of me. I didn't think too much of it at the time. Now I realize he very cleverly avoided being photographed. How I wish I'd have insisted."

The chief brushed it off. "If this guy's smart enough to steal from reputable banks, he's probably had plenty of experience avoiding cameras."

He thought of something else. "You said that you were introduced to this guy at a party hosted by the bank president."

"That's right."

"Who introduced you?"

She had to think about it before saying, "I believe it was Jolynn Carter. She does the same work that I do but in a different branch. There were maybe half a dozen people in her group, and Arlen was one of them. But someone else may have introduced him to Jolynn before I joined them."

"Which branch did Jolynn work at?"

"At the time, she was in number thirty-two, in downtown San Francisco. But I heard that she was transferred to forty-five. Of course, we routinely move around, so that could have changed since I left."

The chief noted everything before looking up. "All right. I'll get this off to the task force."

"Have you heard from Newt?" Jonah asked.

Noble shook his head. "So far, nothing. But the authorities, both state and federal, like and trust Newt. Even though he's retired, he's one of them. I'm sure you'll be hearing from him whenever he has anything to report."

He stood, indicating an end to their meeting.

They shook hands before walking away.

Outside, Jonah took Annie's hand and led her toward his truck. "Lunch at Nonie's?"

"Hmm?"

Realizing that she was distracted, he said, "Never mind. I have a better idea."

He left her in the truck and returned a short time later carrying several bags, which he set in the back seat.

As they left town, Jonah turned on the radio. With Rascal Flatts singing "Bless the Broken Road" in the background, they lowered the windows and allowed the gentle breeze to fill the truck.

The words of the song filled Annie with a quiet

peace. She leaned back against the headrest and studied the rolling hills and the occasional ranch, with split-rail fences meandering along wildflower-strewn fields and meadows.

When she turned to Jonah, her smile had returned. "This is all so pretty. I can see why my uncle refused to join my dad in San Francisco when they were younger. He insisted on returning to his roots here."

"Are your folks still there?"

She shook her head. "My mom passed first. Eleven years ago. My dad's been gone for six years. They were both in banking. Since I'm an only child, it was expected that I'd follow them into the same business, especially since I love it. Or rather, I did until..."

He reached over and closed a hand over hers. "You'll love it again, when this is resolved."

She kept her smile in place. "From your lips, Jonah."

CHAPTER TWENTY-ONE

When they drove past the Merrick ranch house, Annie turned to Jonah. "We're not going home?"

Home. Another word that had slipped so easily from her lips. The thought filled him with hope.

He'd spent the night fighting the feelings that had been unlocked since meeting Annie. But somewhere between then and now, a lot of the questions that had plagued him had been answered. Or maybe they just didn't matter anymore. Whatever the reason, he was feeling confident and strangely calm.

"I thought we'd head to my cabin and do a little hiking. That always seems to ease your mind."

"Oh, yes. I'd love that." She watched as he maneuvered the truck along an overgrown path. "Are you sure you should drive way out here? There's no road."

"None needed. I rarely drive here. But this truck can take us through and around and over any number of obstacles."

Soon they pulled up behind the cabin, where Jonah

turned off the ignition and retrieved the bags before circling around and taking Annie's arm.

"Watch for hidden tree roots or they'll trip you."

"Thanks." She moved along easily beside him.

While she paused to watch the antics of a chipmunk, he stepped into the cabin and within minutes was outside again, handing her one of his wide-brimmed hats and a bottle of water. "All set?"

She nodded, and the two of them set out at a brisk pace.

The sun was already sinking below the peaks of the Tetons by the time Annie and Jonah returned to his cabin. The afternoon had slipped away, and with it, all the tension that she'd been carrying around. Instead of lingering on her troubles, she'd been able to move beyond them to the sights and sounds of the countryside.

As he'd hoped, their hike to high country had resulted in the sighting of a herd of mustangs, and they'd spent a lazy hour under the cover of the woods watching the mares and their frisky young, guarded, as always, by the stallion keeping watch nearby.

Annie was so caught up in all that she'd seen that she couldn't stop talking about it on their walk back.

"That little spotted mare was so sweet. I loved the way she would lift her head and give that little guy a look that would stop him in his tracks."

Jonah was laughing. "I think that look was the equivalent of the hairy eyeball Gram Meg used to give us when our horseplay got too rough."

"The three of you must have been a handful for your grandmother."

"I guess we were. But she knew the men in the family had her back, along with Aunt Liz."

"Still, it all fell to her to keep you three in line."

"For the most part." He opened the cabin door and led the way inside.

They sat just inside the entry and removed their boots, setting them beneath the bench.

"It's getting cool, now that the sun has set. Want me to start a fire?"

Annie shrugged. "That would be nice, if we're staying long enough to enjoy it."

"We're not on any timetable. We can stay as long as we choose."

"What about dinner?"

"I've already texted Billy to let him know we'll be eating here." He crossed the room and knelt in front of the fireplace, holding a match to kindling.

Within minutes, the log caught a trickle of flame and soon a cozy fire was burning.

He stood. "Hungry?"

"Famished." She gave a shake of her head. "After meeting with Chief Crain, I had no appetite at all."

"See what hiking a couple of miles can do?"

"A couple? It felt more like a marathon."

He took her hand and led her to a chair pulled up before the fireplace. "Put your feet up and relax."

He retrieved a bottle of red wine from one of the

bags he'd brought from town and proceeded to uncork it before pouring some into two stemmed glasses.

As he handed one to her, she arched a brow. "Very thoughtful of you, cowboy."

"That's me." He touched the rim of his glass to hers. "Always thinking."

He sank down on the footstool and surprised her by lifting her stockinged feet to his lap and rubbing a thumb along her instep. "It's funny. I've grown up here on this land, watching herds of mustangs all my life. And there have been plenty of times when I felt really happy to see them. But lately, seeing them through your eyes, it all seems new and different. I see them now and feel that tingle, as though I'm seeing something rare and wonderful for the first time."

"They are, Jonah. Rare and wonderful. And magical. Something happens to my heart whenever I'm lucky enough to spot them. But today, having the chance to stand and watch without being seen was really special. I kept hoping they wouldn't melt away as they usually do. Instead, they stayed and grazed and played, allowing us to get a glimpse of their lives up in the hills, away from humans. They reminded me of a big, happy family. Like yours."

"We are happy." He looked thoughtful as he took a drink of wine. "And close. We've always been able to share in good times and bad."

"Have there been bad times?"

"Too many to count." His smile returned. "But the good outnumber the bad."

He stood, gently lowering her feet to the footstool as he vacated it. "I promised to feed you."

"Yes, you did." She was already missing that gentle massage of her foot.

He crossed to the small kitchen area before reaching into the refrigerator and removing several takeout cartons.

Annie stood up. "As long as everything is cooked and ready to eat, I can assemble it. That's how I've survived life in the city. Let me help."

He handed her two bowls and a container before placing another container in the microwave.

Minutes later she had put together their salads of greens, assorted sliced vegetables, croutons, and grated cheese.

She dipped a spoon into a small lidded container and gave a nod of approval. "Oil and red wine vinegar. How did you know it's my favorite?"

"I remember everything about you. What you like. How you taste..." He removed the takeout from the microwave, missing the look on her face as he assembled lemon chicken and bow-tie pasta in a creamy sauce on two plates.

Next he lifted a low table in a corner of the room and positioned it in front of the fire. While Annie carried their plates and bowls to the table, he tossed several cushions on the floor and snagged the wine bottle.

Lounging side by side, they dug in.

*   *   *

"Oh, Jonah." Annie wrapped her arms around her knees and stared into the fire. "You're so lucky to have this retreat. And to think you built it yourself."

"When I started it, I just wanted something quiet." He chuckled. "You may have noticed that we Merricks are a noisy bunch. I've always craved long blocks of silence, in order to work."

He looked around with a sense of satisfaction. "And I learned that I like working with my hands almost as much as with my mind."

"I wouldn't have expected the two to be compatible."

"I know what you mean." He nodded in understanding. "But, in fact, while I'm doing physical work, my mind is free to work out the kinks in the story playing in my head. And then, when I sit at the computer, I'm ready for the stillness that comes with the job."

"Was your family surprised by your success?"

He thought about it for a moment. "They've always been supportive, but I'm not sure anybody expected this."

"I've never seen you doing publicity for your books. I suppose that's why I didn't recognize you when we first met. Except for your photo in the back of your book, there've been no TV interviews or any of those in-depth articles in newspapers or magazines."

"And there won't ever be any, if I have anything to say about it."

"I don't understand. Doesn't publicity sell books?"

He gave a dry laugh. "I'm sure it helps. But I like my life the way it is. I'm as much a rancher as a writer. Here in Wyoming, I get to enjoy the best of both worlds. I'm not willing to sacrifice my privacy for fame."

"So, privacy matters."

He nodded and reached for the wine, topping off their glasses.

Annie grew silent as the fire burned low.

"A penny for them."

She looked up and gave a dreamy smile. "As someone who grew up in the city, I wouldn't have understood your need to stay here on your ranch. But now that I'm here, I can't imagine leaving all this behind for something as fleeting as fame."

He couldn't mask his surprise and his pleasure. "You get it?"

"Of course. Today, watching that herd of mustangs, I found myself fighting tears. I kept thinking that it was almost too mystical to be real. Hiking these hills, watching wildlife most people will only see in movies and magazines, seems like a dream come true to this city girl."

He was silent and watchful as he studied her, hoping to mask the storm raging inside. It mattered to him that she loved his way of life. It mattered to him that she could see and understand all of this. Then again, everything about Annie was beginning to matter to him. But he wasn't ready to put his feelings into words. Not yet.

She put a hand on his. "What's wrong, Jonah?"

"Nothing's wrong." He glanced down at their hands before looking into her eyes. "Everything about you is right."

"I don't under—"

He set aside his wineglass and touched a finger to her lips to still her words.

With his index finger, he traced the curve of her eyebrow, the outline of her mouth before splaying his open palm on her cheek. "Annie Dempsey, you take my breath away."

"And you"—she took his hand and placed it over her heart—"feel what you do to me. My heart's…"

Her words died as his mouth covered hers in a kiss so hot, so hungry, he nearly devoured her. He changed the angle of the kiss and took it deeper, until she wrapped her arms around his neck and returned his kisses with a fervor that matched his.

Jonah buried his face in her hair. "I think…we were meant to be, Annie. When you walked up to my cabin, I knew it was fate."

Her breathing was as ragged as his. "I kept thinking the same. That somehow, in all of Wyoming, I'd just found the one man I couldn't wait to see again."

"And here we are." He kissed her forehead, the tip of her nose, the corner of her mouth before staring at her with naked hunger.

"Kiss me, Jonah. Right now."

"Yes, ma'am." He took her fully into the kiss while

his big hands moved over her, lighting fires wherever he touched.

And then they were lost. Lost in the most exquisite pleasure.

When they came up for air, he fixed her with a look so hot, so fierce, she felt her heart contract.

"Stay the night, Annie."

Before she could react, the ringing of his cell phone had them both looking up sharply.

He studied the caller ID. "I have to take this. It's Gramps." He pressed the button, saying, "Hey, Gramps. What's . . . ?"

He paused before saying, "We'll be right there."

He returned his phone to his pocket. "Gramps Egan just heard from Newt Calder. He said as soon as we get to the house, we're to call him back."

"Oh, Jonah." Annie clasped his hand between both of hers.

They'd gone suddenly cold, Jonah noted.

"Come on." He carefully banked the fire and disposed of the remains of their meal, before setting the dishes in the sink.

Within minutes they were in his truck and heading toward the ranch house.

CHAPTER TWENTY-TWO

When Jonah parked the truck and walked with Annie up the steps, the entire family was waiting on the porch. From the empty plates and cups on side tables, it was obvious that they'd just finished their dessert in the evening air.

Egan stepped forward, offering his phone to Annie. "Newt was sorry you missed his call, but he said to tell you he's home all evening and will talk to you as soon as you call. Would you like us to leave you alone?"

She shook her head as she pressed the number and put the phone on speaker. "There are no secrets here. You all deserve to hear whatever he has to say." She looked around with a nervous smile. "After all, you've generously offered me your home and whatever help I need. How can I not share whatever I learn? We're in this together."

While the phone rang, Jonah took her hand, as if to lend her his strength.

His tender gesture wasn't lost on the others, who watched in silence.

"Newton Calder here."

At the sound of Newton's voice, she said, "This is Annie Dempsey. I'm using Egan Merrick's phone. I have you on speaker so everyone can hear what you have to say."

"Annie, thanks for getting back to me so quickly. Let me begin by saying that I spoke earlier with Noble Crain, so I know you stopped by to see him." Newton chuckled. "I'm glad you're pushing the chief for answers."

Annie asked breathlessly, "Have you learned anything more about Arlen Lender?"

"Only that he seems to have no police record. That may mean he's using an alias."

"The chief said as much." She shared a look with Jonah, who kept her hand firmly in his. "Is there anything else?"

"I'm afraid not. He's still a mystery. But I want to talk about the woman who opened a bank account in your name. I assume you're familiar with the bank's security video showing a woman resembling you."

"Yes. Though she's wearing the same coat, the woman isn't me."

"That's easy enough to say, but it remains to be proven."

At his words, Annie felt a quick shudder of apprehension.

Newton continued. "And I believe I can do that."

She closed her eyes in relief, and Jonah drew an arm around her shoulders, sharing her relief, while the others gathered even closer, afraid to miss a single word being said.

"Let me come back to that after I tell you this. I requested the bank's surveillance of its parking lot and discovered the vehicle used by the woman who opened that bank account in your name. I asked a favor of the federal lab, who enhanced the video enough to reveal two things—a male driver and the license number for that vehicle. They're running the numbers now, and I hope to have the name of the person it's registered to by tomorrow."

His voice lowered. "As we all know, identity theft has become commonplace, and it's usually used to open credit cards. But creating a false persona requires a bit more effort. It's been my experience in cases of false persona, that the thief goes to great lengths to use the right clothing to either remain anonymous, or in this case, make the person easily identifiable to the bank clerk. A bright red coat like one you admit you own leaves an indelible impression on witnesses."

Annie and Jonah exchanged a knowing glance, and the family was reminded of her earlier insistence about that very thing.

Newt continued. "But unless that person is a twin, it is possible to prove the woman in the security video is not you. So I will be sending a text spelling out some specific poses I want you to take while being photographed and videotaped. As an example, I'll be asking you to pose alongside a desk and a chair of certain proportions, so that the lab can measure your height, weight, and hand positions against the person in the video. I believe it will prove conclusively that the person who opened that account in your name was not you."

For the first time since the phone call began, Annie felt something in her chest loosen as she breathed deeply. "Oh, thank you, Newton. Send those directions and I'll get you every photo and video you need as soon as possible."

"Tonight," he said firmly. "And since you happen to have a professional photographer at your disposal, I know they'll be exactly what I ask for. I'll forward them to the lab, and they can get started tomorrow morning."

Everyone turned to Liz, who was smiling and nodding her agreement.

"Newton, thank you again. I'm so very grateful for all you're doing."

He chuckled. "Thank *you*, Annie Dempsey, for giving me this opportunity to step out of retirement once more and pit my skills against a worthy opponent. Although I enjoy being retired, there are times when I miss the thrill of the hunt. Don't lose hope. We'll be in touch soon." With that, he said his goodbyes and disconnected the call.

Annie handed over Egan's phone as the family gathered around her.

When the text came through, Egan handed his phone to Liz, who read it through before taking Annie by the hand and leading her inside, with the family trailing behind them.

For the next two hours, while the others watched, Liz posed Annie in the family's big office beside the desk, standing alongside a chair of a specific height, leaning at the desk and writing with a pen, and even looking directly at the camera.

She then, per Newton's instructions, went through the poses a second time, with Jonah holding a tape measure from Annie's hip to the desktop, which had books added until it was the exact height ordered by Newton, and from Annie's waist to the arm of the chair.

As they worked, Ham turned to Egan. "I think I know what Newt is getting at." He pointed to the tape measure. "Nobody, with the exception of an identical twin, would match Annie's exact measurements. By comparing the security photos to these, the federal lab technicians will be able to prove that the person opening that bank account wasn't Annie."

Egan nodded. "I'm telling you, Newt's the best investigator the state ever had. He cracked more cases than anyone else during his years with the force."

Gradually, as the photo session wore on, the family drifted off to their rooms. It was after midnight when Liz, Annie, and Jonah walked to her studio in the barn and she sent the photos off electronically.

She turned. "Okay. We've done all Newton asked us to do. Now the rest is up to him."

As the three left the barn and made their way back to the house, Jonah offered an arm to both women. Walking between them, he said, "It's funny. When I wrote my first book, I phoned Newt several times to run some scenarios past him to see if they were believable. As always, I was impressed with his sharp mind. Even in a fictional scene, he could point out the glaring errors." He turned to Annie. "Now, facing a real crime with dangerous criminals, I'm so glad Gramps has a friend like Newt. I hope he can ease your mind, at least a little."

He could just make out her smile in the darkness. "Though I haven't met Newton yet, I already trust him completely. Like you, I admire his sharp mind and his eye for details."

Jonah held the back door.

Before going their separate ways, Annie gave Liz a warm hug. "I'm sorry you had to miss your sleep for all this."

Liz returned the embrace. "Annie, I'm so happy I can help in any way. I just know those pictures are going to be an important piece of this puzzle. Now, let's all get some rest. Good night."

Jonah pressed a kiss to her cheek. "'Night, Aunt Liz. And a million thanks."

She turned away, while Jonah and Annie climbed the stairs.

They paused outside her door and he opened it before switching on the light.

In the open doorway, he gathered her close. Against her temple he murmured, "Will you be able to sleep at all tonight?"

She pushed away a little to look into his eyes. "Probably not. I can hardly wait to hear from Newt."

"If he's right, and those photos prove the woman is an imposter, it will force the authorities to broaden their search."

"I know. Oh, Jonah. I want that so much. I want so desperately to be vindicated."

"You will be. Hold on to that thought." He kissed her as gently as he would a sister. But in the space of a heartbeat the kiss deepened, until they were both sighing.

He lifted his head and glanced beyond her. "If you're not going to sleep much, I could always stay..."

That elicited a quick smile. "Nice try."

He shrugged. "Can't blame a guy. After all, we were rudely interrupted back at the cabin."

"Yes, we were." Her smile became a low chuckle. "Sorry about your bad luck, cowboy."

With a devilish grin, she lifted a hand and began closing the door.

He put out a foot to stop her. "Not even a little show of compassion for the guy who drove you to town and took you hiking before feeding you?"

She leaned close and pressed a quick kiss to his mouth

before stepping just as quickly away. "Thank you. And good night."

"I had something more in mind." Though he tried to look aggrieved, his smile said otherwise. "But I'm learning to be a patient man. There's always tomorrow. 'Night, Annie."

She closed the door and listened to his footsteps cross the hallway. She heard the door of his room open and close.

And then, as silence settled over the big house, she walked to the window and stared at the moon, riding high in the darkened sky.

Newt's phone call had given her much more than a hint that she might be able to prove her innocence. Though it was a baby step, it meant that with Noble Crain on her side, and Newton Calder working his magic, and Jonah's amazing family believing in her, the weight of the world had been lifted from her shoulders.

If only her uncle could be as open-minded as this family. Though it caused her a great deal of grief, for now she would be grateful for the support she'd found here in this place.

That phone call had given her what she needed most right now.

Hope.

CHAPTER TWENTY-THREE

With the morning chores completed, the family gathered in the kitchen to enjoy Billy's breakfast. The wiry little man with the bowl haircut and laughing blue eyes always saw to it that they left the table on a high note, ready to tackle whatever the day brought them.

When Egan's phone rang, he studied the caller ID before handing it to Annie.

She couldn't control the little tremor in her voice. "Good morning, Newton. I have you on speaker."

"'Morning, Annie. And good morning, Merrick family. I'm calling for a number of reasons. First, thank you, Liz, for those excellent photos. They were just what I'd hoped for. I've forwarded them to the feds' lab, and they acknowledged that they're perfect for a number of tests they're planning."

Shy Liz beamed her pleasure. "You're welcome, Newt. I was happy to be of help."

"I'll take all the help I can get from all of you.

Now to the news. The federal authorities followed up on the license plate of the car on the bank's security video. It is registered to a Vaughn Park. Does that name ring a bell?"

Annie and Jonah exchanged a look.

She nodded. "I had a visit from a man who called himself Park."

"What kind of visit?" Newt's tone changed slightly.

"I'd consider it a threatening visit. He wanted me to know that Arlen knew where I was."

"Did he threaten you? Did he have a weapon?"

"No to both. But I was afraid of him. He gave the impression that I was in danger."

"The feds have his name now. If he has a criminal record, he'll be in their database. In the meantime, we'll keep digging."

"What can I do to help, Newton?"

At her question, he paused. "Scour the Internet. So far you have two names to look for, and they're probably part of a wider network. Look for identity thefts involving large sums of money stolen from private banking accounts. The more people we have searching, the more likely we are to come across something. Remember, the smallest clue could lead to something bigger. Whenever I uncover more information, I'll send it along. You do the same."

"I will, Newton. And thank you for everything."

"I'll be in touch. Now, Annie, give me your phone number. It's time to eliminate the middle man." He chuckled. "Sorry, Egan." To Annie he added, "From now on I'll contact you directly."

When she gave him her number, he said, "Okay. Add my number to your phone. If you think of anything at all, day or night, call me."

After he rang off, she pulled out her cell phone and punched in his number before handing Egan his phone.

Jonah caught her hand. "You heard Newton. It's time to get to work. I have both a desktop and a laptop at the cabin. If the two of us put our heads together, we ought to be able to find something on Vaughn Park and Arlen Lender."

"Even if Lender is using an alias?"

He sandwiched her hand between both of his. "It's worth a try."

She nodded. "I agree. Doing something is better than doing nothing."

While the others voiced their agreement and gathered around to offer whatever help they could suggest, Hammond stood a little apart, studying Jonah and Annie with that sharp-eyed stare.

Something about his great-grandson and this woman had altered slightly in the past day or so. Though it had been a gradual change, there was a new intimacy between them that hadn't been there before.

Over the years he'd learned the signs, and this time he was sure of it.

His great-grandson was falling. In fact, he'd already fallen hard, if the look in Jonah's eyes was any indication.

*   *   *

As Jonah and Annie prepared to leave for his cabin, Billy handed Jonah a large handled bag.

At Jonah's questioning look, he smiled. "Supplies to keep up your energy, while you and Annie scour the Internet."

"Thanks, Billy." Jonah shook his head. "Why am I not surprised? While the rest of us are thinking only of our destination, you always remember the fuel we need to keep us going on our journey."

"That's my job." The cook paused. "How long do you and Annie plan on working over at the cabin?"

Jonah shrugged. "I guess we'll be there as long as it takes. But if we learn anything at all, we'll call home and share it with the rest of you."

Billy nodded. "Good luck. But in case you pull a late-nighter, I added a little something."

Jonah joined Annie at the back door, where she was slipping into her hiking boots.

With a wave of their hands, they called their good-byes to the family as they walked outside and started along the trail that led to Jonah's cabin.

Watching through the window, Meg turned to Egan with a sigh. "I'm glad Jonah has become Annie's champion. That sweet young woman deserves a break." She caught her husband's hand. "Oh, I pray they find something to give them hope."

"Don't worry, Meggie girl." Egan drew her close

and pressed a kiss to her forehead. "The most important thing is, Newt believes in Annie's innocence. Now they just have to band together to prove it. I do believe that, with the two of them following up on Newt's information, they'll find something to unravel this mystery."

In the cabin, Jonah sat at his desk scrolling through names and faces on the Internet that matched the ones Newton had given them.

Across the room, Annie did the same using his laptop.

He flexed his stiff shoulders before picking up his mug, only to find it empty. Heading to the kitchen, he filled it with fresh coffee, before crossing the room to fill Annie's.

"Thank you." She barely glanced up before continuing to scroll.

He pulled out his phone and was amazed to find that it was past noon. "We've been at this for hours. We need a break."

Annie paused to glance over. "You go ahead. I'm not hungry."

"Neither am I. But I'm restless. Want to hike for a while?"

She brightened. "I'd love to. If I stay here much longer, my eyes will cross."

He reached for her hand and helped her up before taking the laptop from her and setting it on his desk. "Come on. The work will still be here when we get back."

He reached into the refrigerator and withdrew two bottles of water.

With a smile, Annie accepted one and followed him from the cabin. The minute they started toward the high meadow, their smiles deepened. With every step, their lungs expanded and their hearts grew lighter. This was the perfect break after a morning of confinement staring at computer screens.

The afternoon had fled. The sun was already dipping behind the peaks of the Tetons, leaving the countryside in soft lavender twilight.

"Another wildcat sighting! And this one so close I could see those amazing, terrifying eyes. I feel so lucky." Annie's smile was radiant as she tucked her arm through Jonah's.

"You wouldn't feel lucky if he'd pounced."

"But he didn't. At first he just watched us. Then he disappeared up the tree."

"And we turned tail and went the other way as fast as possible like a couple of roadrunners."

Annie was giggling. "Hey, we're not foolish enough to tempt him. But oh, Jonah, wasn't he magnificent?"

"Yes. He was." He wrapped an arm around her shoulders, loving the way she'd blossomed as soon as they'd begun their trek to the hills. "Have you always been in love with the outdoors?"

She nodded. "I was on my high school track team, but I wasn't fast enough to keep it up in college.

So I got my outdoor fix by jogging after classes. The more I ran through parks, the more I found myself feeling a kind of quiet joy I'd never felt on the school track. When I started working, I'd jog or hike before dinner and on weekends. But this"—she spread her hands wide to indicate the beauty of the countryside—"this is a hiker's paradise. I just want to see it all."

"You'd need a lifetime to do that."

"I can't think of a better way to spend my life."

Her words pleased him more than anything he could think of. "Really? Think you could ever leave the big city behind and feel at home in the middle of nowhere?"

"This is hardly nowhere. Look around you. It's paradise."

Feeling an odd sense of contentment, he took Annie's hand as they continued toward the cabin. Along the way, she kept up a running commentary on all they'd seen on their hike.

"Do you have names for all the stallions that guard their herds?"

He grinned. "Names are for pets. These wild horses could never fall into that category."

"Kirby told me that Casey saved the life of the black stallion he named Storm."

"That's different. Storm was a newborn when Casey found him, all alone and vulnerable. He carried him home and raised him until he was old enough to be turned loose with his herd. If you ask me, I believe Storm was the main reason why Casey became a veterinarian. That stallion has been the subject of several scholarly papers Casey wrote for the wildlife society."

"I'm impressed. Kirby told me your brother is a well-respected expert on Wyoming wildlife."

"He is. That's been his love since he was just a kid. Again, thanks to Storm."

She paused. "And you're so proud of him you're practically exploding with pride."

He shrugged. "That's the truth. I'm proud of all my family."

"You should be. I know they're proud of you."

When they reached the cabin, Jonah held open the door. As Annie stepped inside, she paused at the bench just inside the door to remove her hiking boots. Jonah did the same.

She stripped off her socks, wiggling her toes. "Oh, this feels so good."

"Yeah." He was grinning at her. "Why is this the first thing we think of after a long hike?"

She walked barefoot to the kitchen. "Because our poor feet have been laced up in hiking boots for hours, and they deserve to be free."

He crossed to Annie. "I don't know about you, but I've worked up an appetite. You hungry?"

"Oh, yes. Now I'm ready to eat whatever Billy sent."

Jonah removed the container from the refrigerator and opened it with a smile. "Steaks, marinated and ready to grill over the fire. Twice-baked potatoes that just need to be heated. And thick slices of tomatoes straight from Billy's greenhouse."

Annie was laughing as she put a hand over her heart. "My hero. If you grill the steaks, I'll heat up the potatoes."

He pretended to consider a moment before saying, "Somehow, my job seems a lot more involved than yours."

"Big strong men should always be happy to take over the grill."

"Hmm. And pretty women get a pass?"

"Definitely. And thank you for calling me pretty."

"As if you didn't know." He chuckled before dragging her close to press a light kiss to her temple. "You're not just pretty, Annie. You're so dazzling I'm blinded by you."

She put a hand to his chest to steady herself. "You're pretty dazzling yourself, cowboy." She took in a deep breath. "Now, before we get sidetracked by all this sweet talk, feed me."

He kissed the tip of her nose. "Okay. There's wine left over from last night. I'll let you pour."

"Happy to."

He crossed to the fireplace and held a match to the tinder. Within minutes the log was blazing. A short time later, he placed a grill over the low, steady flame and added the steaks.

While they grilled, he and Annie sat on cushions

nearby, sipping wine and staring into the flames as they reveled in the wildlife they'd seen on their hike. When the steaks were ready, Annie added the prebaked potatoes, which had needed only a few minutes to heat in the microwave, and then she arranged the tomato slices on a plate.

As they had the night before, they set their plates on a low table in front of the fire.

Jonah topped off their wineglasses and took her hand until she was standing beside him. "I know we didn't find much on the Internet today, but I have a feeling that with Newt's help, we're getting close."

"I feel it, too. Oh, Jonah, just having him on our side gives me such hope."

"'Our side.' I like the sound of that." He touched the rim of his glass to hers. "To hope, to success, and to our side."

They sipped and shared a smile before he leaned over to brush a light kiss over her lips.

She saw his look of fierce concentration as he suddenly set aside his wine and reached for hers, placing the glasses on the mantel.

Without a word, he drew her into the circle of his arms and kissed her again. This time it was no light press of mouth to mouth. He drew her fully into the kiss until they were both breathless.

"Jonah..." She touched a hand to his face and he caught it, pressing a kiss into her palm.

At that sweet, unexpected gesture, she felt her heart

stutter. For a moment she could do nothing more than stare at him.

With a muttered oath, he dragged her close.

On a sigh, she wrapped her arms around his neck, her fingers tangling in his hair as she offered her lips.

And then they were lost in a kiss so blazing with need, everything else was forgotten.

CHAPTER TWENTY-FOUR

Jonah." It was the only word Annie could manage over the pounding of her heart.

Their bodies were pressed so tightly, their two hearts beat a frantic tattoo, threatening to break clear through their chests.

"Our dinner…"

"Will keep." His mouth, that wonderful, clever mouth, began trailing hot kisses across her face, down her throat, nuzzling the little hollow between her neck and shoulder.

She arched her neck, loving the feel of his lips on her flesh and the quick skitter of tingles along her spine. Her skin felt so hot she wondered if she would set the cabin on fire with the heat they were generating.

"I've thought of nothing but this, just this, all day." The rumble of his deep voice vibrated through her, and she knew it was the same for her. Though she'd tried to be cool, to concentrate on the important work at hand, and then their glorious hike in the hills, this sexual tension between them had intruded on all her thoughts. This was what she'd wanted. The feel of his hands on her. His mouth on hers. And this keen edge of excitement that had her breath burning her lungs, her pulse leaping higher with every touch, every kiss.

He reached for the buttons of her shirt, and he seemed to hesitate for the slightest moment, as though waiting for her reaction.

She put a hand on his. "Let me help you."

"No." He kept his gaze fixed on her as he unbuttoned her shirt and slid it from her shoulders. "I've been wanting to do this for too long."

His eyes crinkled into a smile at the bit of fabric that barely covered her breasts. "Leave it to a city girl. Wearing silk and lace under flannel."

"Doesn't everyone?"

She felt the warmth of his laughter as he reached behind her and unhooked her bra, watching it float to the floor.

"God, Annie, you're so beautiful you take my breath away." And then his hands were on her, and she felt her flesh grow hotter, her bones beginning to soften under his touch and melt like wax.

Still, it wasn't enough. She wanted her hands on him. Was desperate to touch him as he was touching her.

She nearly tore the buttons of his shirt as she slipped it from his shoulders. For a moment all she could do was sigh at the sight of all that muscled flesh. Now at last she was free to run her fingers over his torso. Unable to resist, she buried her mouth in the hair of his chest and breathed him in.

With a hiss of pleasure, he dragged her close and savaged her mouth until they were both struggling for breath.

His hands tugged at the snap at her waist, and her jeans joined the rest of their clothes.

His smile of pure appreciation turned into a deep-throated chuckle. "A thong, Ms. Dempsey?"

She gave a lilt of laughter. "Or, as I like to call it, my big-girl panties."

He was laughing as he drew her close. The minute they came together, his laughter faded. With a moan of pleasure, he ran his hands over her.

"At last, I can do what I've only dreamed of. I'm finally free to touch you everywhere."

And he did.

With murmured words and soft sighs, they lost themselves in the rising passion.

His mouth found her breast and he closed his lips around one erect nipple, nibbling and suckling until she was nearly sobbing with need.

"Jonah." His name was torn from her lips. "The bedroom..."

"Too far. I'll never make it."

They lowered to the floor, softened by the cushions.

Her breathing was labored, her heartbeat pounding beneath his hand.

Now he moved over her at will. With teeth and tongue

and fingertips, he explored the soft angles and planes of her face, the smooth line of her throat, the trembling muscles of her stomach. He teased her nipples until she writhed and moaned, desperate for release from the madness that had taken over.

Except for their sighs, and the sound of their labored breathing, the night had grown still. The world beyond this cabin no longer mattered. Outside a coyote howled, and an answering song sounded in the distance. In a nearby tree, an owl called to its mate.

The man and woman locked in an embrace took no notice. The air between them was charged with an electric current flowing from one to the other.

He pressed feathery kisses down her neck, across her shoulder, and lower, to her breasts. The look of pleasure in his eyes had her pulse rate soaring.

Just as she began to relax in his arms, he found her, hot and wet, and without warning, took her up and over. Her eyes went wide, then glazed over as waves of sensation washed over her, carrying her along in its tide.

"Jonah. Please. Now."

She wrapped herself around him and lifted to him. He entered her, unleashing a firestorm of passion that took them over completely.

Their breathing shallow, their heartbeats thundering, their bodies slick, they began to move, to climb.

With shuddering breaths and urgent whispers, they moved together, so caught up in the moment, the world had completely slipped away.

"Annie. My beautiful Annie." The whispered words were torn from his lips.

At the sound of her name, her lids fluttered and she saw herself reflected in those dark, fierce eyes staring into hers.

With unbelievable strength, she gripped him as they moved together, climbed together, until they reached a shattering climax that had fireworks going off behind her eyelids.

It was unlike anything she'd ever known.

"Are you all right?" He lay over her, his face buried in her neck.

"I'm fine." It was all she could manage without crying. But her throat, she realized, was clogged with unshed tears and she had to struggle to hold them back.

He lifted his head a fraction, his words muffled against her ear. "Sorry. I was rough. I should have realized…"

"Rough?" Her tears were forgotten as a little laugh broke through. "I nearly tore your clothes off. You had me so hot I thought I might explode."

At her admission, he leaned up on one elbow. "Me too. But I was trying to slow things down."

She wrapped her arms around his neck and drew his face down for a long, slow kiss. "It was… very special."

"Yeah. For me, too."

He paused, considering. "Sorry about our dinner. By now everything's bound to be cold."

"I like cold steak."

"So do I. But I love hot sex with you more."

They shared a laugh.

He rolled to one side and gathered her close. She snuggled against him, loving the way she fit so perfectly in the circle of his arms.

He played with the hair at her temple, twirling it around his finger. "Do you know how long I've been dreaming of this?"

She arched a brow. "How long?"

"Since the night you walked into Nonie's. I felt as though I'd been struck by lightning. A jolt of pure electricity shot through my system, and for a minute all I could do was stare."

She smiled. "I felt it, too."

He peered into her eyes. "You did?"

She gave a dry laugh. "How could I not? The way you were staring at me, I felt like a spotlight was shining directly on me."

"It was. Everything in that place had faded away. The noise. The music. Even the crush of people. There was only you."

"And you. That sexy cowboy, staring holes through me while I ordered my takeout."

"I figured you didn't notice."

"Oh, I saw you."

He murmured against her temple, "You said your name. Annie. And I remember thinking it was the most beautiful name in the world. And I knew, without a doubt, that I would see the beautiful, mysterious Annie again. Or die of loneliness."

Her eyes crinkled with laughter. "My, my, cowboy. How dramatic. Spoken like a writer."

"Spoken from the heart." He took her hand in his and laced his fingers with hers. "Would you mind staying the night here?"

For the space of a heartbeat, she hesitated. Then her smile came. Slowly, almost shyly. There was no hesitation as she touched a hand to his cheek. "There's nothing I'd like more."

He pressed his forehead to hers. "Thank heaven. I was afraid you were about to break my heart."

He paused a moment. "Would you like to eat now? Or would you rather just lie here awhile?"

"Let's just lie here. We can eat later."

"I like the way you think, Annie Dempsey."

"I like the way you make love, Jonah Merrick."

He grinned. "We're quite the pair."

He snagged an afghan from the footstool and draped it over both of them. And while the fire burned low, they lay together, wrapped in the glow of their lovemaking, sharing stories about their childhood, eager to know everything about each other, as lovers do. Their favorite food, and color, and season of the year. Their childhood fantasies. Their best friends.

"I love hearing about your childhood here on the ranch."

"And I love the image of ten-year-old Annie Dempsey beating every kid in the class on a math quiz."

"I was such a nerd. I used to spend the entire weekend figuring out a math puzzle for extra credit in class."

"Well, when I wasn't chasing after my brothers, I had my nose buried in a book."

Annie was laughing as she wrapped her arms around his waist and pressed her mouth to his throat. "We have nothing in common."

He gave a quick moan of pleasure. "I can think of one thing." He had that wolfish look she'd come to love. "But I'm afraid our supper is going to get even colder."

She had the look of a woman in love as she met his eyes. "Who needs food?"

"I knew we'd find common ground."

This time there was no frantic need, no desperate rush. Instead, with whispered words and slow, deep kisses, they took each other on a lazy, delicious journey, knowing they had all the time in the world.

CHAPTER TWENTY-FIVE

W̲ake up, sleepyhead. I come bearing gifts."

Annie opened her eyes slowly, then sat up to accept a cup of steaming coffee from Jonah's hands, sipping and sighing with pleasure.

Sometime in the early hours of the morning, after a night of loving, Jonah had carried Annie to his bed where they'd alternately talked and loved and had even picked at their cold supper at one point, until sleep would take them. Then they'd wake and talk again, sharing stories of their lives before meeting.

Jonah regaled Annie with tales of growing up wild and free on the ranch, and of his love for books, especially stories of the old west.

Over the rim of her cup, she continued the conversation they'd started during the night. "I believe you were complaining about being the youngest."

Jonah leaned over to press a kiss to her forehead. "Brand never let me forget that I was the 'little brother' and that he was in charge." He leaned up on one elbow, running his finger across her shoulder as he talked, sending little shivers along her spine.

"When did he finally accept you as an equal?"

"I'll let you know when it happens."

They shared a laugh.

"The truth is, I don't know exactly when or how it happened. I guess when Casey was studying veterinary science, and I was away at Yale and—"

"Wait." She stared at him with a look of disbelief. "You actually left the ranch to attend school in the East?"

"Just a year of graduate study. That was all I could take, before I knew I had to head home." He smiled and brushed her mouth with his. "If I'd had you waiting for me, I wouldn't have lasted a month. Anyway, when the three of us were back together, the dynamics had shifted, and we felt more like equals than older or younger."

"That's nice." She set aside her cup and wound her arms around his neck, pulling him down for another slow kiss. "So's this."

That was all it took for them to lose themselves once more in the simmering passion.

"I knew I was the nerd of the class, but it didn't bother me."

As they lay side by side, Jonah asked her about her school days.

At her words, he shook his head. "It's hard to believe you weren't one of those golden California girls turning the head of every guy for miles around."

"At the tender age of a preteen, nothing mattered more to me than being smart. I was so competitive. Whenever there was a math quiz, while the rest of the class groaned, I was ready to take on everyone, just to earn the highest grade."

Jonah was laughing. "Every class has one."

She joined in his laughter. "That was me. Obnoxious. Driven. I was absolutely fascinated with numbers. My best friend Lori was always asking me to help her with her math."

"And you were happy to oblige."

She nodded. "It was the most natural thing in the world for me to follow my parents into finance. Though they both held positions of importance, when I expressed an interest in the same career, they insisted that I start with the lowest job and work my way up without any help from them. At first I thought they were being mean. It was only afterward that I realized what a gift they'd given me. I never had to worry that my success was the result of their interference. I knew for a fact that it came from my own hard work."

"Smart people, your parents." Jonah listened, all the while watching her eyes, loving the way they sparkled as she talked about her friends and family.

"Even though they wanted me to follow them into banking, they wanted me to feel a sense of independence and accomplishment."

"And look at you, Annie Dempsey. An independent woman." He framed her face with his hands. "It's one of the many things that I l—" He caught himself and said, "That intrigues me about you." He dipped his head and kissed her, gently at first, then drawing her fully into the kiss until, with a sigh of pleasure, they came together in a firestorm of passion before, spent, they slept once more.

As the mattress dipped under Jonah's weight, Annie sat up, shoving hair out of her eyes and pulling the blanket to her shoulders. "Do I smell coffee?"

"You do." He was barefoot and naked to the waist. He'd pulled on his discarded jeans, leaving them unsnapped at the waist.

He offered her the cup and she drank greedily.

"Oh. Mmm." She took several more sips before handing it back to him. "That's heavenly. Thank you. How long have you been up?"

"Just long enough to make coffee and see what else Billy sent. We have strawberries, ham and eggs, and cinnamon biscuits."

"Bless Billy. A breakfast fit for a king."

"Or a queen." He ran a finger along the top of her bare shoulder. "I'm sorry I didn't let you get much sleep last night."

She touched a hand to his cheek. "Do you hear me complaining?" She stretched. "Best night ever."

"For me, too." He set aside the cup and slipped out of his jeans before climbing into bed beside her.

She shot him a look of surprise. "I thought you wanted breakfast."

"I did. But I just remembered something important."

At her silent question, he gave a wicked smile. "You're not wearing anything under this blanket."

"A gentleman would have pretended not to notice."

He laughed and pulled her into his arms for a long, slow kiss. Against her mouth he growled, "I never claimed to be a gentleman. I'm just a low-down, rotten, love-crazed cowboy, ma'am."

"My kind of guy," she managed to whisper before she lost herself in the pleasure he was offering.

After a long, lazy shower together in the tiny bathroom, they dressed and decided they would fortify themselves with Billy's breakfast before returning their attention to the computers.

Jonah started a fresh pot of coffee. "Did you take your friend Lori into your confidence before leaving town so suddenly?"

Barefoot, Annie was hulling the strawberries and arranging them on a plate, along with the cinnamon rolls. She paused to look at him. "I called her in a panic and told her that I was in trouble and had to leave San Francisco right away. I know I hurt her when I told her I couldn't explain, but I warned her that she might read some terrible things about me that she shouldn't believe. She got really upset and asked me where I was going. I said it was safer for her if she didn't know. That way, she wouldn't have to lie if Arlen happened to contact her."

"She knew Arlen?"

"She hadn't met him, but I'd told her about him."

"Why didn't she meet him?"

"Looking back, I realize he always had one excuse or another whenever I made plans to meet her and her boyfriend, Nick. But at the time, Arlen seemed so sincere about hoping to get together another time that I always just let it go."

"Have you contacted Lori since you got here?"

She shook her head. "I texted her but then deleted it. I was afraid she would somehow be dragged into this mess just by being associated with me. I hate that I'm keeping all this from her, but Lori is the sweetest friend ever. I couldn't stand it if I was the cause of any trouble for her."

Jonah hurried over to press a kiss to her cheek. "I'm sure Lori will understand her friend's tender heart."

She leaned into him for a moment, drawing on his strength. "Oh, I hope so."

He tossed the last of the logs onto the fire before crossing to the bench by the door to pull on his boots. "I should be able to chop a couple of logs and be back inside by the time you scramble up some eggs and fry the ham."

Seeing her worried frown begin to fade, he ambled over to press a kiss to her mouth and kept his tone light. "You look like you really know your way around a kitchen."

"That's me. A regular domestic goddess," she said

with a laugh. "Fortunately for you, one of the few things I know how to make is scrambled eggs."

He pulled her close. "Want to forget all this and just go back to bed?"

"I could be persuaded."

He gave her a devilish smile. "Maybe we'll fortify ourselves with some breakfast, and then spend the day like a couple of lovesick fools."

"Works for me, cowboy."

He kissed her again before sauntering to the door. "I'll be right back."

Annie started cracking eggs into a bowl while Jonah ambled outside to the woodpile at the rear of the cabin.

With the sound of the ax biting into wood outside, Annie hummed as she poured the eggs into a skillet and carried it to the stove.

Feeling the rush of cool air, she turned with a smile. "That was the fastest..."

Her smile died when she saw not Jonah, but Park, the angry, threatening stranger who had stormed her apartment in town with a message from Arlen Lender. On his face was a smug sneer that had her adrenaline surging through her system. He looked entirely too sure of himself.

"What...? Where...?"

He advanced so fast there was no time to react. He threw one muscled arm around her and pressed a dirty rag over her nose and mouth to muffle her scream. She clawed frantically at his arm, but he only tightened his grasp. She felt a sudden sharp sting as a needle was plunged into her upper arm. She fought harder until her hands dropped uselessly at her sides. Her vision blurred while her entire body went limp.

She felt herself falling, but instead of a hard landing, she was suddenly floating through the air.

She felt the coolness of the woods, and then she thought she heard the sound of an engine as she was dropped unceremoniously onto a cold surface before something that smelled of horses and sweat covered her from head to toe, nearly smothering her as she drifted into unconsciousness.

Jonah lifted the ax high and brought it down with such force the blade bit clean through the log, sending pieces scattering. He set a second log in place and did the same with ease. All the while, his mind was on Annie. Laughing. Loving. Sharing secrets from her childhood.

Last night had been everything he'd hoped for, and more. Though he'd been slowly losing his heart from the minute he'd first seen her at Nonie's, all his feelings had become crystal-clear during their long night of loving.

She was the one.

There had been plenty of women in his life. But none of them had ever electrified him the way Annie did. Since meeting her here in the woods, she was his last thought before sleep took him. His first thought when he woke. All day, while he tried to work, thoughts of Annie played through his mind.

At first he'd thought she was a passing fancy. A pretty face that intrigued him. They might enjoy a fling, and after satisfying their curiosity, they would go their separate ways. But then she'd come to stay at the ranch, and he'd had a chance to watch her interact with his family. To joke with his brothers and befriend their wives. To charm not only Billy but also the toughest critic of all, Ham. And now, after a night of unbelievable pleasure, he knew in his heart that he would never have enough of Annie. A lifetime wouldn't be enough.

And if she were to leave him, the pain of loss would stay with him forever.

Crazy, he thought. Some people needed years to decide, but he hadn't a single doubt that she was the one.

What better time and place to let her know his feelings than right here, right now? This cabin was his own private space, away from his family who, though much loved, could be intrusive. And it was where he and Annie had finally found the freedom to express their love.

He didn't know yet just how or when he would tell her. But when he saw an opening, he would let her know what was in his heart.

Grinning as his plan began to form, he collected an armload of wood and made his way around to the door of the cabin.

He nudged it with the toe of his boot. When it didn't budge, he was puzzled. He'd deliberately left it slightly ajar so he could easily haul the logs inside.

Annie must have found it open and closed it. Or maybe the breeze blew it shut.

He dropped some of the logs, freeing one hand to turn the handle before stepping inside.

The first thing he noticed was the black smoke billowing from the skillet on the stove.

"Hey, domestic goddess, you're burning the eggs."

He was laughing as he strode across the room and deposited the logs beside the hearth before yanking the skillet from the stove and turning off the hot burner.

Seeing that the contents had burned to ash, he set it in the sink and turned on the water, sending up another cloud of smoke.

Wiping his hands down his pants, he looked around. "Annie? Where are you hiding?"

When he got no answer, he walked to the bedroom. Finding it empty, he crossed to the open bathroom door.

Empty.

Puzzled, he made another turn around the cabin.

He could feel the hair at the back of his neck standing on end. A feeling of dread started twisting in his gut.

"Annie?"

Forcing himself to concentrate, he noted that her hiking boots were still by the bench. He'd teased her about being a city girl, but one thing was certain. She would never go outside barefoot.

Still, to satisfy his curiosity, he stepped out the door and took his time studying the ground, spotting large footprints in the damp earth. Too large to belong to Annie. A man's prints.

One set of prints had approached from the far side of the cabin. The same set of prints could be seen going in the opposite direction, away from the cabin door and back around to the far side. This set of prints, he noted, was deeper. Carrying something heavy.

The thought burst into his mind.

Annie would never go outside barefoot *willingly*.

With a low moan of anger mixed with fear, he retrieved his cell phone from his shirt pocket and dialed the police chief's number.

"Chief Crain here."

"Noble. Jonah Merrick."

"Hey, Jonah. I was just going to—"

"I need you to come to my cabin in the woods, Noble. Annie has gone missing."

"Missing? Are you sure?"

"Noble, my next call is to Newton Calder. Annie's been taken. And I need both of you now."

Before the chief could ask any more questions, he hung up. As promised, he phoned Newt and then placed the hardest call of all. To his family.

CHAPTER TWENTY-SIX

The rough jostling of the vehicle woke Annie. Nausea rose up in her throat, probably caused by the drug that had been injected into her arm. She could feel the coarse fabric that covered her head, casting her in pitch-darkness. From the strong animal smell, she realized it was a saddle blanket, probably snatched from Jonah's lean-to behind the cabin.

Getting her bearings, she realized her abductor had left her hands unbound—probably thinking it was safe due to the strong effects of the drug. She eased the saddle blanket down until she could see daylight. She was lying on the back seat of a car that was heading uphill and not following a smooth trail, but rather going in some sort of haphazard direction over rocks and small brush in its path. The pitch and roll of the vehicle added to her distress.

From her vantage point, she could see her abductor's head. They were alone. No other passengers.

Where was Park taking her? Had Arlen somehow made his way to Wyoming?

She tried to imagine the slick man in the thousand-dollar suits and Italian leather shoes spending even one day in the wilderness. She knew Arlen would prefer to remain in comfort and let someone else, like this thug, carry out his orders.

The driver swore as he swerved around some obstacle or other before punching the accelerator and sending the vehicle surging ahead, causing Annie to moan as bile rose up in her throat.

A short time later they came to an abrupt halt.

When Park opened his door, Annie closed her eyes and prayed he would leave her alone in the car long enough to get her bearings and possibly make an escape.

She heard the crunch of footsteps moving away and tossed aside the blanket, eager to try to make a run for it.

She struggled to sit up and could feel her head swim. Her fingers refused to work as she fumbled to open the passenger door. Her feet were leaden. Before she could even attempt to stand, Park was already returning. Caught, she froze, eyes wide as he shot her a sly grin.

"Sleeping Beauty is awake. And it looks like you were thinking of making a getaway." He swung a big hand, slapping her across the cheek with such force her head snapped to one side and she saw stars. She teetered on the edge of the seat. Before she could fall, he picked her up like a sack of grain and tossed her over his shoulder, carrying her inside a rough shelter where he dropped her to the floor in a heap.

While she dragged in a series of painful breaths, he closed the door and set a wooden brace against it.

Dazed, she looked around. They were in a shack with a dirt floor and a roof that sagged so badly it looked as though it would collapse on them in a strong wind.

Park picked up a backpack and sat on the floor with his back against the wall. Opening the pack, he withdrew a bottle of whiskey and took a long drink before leaning his head back and staring at her.

"May as well get comfortable. We got nothing to do now but wait." His lips peeled back in an imitation of a grin. "Unless you can think of a fun way to pass the time."

The smile he gave her had her skin crawling.

Jonah's cabin was crammed with people. Hammond sat in a chair in front of the fireplace. Egan and Meg shared the bench, which Jonah had carried from the front door to a place beside the hearth. His grandparents held hands and tried to hide the nerves that bubbled just below the surface.

Billy had staked a claim on the kitchen, where he brewed endless cups of coffee. Bo, Liz, and Chet stood beside the kitchen sink, talking in low tones.

Brand and Avery had arrived with Casey and Kirby, trying in vain to think of comforting words for Jonah, who paced back and forth like a caged panther, his features grim, hands clenched at his sides as though holding himself together by a mere thread.

As soon as Noble and Newt had arrived, Jonah had taken them outside to point out the man's footprints and had led them to a set of tire tracks he'd located running alongside the cabin and disappearing deep in the woods. Thankfully, Liz had brought along her ever-present camera and went along with them, photographing everything with the promise to forward the pictures to the FBI lab. Chief Crain had kept everyone away from the area of footprints and tire prints, explaining that he'd already ordered up a task force of state and federal investigators, who would be going over the entire area with a fine-tooth comb.

Newton, with his jaunty cap over a shock of white hair giving him the look of an aged Sherlock, explained. "Once the feds come into a case, the rest of us have to step back and allow them to take the lead."

Now they were all together inside the cabin as Noble laid out what he and Newton had determined so far.

"This was no random kidnapping. It appears to have been carefully planned. Judging from the speed with which Annie was taken, her kidnapper must have been watching and knew the exact moment Jonah left her alone."

His words had Jonah's eyes narrowing in fury at the knowledge that a stranger had been watching them all through the night and into the morning. A voyeur, no doubt, who had taken great delight in viewing their most intimate acts.

Noble turned to Jonah. "I believe you said Annie was alone no more than ten or fifteen minutes while you were chopping wood, and that for convenience, you left the door ajar?"

Everyone turned to Jonah, who nodded.

"It offered the kidnapper the opportunity he'd been waiting for. No door to force. No one around to shout a warning. And if he caught Annie by surprise, which the burned eggs seem to confirm, he could stifle any cry while subduing her with anything from chloroform to an injection. It was a simple matter to carry her off to his vehicle, hidden deep in the woods."

Jonah's voice was strangled. "And they could be any-where by now, while we stand around here."

"Necessary background work," Noble said softly.

"I understand. But how do we search for Annie when we don't even know who took her or what he was driving?"

"We will," Noble said firmly. "The task force is on the way. We have very clear tire marks in the damp earth. They'll be able to identify the make and model of the vehicle within hours."

"Hours." Jonah spat the word like a curse. "And this guy is already miles away."

His family could see the rage and frustration in his eyes and were helpless to offer any comfort.

"Jonah, Newton and I are in agreement that you will

probably receive a call from Annie's kidnappers some-time today. They may ask for money, but we can't be sure what type of game they're playing. For that reason, one of the members of the federal task force will have to stick by you until this is resolved."

Meg's nurturing nature kicked in. "Noble, we have to notify Annie's uncle. As far as we know, he's her only living relative."

Noble agreed. "I'll call Des."

Jonah gave a vehement shake of his head. "I should be the one to call, Noble. I was the last to see Annie. I'll need to explain why."

The chief cleared his throat. "I know this will be awkward. It's no secret that you folks haven't spoken in years."

Jonah's tone was firm. "This is my responsibility."

The chief paused before nodding. "I guess I can allow it. Afterward, if he wants to talk to me, let him know I'm available anytime."

They heard the rumble of vehicles and peered outside to see a group of men and women moving around the outside of the cabin. Noble and Newton stepped out the door and spoke briefly to them before returning.

Noble nodded toward the window. "The state and federal agents will be busy here for some time. It would be best if you folks returned home." He turned to Jonah. "No need to worry about banking the fire or securing the cabin. They'll see to it that the place is secure before they leave. And they may leave a few key people here overnight if they see a need for it."

They shook hands all around before the family walked outside and began climbing into trucks for the trip back to the house.

Bo turned to his youngest son, who hung back, looking around as though hoping to see Annie appear at any moment. "You coming?"

Jonah's eyes mirrored his pain. "I'd rather walk home, Pop. Maybe the fresh air will clear my head."

Bo put a hand on his arm. "I'll walk with you."

"No." He spoke sharply, before struggling to soften his tone. "Thanks, Pop. I appreciate the offer. But I need to be alone."

"If it's any comfort, son, I know the feeling." With a last look at Jonah, Bo climbed into the truck and felt again that never-forgotten pain of loss. Sometimes it was little more than a momentary ache. At other times it was as raw and deep as those first days and weeks after the fire, when the death of his beloved Leigh had left him shattered beyond repair.

The Merrick family had assembled in the great room to meet with Des Dempsey, after he'd surprised them by agreeing to drive to their ranch.

From the stilted attempts at conversation, it was obvious they were all feeling the strain of such an awkward meeting. It would be the first time these two rival families were together in over twenty years.

Bo was pacing, his hands behind his back, his expression grim.

Meg and Egan sat together on one of the sofas, holding hands as much for courage as for comfort.

Hammond was in his favorite armchair, his white lion's mane of hair and fierce dark eyes giving him the look of a biblical patriarch.

Brand and Avery and Casey and Kirby took seats on one side of the room, looking like they would spring up and surround Bo if he and Des should come to blows.

Jonah stood alone, his face unreadable. He'd barely spoken in the hour since he'd returned home and found federal agents already setting up equipment in the family office in anticipation of contact by the kidnappers.

At the sound of wheels crunching on gravel, everyone tensed.

A minute later, Billy opened the door to the great room to say, "Your visitor is here. Would anyone like coffee or tea?"

At the sight of the figure behind Billy, there was a moment of complete silence.

It was Meg who managed to say, "Nothing right now, but maybe you could prepare some tea and coffee in a little while, Billy."

Before she could get up, Bo walked past her to the man who stood framed in the doorway.

"Des." Bo paused before sticking out his hand.

"Bo." Des hesitated before giving a quick handshake.

Both men lowered their hands to their sides, where

they were clenched into fists. The two men stood, each taking the measure of the other.

Though both of them were nearing fifty, Bo's years of ranching had kept him lean and muscled. Except for some graying at the temples, his hair was still dark and curling over the collar of his denim shirt.

Des Dempsey wore his usual suit and tie, since he'd come from the bank. Though his tie was carefully knotted, his suit jacket couldn't hide the fact that his waist had thickened. His copper hair was threaded with gray. His laughing eyes, once his best feature, appeared both wary and weary as they narrowed on Bo with keen interest.

"I'm sorry my wife, Bev, couldn't come. She's recovering from chemo, and I thought whatever this was about, I'd try to shield her from anything that could upset her."

"Of course." Bo led him farther into the room. "I'm sorry to hear that she's going through this."

Des gave a little shrug. "It's hard. But she's hanging in there. I just hope, when the treatments are over, I can take her away for a while."

He greeted the older members of the family. "Ham." The two exchanged a quick handshake.

"Miss Meg."

Meg was on her feet to offer him a hug, which he endured stiffly.

"Des, I'm so sorry to hear about Bev's illness. I hope you'll tell her I send my best."

"Thank you, I will." He and Egan looked one another up and down before awkwardly shaking hands.

Des arched a brow when he spotted Bo's sister. "Liz. I haven't seen you in years."

"I like to stay close to home." She managed a polite smile.

"So I've heard. Sorry about…"

They both knew he was thinking about her humiliation at the hands of her fiancé, leaving her the topic of conversation in the little town of Devil's Door for many years.

To spare Liz, Chet stepped forward with his hand outstretched, forcing Des to turn to him. "Hey, Des."

"Chet."

Bo led Des toward the others. "My son Brand and his wife, Avery. And Casey and his wife, Kirby. And my son Jonah."

"The writer," Des muttered before acknowledging all of them with a nod. "Seems like yesterday you boys were all just tykes."

Bo pointed to a high-backed chair. "Have a seat, Des, and we'll explain why we asked you here."

"I hope you'll make it brief. I have appointments this afternoon." He sat, stiff-backed, looking as uncomfortable as they all felt. "I'm guessing it has something to do with my niece Annie."

Bo crossed his arms over his chest and allowed Jonah to take charge.

"I'm sorry to be the one to tell you bad news,

Des. Annie has gone missing. We believe she's been kidnapped."

"What?" Des was on his feet, his face reflecting his shock. "Is there a ransom note?"

"There's no word yet." Jonah lifted a hand. "And we don't know where she's been taken or by whom."

"Then how do you even know... ?"

"Both Chief Crain and the crime task force concur that Annie has been kidnapped."

"Crime task force?" From his expression, it was plain that Des couldn't seem to wrap his mind around what Jonah was saying. "So this has something to do with the theft..."

"I called as soon as I discovered her missing..."

Des held up a hand to silence him. "When I offered to put up Annie at Mandy and Jamie Ward's B and B, she told me that you had persuaded her to stay at your ranch because it was the safest place to be. How could someone manage to break in here, with all of you around her, and kidnap my niece?"

Jonah clenched his hands at his sides, struggling to keep his tone even. "We weren't here. Annie and I spent last night at my cabin. It's a little office I built about a mile from here, in the woods."

Des was looking at him as though he were speaking gibberish. "You're telling me that you and my niece spent the night alone in a cabin in the woods, knowing she's in danger, and now she's missing? Just where were you when she was supposedly kidnapped?"

"Around the back of the cabin chopping logs for the fire."

Des grabbed Jonah by the front of his shirt and dragged him close. "And in the time it takes to chop wood she just disappeared into thin air?"

The entire Merrick family was on their feet, surrounding Des and Jonah with looks so hostile he abruptly released his hold and lifted his fists, ready to fight all of them.

Jonah raised his hand in an attempt to soothe the tension. "I don't blame you for your reaction. Any one of us would feel the same way. Frankly, I'd feel a whole lot better if I could just punch someone or something. So if you'd like to take a shot, have at it, because this is all my fault."

Des took a closer look at this young man, seeing all the rage and frustration seething within him.

He took in a calming breath before saying, "Why don't you walk me through what happened. What you two said and did. Maybe you exchanged some harsh words?" His tone turned hopeful. "Maybe Annie just needed to get away."

Jonah shook his head and stalked to the floor-to-ceiling windows offering a stunning view of the Grand Tetons. Ordinarily just the sight of those majestic mountains would be a soothing balm. Today, he couldn't even see them through the misery that clouded his vision.

With his back to the others, he said, "Annie and I were laughing together. We were sharing a private joke, since she admitted she can't cook. But she offered to scramble eggs while I chopped some wood. I called her a domestic goddess, before going outside..." His words trailed off before he managed to add, "When I came back inside, she was gone. Vanished. But from the footprints and the tire tracks I saw, I knew she was taken"—his next words were barely audible—"against her will."

Des looked first at Bo, then at the others, who were all staring at Jonah with looks that ranged from stunned to sympathetic.

Meg's gaze was fixed on her grandson with a look of tenderness as she walked to him and put her arms around him. Softly she said, "I should have, but somehow I didn't realize how it was between the two of you until now. We'll find her, Jonah."

"I have to find her, Gram Meg." His words were muffled against her soft cheek before he pushed away and strode toward the door. "I have to find her, or die trying."

CHAPTER TWENTY-SEVEN

Annie sat as far from her abductor as she could manage, considering the small space of their shelter. She'd crawled to the opposite wall, forcing herself to sit up, praying the last dregs of whatever he'd used to knock her out would soon be gone. She was beginning to get some feeling back in her hands, but her feet were still too numb to allow her to stand.

Her vision was clear, but she still battled the feeling of nausea. Each time she saw Park take another swig of whiskey, she had to look away and swallow hard, fearing she might be sick.

"Want some?" He held up the bottle. "I guarantee it'll make you feel better."

She swallowed back the bile rising in her throat.

Seeing her, he chuckled. "You're looking a little green, girly. Come on. Try it. It'll put a bloom in your cheeks and heat in your belly."

When she refused to answer, he shrugged and took another swig before capping the bottle and setting it aside. He lumbered to his feet and walked to the door, and for a moment Annie felt her hopes rise. If he left her alone for even a minute, she would take a chance and escape, even if she had to crawl.

He opened the door and paused with his back to her. She heard the sound of his zipper and felt all her hopes dashed as, moments later, he finished his business and stepped back inside, firmly closing the door behind him.

Billy wheeled in a trolley with tea and coffee and sandwiches and parked it to one side before inviting everyone to help themselves.

No one showed any interest.

At a knock on the great room door, they looked up to find Chief Crain in the doorway.

"Newt is off following a lead."

The others perked up as Jonah asked, "Does this mean they've found Annie?"

Noble shook his head. "No. Sorry. But Newt thinks this is a solid lead and said to tell you all to stand by."

Seeing their looks of defeat, he added, "I'm heading to your office, Bo. The task force is ready whenever the kidnappers make their call."

He turned to Jonah, who stood alone near the windows, looking fierce enough to single-handedly fight a den of wildcats. "When your cell phone rings, don't answer. Just head to the office and follow the team's instructions."

Jonah nodded. "We've gone over the details four times now."

When Noble Crain walked away, Des Dempsey cleared his throat. "In all these years, Bo, I never had the chance to tell you how sorry I was about the fire and"— he coughed—"and losing Leigh."

"I figured you were too busy gloating." The words were out of Bo's mouth before he could stop them.

A pall of silence fell over the occupants of the room. They braced for the fight that Bo had been spoiling to have for all these years.

Ham started up out of his chair before looking around and sitting back down.

"Why would you say a thing like that, Bo?" Des looked more shocked than angry. "I've heard rumors, of course, through the years. But I never understood how you could think I'd enjoy your misery."

"I know that you and Leigh were planning on getting married when I came along." Bo's eyes narrowed. "Believe me, I didn't plan on getting in the way of your happiness. It just happened. I saw her and was struck by something beyond my control. One minute was all it took for me to know she was the one. And I guess it was the same for her."

Des nodded. "She came to me and told me how she felt. When she gave me back the ring, I have to admit I was jealous. I said some things I'm sorry for. It hurt my pride to lose her to another man."

"And to get even, you refused to give my family a loan that we needed to keep our ranch afloat."

Des frowned. "I'm not proud of that, Bo." He turned

to Hammond, and then to Meg and Egan. "I'm really sorry for what I did. It was mean and petty." He managed a wry smile. "I was young and stupid, and it cost me my best customers."

"That it did, boy." Hammond actually grinned. "And the bank over in Stockwell made a bundle on us over the years."

Now Des's smile wasn't forced. "You know, Bo, you actually did me a favor. A couple of years later, when I met Bev, I realized I'd never felt about any woman the way I feel about her."

"That's good." Bo stepped closer, looking directly into Des's eyes. "That's how every man should feel about the woman he marries." Now it was his turn to clear his throat and try to talk about something that was clearly painful. "About the fire..."

The family went completely still.

"Even though most folks thought it was caused by sparks from the fireplace, I harbored a lot of anger in my heart, thinking you could have had a hand in it."

Des was shaking his head. "I give you my word, Bo, I'd never consider such a thing."

Bo nodded. "I guess I realize that now. And hell, I'm just sorry I've wasted so many years over something that I never should have considered, for even one minute. I was a broken man, but that's no excuse for what I was thinking." He stuck out his hand. "I hope you can forgive me, Des, and we can put this behind us, especially in light of our common concerns over Annie."

This time Des grabbed his hand and held it. "Done. Not just because we should have had this conversation years ago, but as you said, so we can concentrate all our energy on finding Annie. Together."

The two men were nodding vigorously as they stepped apart.

Annie leaned against the wall of the shack, keeping an eye on Park. He'd already downed half the bottle of whiskey and was beginning to slur his words.

The tingling in her toes proved that the drug was wearing off. If only he would leave, she could slip away. But the way he was staring at her had all her senses on high alert. She knew that look. Had seen it on enough men in her life to know what he was thinking. This could very quickly get out of control. He was dangerous enough without adding alcohol to the mix. And the gun she'd seen in his pocket added another layer of danger.

As if reading her thoughts, he lumbered to his feet and stumbled across the narrow space to stare down at her, fingering the pistol in his pocket.

"I figured I'd have gotten my marching orders from Arlen by now, but since we've got some time..." He released his hold on the gun and dropped down beside her. "Let's you and me get to know each other, girly."

He leaned in, pressing his mouth over hers.

As his sour breath filled her lungs, Annie shrank back, wiping the back of her hand over her mouth.

Park fisted a hand in her hair, forcing her to face him. "You think you're too good for me? Is that it? Now you listen, girly. You can make this easy or—"

As he ground his teeth against hers, she raked her nails across his cheek, causing him to pull away with a vicious curse.

He touched a hand to his cheek and it came away stained with his blood.

He swore again and slapped her hard enough to cause her head to slam against the wall.

Stunned, she sucked in a breath, hoping to clear the spots dancing in front of her eyes.

"So, you like to fight, do you?" An evil smile split his lips. "Even better. I get off on women like that."

He raised a fist and Annie realized, too late, that no matter how hard she fought back, she had no defense against his brute strength.

Before he could strike another blow, his cell phone rang.

Breathing hard, he fumbled for his phone. "Yeah."

At the voice on the other end of the line, his manner changed. He stood up and leaned an arm against the wall, listening intently.

When Jonah's cell phone rang, he held up his index finger, indicating the call was coming from an unknown caller. At that signal, the family fell deathly silent.

Following the orders set up by the head of the task force, he raced down the hall to the family's office, currently filled with high-tech equipment and trained personnel.

The rest of the family followed, crowding around the doorway to watch and listen.

The director of the task force, Agent Mavis Johnson, signaled for Jonah to accept the call, while the staff began recording.

"Hello." Jonah felt oddly calm in the midst of the storm. This was what he'd been waiting for. Now, finally, he would learn where Annie was and the fate awaiting her.

"Jonah Merrick?"

Agent Johnson counted down three, two, one, before pointing at Jonah to respond.

"Yes."

There was a soft chuckle on the other end of the line. "Very good, cowboy. They've trained you well. I know you're probably waiting for a ransom demand. I know, too, that this is being recorded. It won't do you any good. The authorities may be smart, but I'm smarter. I'm using a burner phone. By the time they trace it in a dumpster, I could be in another country."

Jonah's calm feeling dissolved, replaced with rising anger. The confident tone on the other end of this call had alarm bells going off in his brain. Arlen Lender had anticipated all of this. Was, in fact, enjoying his audience and was showing off for them.

The voice continued. "From the number of cops crawling around that cabin in the woods, it's obvious you're as stupid as Annie Dempsey. She was warned to keep quiet, but she chose to go to the authorities and then thought she could run and hide. You can see how well that worked for her. Now she has to pay the price for defying me. I'm bigger, smarter, and more influential than the state police or the federal government. Their little two-bit dog and pony show will never shut down my organization. I'm too smart for that. But just in case anyone else is thinking about breaking ranks and ratting me out, hear my message loud and clear. There will be no ransom request. For disobeying my orders, Annie Dempsey is going to die. So pack up your expensive equipment and go home, everybody. The show's over."

Park was sweating profusely as Arlen's voice thundered over the phone.

Annie could overhear every word.

"Just as I figured, there are cops swarming over that cabin like locusts. You'd better hope, for your sake, that you followed orders and left nothing that could ID you."

"I did everything you said, Arlen."

"Good. I just called the cowboy. By now, every cop in Wyoming will be out looking for the bitch. Time to waste her and bury her inside the shack before you set it on fire."

"Won't the fire bring the cops?"

"Then you'd better be long gone before they get there."

Seeing Park wipe a hand across his glistening face,

Annie used that moment of distraction to slip her cell phone from her back pocket. She'd thought, this high in the hills, there would be no reception. But since Arlen got through, so could she. She looked down, fumbling to press the speaker button, hoping someone, somewhere, could pick up the conversation.

Seeing the slight movement, Park swore and rushed over to grab the phone from her hand.

"What was that?" Arlen's voice roared.

"The bitch was trying to use her phone. Don't worry, I've got it."

"Her phone? You didn't search her?"

More sweat popped up on Park's face. "There wasn't time. I had to get her away before the cowboy came back. Then"—his face became dark with fear and fury as he realized his blunder—"I...I forgot."

"You know the rules." The sudden icy calm of Arlen's tone was even more frightening to Park than his boss's screams of anger. "Time's up. Get rid of her and get out of Wyoming without a trace."

"Where will we meet?"

"I'll call you with that information later." The smooth-as-silk voice left Park trembling.

That tone of voice, that quiet dismissal told him his fate had been sealed.

CHAPTER TWENTY-EIGHT

At Arlen Lender's words, the entire room at the ranch had gone silent.

Jonah stood staring at the phone in his hand, as though expecting it to ring any moment with another call saying it had all been a misunderstanding.

He desperately wanted a ransom request. A location. A measure of hope, no matter how slim.

Annie was out there somewhere, alone, frightened, her life in the balance. And the so-called experts were looking as perplexed as he felt.

Chief Crain pushed his way through the crush of family and walked down the hallway, speaking rapidly into his phone.

Agent Mavis Johnson began moving around the room from monitor to monitor, asking questions, causing heads to shake in defeat.

Suddenly one of the officers wearing headphones gave a shout and the agent rushed to his side as he held up a hand for silence.

Mavis Johnson turned to the others. "We just got a ping from Annie Dempsey's cell phone."

Jonah's heart started racing. "Did she speak? Is there a message? What's she saying?"

The officer monitoring the call shook his head. "It was cut off quickly, which tells us that her abductor probably found out about it and took it from her. But the location is fixed and we're already on it." His eyes were trained on the monitor as the others gathered around.

He pointed. "Got it. In the hills, about six-point-eight miles from the cabin where she was abducted."

Just then, Chief Crain came hurrying into the office. "The state lab has identified the vehicle used in the abduction from the tire tracks. It's a Range Rover."

Agent Johnson nodded. "That's a start."

"There's more." Noble held up a hand for silence. "We have good reason to believe the vehicle is gunmetal gray with tinted windows..." A flush stole over his cheeks. "Since my wife, MaryAnn, spotted one yesterday with California plates rolling through town and thought maybe a celebrity was visiting." He winced. "You know how my wife would love to brag about having a movie star in town."

He didn't need to say what the Merrick family already knew. His wife loved to share any bit of gossip she could glean.

A small ripple of nervous laughter followed that admission.

He continued. "And one more bit of good news. Julie

Franklyn told Newton that a man came by her salon a couple days ago asking where her former tenant had gone. She was able to give a very good description of the man, because she thought he needed a haircut. She's working with the state police sketch artist. We'll get that out to all law enforcement ASAP."

"All right." Jonah couldn't keep the tiny thread of hope from his tone. "We've got a description of the vehicle, and we know approximately where Annie is. Let's go get her."

He spun around, heading for the doorway.

"Hold on." Agent Johnson used a tone of voice that commanded respect.

Everyone froze.

"This is not your operation, Mr. Merrick. You're ordered to stand down and let the experts handle this."

"But…" He turned to her, eyes blazing.

"No buts, Mr. Merrick. I'm in charge." She fixed him with a look guaranteed to freeze his blood. "See that you remember that."

Park was sweating bullets as he caught Annie by the wrist and yanked her to her feet.

His other hand closed into a fist, and she braced herself for a beating.

Instead he hauled her along to the door of the shack. "Since I need to get something out of the car, and I can't leave you alone here, bitch, you're coming with me."

She had to run to keep up with his quick strides as he opened the back hatch and pulled out a spade before returning to the shack.

She couldn't resist taunting him. "Your partner in crime didn't sound too happy."

He swore before giving her a shove that sent her sprawling. "Sit there and shut up."

As she crawled to the far side of the shack, she sagged against the wall watching him dig a hole.

He shot her an evil grin. "Maybe I should measure you before I dig your grave."

A shudder raced down her spine and her mind seemed to freeze as she realized the enormity of what was happening.

Seeing her pallor, his smile widened. "Sorry there isn't time for that little party I'd planned, but hey, when I get back to civilization, there will be a warm and willing female waiting for me."

"If you live long enough to party."

He slanted her a hateful look.

"Your boss didn't sound too happy with you. And who knows? Maybe somebody is digging your grave right now, too."

She could see that she'd hit a nerve. Park paused and pulled a filthy handkerchief from his back pocket to mop at his dripping face.

"Know what else I'm thinking?"

"Shut up." He held up the shovel in a menacing manner, and Annie could see the veins popping at his temples. His hands, she noted, were actually trembling.

In the silence that followed, he went back to his digging, all the while gritting his teeth and swearing under his breath.

When the hole was nearly finished, he grunted at the exertion and set aside his shovel. Pulling his cell phone from his shirt pocket, he turned away, punching in a number and then speaking to someone in a voice so low Annie couldn't make out the words. But whatever he was saying, he sounded desperate.

She glanced at the open doorway. Though there wasn't much of a chance that she could make it very far, it might be the only chance she would get.

She stood up and tentatively lifted the shovel, testing its weight. Then, with a mighty swing at Park's head, she heard his cry of pain as he fell face-first into the open grave.

Without bothering to look back, Annie dashed through the open doorway and headed into the woods.

Though she was barefoot, and every stone and twig and root cut into her tender flesh, she never made a sound. All her energy, all her being, was concentrated on making good her escape.

Jonah stood in the family study, watching and listening as Agent Johnson spoke to endless voices on endless phones, ordering reinforcements on the ground and in the air.

The trained agents who'd remained at his cabin were now ordered to head toward the spot where Annie's phone had given off its signal. State police helicopters were dispatched to the site.

Battling feelings of rage, of hopelessness, of helplessness, he walked out of the room and beckoned his family to follow.

Once in the great room, he closed the door and turned to face them.

His voice, low with passion, had them gathering around to hear every word.

"I know we're supposed to just wait here and hope for the best." His eyes blazed with the fire burning inside. "But we know this land better than these so-called experts. I've hiked those hills with Annie"—his voice nearly broke, but he forced himself to go on—"and I believe my only chance of saving her is to leave now and find her before her abductor can carry out Lender's orders."

Brand put a hand on his shoulder. "I'm with you, bro."

Casey nodded. "Me too."

"Now, you listen to me, boy." Ham's voice had them all turning.

Jonah was already shaking his head in denial. "You're not going to talk me out of this, Ham."

"Is that what you think, boy?" The old man gave him a steady look. "I was about to say, you're not leaving here without me."

"But..."

Bo turned to his father, and Egan spoke for both of them. "We're in, too."

Chet nodded toward Liz and closed his hand over hers before saying, "Count us in."

"And us," Meg said firmly. "Avery, Kirby, and I refuse to be left behind just because we're women. We're smart and strong and…"

Billy turned away from the food trolley to join the others. "I'm not staying behind. We're family, and that's what family does."

"And what about me?" At Des Dempsey's voice, they all turned. "Annie's my niece. And as Billy said, this is what family does. I'm in."

Jonah swept them a look of love and gratitude. "Then let's not waste any time. We'll go up-country with horses, trucks, and ATVs. We'll come in from all directions. And if we're quick enough…" He left the rest of his thoughts unspoken.

As they headed toward the barn, Jonah felt a faint thread of hope coursing through his veins.

They had to make it in time. They had to.

The words played through his mind like a prayer.

If they didn't…

He brushed aside the quick ripple of fear. It was impossible to imagine his life without Annie in it.

CHAPTER TWENTY-NINE

Annie heard Park's howl of pain and outrage echoing in her ears.

She chanced a quick look over her shoulder. In his drunken state, he had picked up the shovel, carrying it with him, until he seemed to realize the foolishness of it and tossed it aside.

Even that brief moment gave her a chance to put more distance between them, and she raced headlong into the thick foliage that she hoped would slow him even more.

Her feet, accustomed to the cushion of heavy socks and hiking boots, protested every step she took. Despite the pain, she never slowed her pace.

When she came to a steep drop-off, she skidded to a halt. Sticking close to the edge, she followed the rim until she'd circled halfway. Dropping into some underbrush for cover, she paused to catch her breath and to watch and wait.

Within minutes, Park raced up with fire in his eyes.

It might have been his fury, or possibly the effects of all the whiskey. Whatever the reason, he failed to see the drop-off in time and went crashing through tree branches and thorny vines, screaming and cursing all the way until he came to a painful landing below.

Then there was only silence.

Annie darted away, hoping against all odds that she was headed in a direction that would lead her to safety and not deeper into the wilderness.

After dividing up their cache of rifles and handguns and deciding on the general location to head toward, Jonah, Chet, and Liz set out on horseback, while Brand and Avery, and Casey and Kirby commandeered two all-terrain vehicles. Bo drove a truck with Des and Hammond in the front passenger seat and Meg, Egan, and Billy in the back seat.

Jonah gave a thumbs-up to Chet and Liz before urging Thunder across a meadow. Once he'd traversed the field of tall grass and wildflowers, he started up a steep incline into high country.

Though Jonah was relieved to finally be doing something, he couldn't keep the troubling thoughts from invading. How was Annie handling this terrifying situation? Had she been drugged? Worse, was she injured or harmed in any way? Was her abductor a brute? Was she feeling alone? Abandoned?

He swore and struggled to find something hopeful to cling to.

The Annie he knew was a strong woman. Hadn't she defied Arlen and taken her story to the authorities?

Feeling better, he thought again about the things she'd revealed on their night together. She was smart. She'd been born to wealth and comfort, and yet she'd worked hard to get to the top of her profession.

Smart and strong.

Hadn't she hiked these very hills enough times to have some sense of where she was?

He tried to put himself in her place. If there was the smallest chance of escaping, he knew he would risk it.

So, he knew, would Annie.

The thought came through so clearly he almost smiled.

The Annie he knew, his Annie, wouldn't give up without a fight.

He urged Thunder into a gallop. He had to reach her in time. Had to. Or his life going forward would be nothing but an empty shell.

Noble Crain strode down the hallway toward the great room. Following in his wake was Agent Johnson, who was actually smiling for the first time in hours.

Noble opened the door and exclaimed proudly, "We have a lead on Arlen..."

He stopped so abruptly, Mavis Johnson bumped into his back, shoving him forward.

Seeing the room empty, Agent Johnson shot him a look of surprise. "Where are all the Merricks?"

Noble Crain huffed out an exasperated breath. "I guess I should have assigned them a guard."

"A guard? In their own home?"

"As you may have noticed, the Merrick family doesn't take kindly to being told what to do."

She arched a brow. "I thought Jonah handled the phone call exactly as we'd suggested."

"Yes, he did. But when you determined Annie's location, you may have noticed that he was all set to go find her, until you said he needed to step back and let the authorities handle things."

"You think that's what he . . . ?"

Noble nodded. "Not just Jonah, but his entire family, and Des Dempsey, too. I'd be willing to bet my year's paycheck they've already taken matters into their own hands. Unless I miss my guess, they're probably halfway there already and about to meddle in things better left to the professionals."

Mavis Johnson's hand went to the weapon at her hip. "We have to stop them. They could make a mess of the entire operation."

"It looks to me like we're too late to stop them. But if we hurry, we might still be able to join up with them."

As the agent made a dash for the team in the other room, Noble stood watching, a half-smile curving his mouth.

Leave it to the Merrick family to meddle. In all the years he'd known them, they'd always done things their own way, and to hell with the rules.

*   *   *

After making her way through the thickest part of the woods, Annie paused for a moment to look around and get her bearings.

Behind her were the towering peaks of the Tetons. Spread out before her was the high meadow where she and Jonah had seen the spectacular herd of mustangs that had brought her close to tears.

A feeling of hope surged through her, spreading warmth through her veins. She knew this place. Had hiked here. Despite the lack of proper gear, she could do this.

On one of her first solo hikes, Jonah had told her how to look for familiar landmarks. The first and simplest was the Tetons. As long as they were behind her, she was heading in the right direction.

She started across the meadow at a run, desperate to get as much distance as possible from Park. If he made it out of that ravine, he would be more dangerous than ever. If the fall hadn't caused any serious injuries, it would have surely sobered him. And she feared that a sober yet incensed Park could be an even more dangerous adversary than a drunken Park.

Annie's abductor had been forced to waste precious time escaping the ravine. Using vines and branches, and carving footholds in the earth, he'd finally crawled up the steep incline and lay panting in the tall grass. A look in all directions convinced him that the damned female was long gone.

He wasn't about to give up. He knew that his only chance of surviving Arlen's fury was a photo of her dead body in the grave he'd dug back there, and then a final photo of the shack on fire.

Without those, he'd signed his own death warrant. Arlen Lender wasn't a man who accepted dissent among his team members. And he certainly never accepted failure.

Seeing bright sunlight up ahead, Park pushed himself to move faster. Once he cleared these woods, it would be a simple matter to spot Annie Dempsey in an open field. She may be smart, and fast, but she was unarmed. One bullet would end this chase.

With any luck, he could still be on the road within the hour.

Jonah, astride Thunder, had been moving steadily upward. As he rode, he kept a sharp eye out for anything out of the ordinary.

Even so, he nearly passed the tumbledown shack that blended into the foliage. But then he caught sight of the Range Rover hidden in a stand of trees.

In a flash, he was out of the saddle and racing toward the vehicle. Finding it empty, he made his way to the shack, his heart pounding.

When he stepped inside the empty shack, he saw the hole in the ground and his heart nearly stopped.

Peering over the edge, he was relieved to find it empty as well.

Looking around, he dropped to his knees to touch a hand to the dark, wet stains in the dirt.

Dear God. Blood.

He retrieved his cell phone and dialed Chief Crain. When he heard Noble's voice, he said, "I found the Range Rover and a shack in the northwest corner of Devil's Door woods. I believe Annie's abductor was digging a grave when she may have escaped, since both of them are gone. Send some of your men here. I'm heading south, to the high meadow."

He hung up before Noble Crain could issue a protest. Then, as he mounted Thunder, he phoned Chet, followed up by a call to his father and a text to his brothers to alert all of them to the change in plans.

Annie could no longer feel her feet, though she kept doggedly running.

Behind her, Park found it a simple matter to follow the bloody trail in the grass.

Every once in a while, he would stoop to feel the droplets with his fingers. Still warm and wet. Even though he couldn't see her, he knew she was just minutes ahead of him and, with those bare feet torn and bloody, slowing down with every mile.

It was only a matter of time now.

Though his bleeding head was spinning from that assault with the shovel, he was pushing through the waist-high grass when he thought he spotted something. Pausing, he caught sight of a figure up ahead, dark hair flying, and then suddenly she dropped out of sight.

She'd fallen. He picked up speed, running now as he felt success almost within his reach. The bitch would pay for messing with him.

At a signal from Kirby, seated behind him on an ATV, Casey cut the engine and waited until Brand pulled up alongside him. Avery was sitting behind Brand and waving her hands.

With both engines off, the sudden silence was shocking.

Avery pointed to her cell phone. "We got a text from Jonah."

Kirby retrieved her phone from her pocket and saw the same text. "Change of plans. Jonah's heading this way." She looked over and gave a little gasp.

"What is it?" Casey demanded.

"I think I just saw something up there."

"What?"

"I don't know. Maybe a man's head. Maybe just a bird on a tree branch."

Brand looked at Casey. "We have to check it out, especially after Jonah's text. But let's go on foot so our engines don't give us away."

The others nodded their agreement, and they all climbed off their vehicles to start walking through the tall grass.

Across the meadow, Bo hit the brake and put the truck in park while he explained to the others what Jonah had said.

"Jonah found the Range Rover and a shack with a hole big enough to be a grave. Both were empty. He said he's heading this way and wants us to wait here."

They opened the doors of the truck and everyone stepped out, spreading apart and keeping watch for anything that looked suspicious.

Minutes later, Chet and Liz rode up and dismounted. After a whispered conversation, the group agreed to form a semicircle and begin walking toward the highest point in the meadow.

Annie had fallen face-first in the grass and lay for a moment, feeling light-headed.

Pushing herself to a sitting position, she took in several deep breaths and managed to stand.

Out of the corner of her eye she caught a blur of motion and turned to see Park racing toward her. Panicked, she turned and started to run. Before she'd taken two steps, he hurled himself at her, taking her down. The full force of his bulk knocked the wind out of her and she lay struggling to breathe.

"Finally." He rolled off her and got to his feet, standing over her with his pistol drawn. "Did you really think I was going to give up and just let you go?"

"Why not? You have nothing to gain by chasing me down."

"Nothing to gain? You heard Arlen. I'm going to bury you and then burn that shack over your grave. And that's me winning, bitch."

"You'll still lose, Park. I heard Arlen's voice. He doesn't like stupid mistakes. And you made a big one by not finding my cell phone."

"He'll get over it. You know that call I was making?"

"When I escaped?"

His eyes narrowed on her. "That was Arlen's partner, and my bed partner, Jolynn Carter."

"The banker who introduced Arlen to me?"

"Just the way Arlen coached her. I told her I'd take care of everything if she'd smooth things over with Arlen." He waved the pistol. "Now, let's get moving. I need to finish my job here so I can get back to the city."

A terrible wave of fury swept through Annie. She'd come so close. And now this monster was about to deny her the freedom she'd fought so hard to earn. As he gave her a shove, she let out a mighty scream and swung her arm, slapping aside the gun.

Caught by surprise, he watched as it tumbled to the ground. With a vicious oath, he dropped to his knees to retrieve it.

As he straightened, she picked up a thick tree branch and swung it against his head. He staggered, shaking his head to clear it.

With a furious string of curses, he started to get up and she swung it a second time, hitting the back of his head with as much strength as she could muster.

Moaning, he fell to his knees.

"I'm not going back to that grave. You hear me? I'm not going." For good measure, Annie hit him a third time, leaving him lying motionless.

As she reached around him to retrieve the gun lying in the grass beside him, his hand shot out, covering hers.

Like a feral animal, he was on his feet and standing over her, the gun pointed at her head.

"You're right, bitch. You're not going back to that grave. You've saved both of us a long walk. I'm going to kill you right here." His finger tightened on the trigger. "Right now."

CHAPTER THIRTY

Reflexively, Annie closed her eyes, bracing for the explosion that would end her life. Then, refusing to take the cowardly way out, she opened her eyes to face her executioner and saw, from the corner of her eye, sudden movement.

Jonah and Thunder came racing up from behind Park. In a blur of motion, Jonah leapt from the saddle, landing on Park and taking him to the ground.

The collision caused the gun in Park's hand to fire wildly, the bullet landing in the grass nearby.

The report of the gunshot echoed and re-echoed across the meadow, bringing all the family running toward the spot.

Before Park could fire off another shot, Jonah's fist landed in his face, breaking his nose and sending a fountain of blood streaming.

With a roar of pain, Park swung the hand holding the pistol, catching Jonah on the side of the head and knocking him almost senseless.

With his ears buzzing, Jonah shook his head to clear it.

When Annie saw Park taking aim and realized that Jonah was too dazed to react, she picked up a rock and heaved it at the gunman's head.

With a grunt of pain he turned, aiming his gun directly at her.

"No!" Jonah swung out his arm, knocking the pistol from Park's hand before pummeling him until the gunman doubled over in pain.

When Park dropped to the ground, his fingertips brushed cool metal nestled in the grass.

Snatching up the gun, he got to his feet and with an evil smile aimed it at Jonah. "Say goodbye, cowboy."

Annie was filled with an overwhelming sense of outrage. She'd come so far. Had fought so hard. And now, Jonah would be forced to pay the price.

Desperate, she came at Park like a wild creature, her fists pounding his head. When he turned to defend himself, she raked his face with her nails.

He lifted the gun.

Before he could fire, he saw a crowd of people in his peripheral vision and then a man's gruff voice called, "Drop it right now or we'll kill you where you're standing."

Park looked over to see a line of men and women circling him and half a dozen guns and rifles aimed directly at him.

"Okay. Don't shoot." With blood streaming down his

face from Annie's nails and from his broken nose, he looked more like a victim than an attacker.

Park dropped the pistol and dropped to his knees before raising his hands.

Just then, an armored police vehicle rolled up and came to a halt beside the bystanders. Half a dozen officers in full battle gear disembarked and formed a protective circle around the crime scene.

Some distance away, a police helicopter was landing, blades flattening the grass, engines drowning out the voices as the occupants jumped to the ground and closed the distance at a run.

The scene was one of controlled chaos. While Park was taken into custody and read his rights, the Merrick family gathered around Jonah and Annie, who simply stared at one another for long minutes.

"Did he hurt you?" Jonah's look was fierce, the words forced from clenched teeth.

"No. He..." Ashen-faced, she swallowed, feeling such a welling of emotion she wondered if she could speak at all. "He was ordered to kill me and bury me in a shack..."

"I know." Jonah's face contorted in pain. "I saw the grave."

"You did? Oh, Jonah. I didn't know what else to do, so I hit him with the shovel and ran."

"You hit him with the shovel?" His lips curved into a grin of amazement. "Who are you? And what have you done with my prim little city woman?"

"She's still here. But when I saw Park aim that gun at you, something inside me snapped. It's one thing to fight for my life, but when it was your life, Jonah, I knew I would die before I'd let him win." She sniffed, fighting tears.

Seeing that she was about to break down, he murmured, "It's okay, baby."

With a wave of relief, Jonah gathered her into his arms and held her as the tremors that began in her hands started moving through her limbs, leaving her shivering and light-headed now that her ordeal was actually over.

Against his throat she cried, "I thought I was going to die and I'd never get to see you..."

"Shhh." He pressed soft kisses to her cheek, her temple, the corner of her trembling lips. "I was so afraid I'd be too late."

"A minute more and..."

"All right, now." Agent Johnson's voice, all business with the arrest of the abductor, broke through their halting words. "We'll be taking the kidnapping victim back to town by copter. We'll need a statement and as much information as she can give us to make the necessary arrests of the other members of this band of criminals."

Annie's hands tightened at Jonah's shoulders. "I want to stay with you."

He nodded and turned to his family for confirmation before saying to the federal officer, "We're taking Annie back with us. What she needs now is rest and food, and when she's feeling up to it, you can interview her at the ranch."

"In case you haven't noticed, Mr. Merrick, you're not in charge here." The agent motioned for two officers, who stepped to either side of Annie, closing their hands around her arms and leading her toward the waiting helicopter.

Jonah started after them. "I'm going with—"

"You'll go home with your family, Mr. Merrick." Mavis Johnson stepped directly in front of him, preventing him from moving.

Chief Crain touched a hand to her. "Excuse me, Agent Johnson. Could I have a word?"

She glowered at him. "In a minute." She turned back to Jonah. "I'll have a few choice words, to say to you and your family after I have the victim's statement."

Jonah's tone was pure ice. "That victim has a name. It's Annie Dempsey."

The agent shot him a cool look as the Merrick family pushed their way through the crowd of uniforms. Seeing that Jonah looked ready to fight off the entire company of police officers, Bo and Egan took him by the arms and led him away from the federal agent to prevent him from saying or doing something he might regret.

Chet grabbed Thunder's reins and he and Liz mounted their horses, leading Jonah's horse behind theirs as they headed home.

Brand and Avery, and Casey and Kirby climbed aboard their ATVs and turned toward the ranch with a roar of engines.

The rest of the family, keeping Jonah in their midst, crowded into the truck, with Bo at the wheel, and drove away through the tall, waving grass.

Mavis Johnson had fire in her eyes as she started toward her vehicle. "I had questions I wanted answered. The nerve of those people..."

Chief Crain merely nodded. "You're on Merrick land now, ma'am, where they're a law unto themselves."

"I make the rules, Chief Crain."

"Yes, ma'am. And the Merricks break them." He waited until she'd stalked away before allowing the little smile that had been threatening.

Though he agreed that rules were meant to be followed, he couldn't fault the Merrick family for following their own path. Especially since there was no denying that it had been their quick action that had prevented what could have been a real tragedy. Those precious minutes when they'd arrived, after ignoring the rules laid out by Agent Johnson, had meant the difference between life and death for Annie Dempsey. In their mind, as well as his, that's all that mattered.

He only hoped, when she'd had time to cool down, the federal agent would come to the same conclusion.

At Agent Johnson's orders, Annie fastened her shoulder and lap belts. She felt her stomach lurch as the helicopter lifted off and she saw the ground begin to disappear below the helicopter.

No sooner were they airborne than the agent began her interrogation, or as she'd insisted on calling it, a "debriefing." With Mavis Johnson and several officers listening carefully, Annie was forced to give a detailed description of everything she could remember, from the time Park had entered Jonah's cabin and drugged her to those last moments when Park had surrendered.

By the time Annie had finished giving her statement, they were landing on the football field behind the Devil's Door high school.

Satisfied with the information she'd been given so far, the agent agreed to allow Annie to return to the Merricks' ranch.

As Annie settled inside the car dispatched to drive her, Mavis Johnson leaned in to say, "It will take us some time to follow up on all you've given us. In the meantime, be warned. Unless or until you are completely cleared of any suspicion, you are still considered a person of interest."

The minute Jonah saw the police car moving along the asphalt driveway, he was out the door and waiting.

He had only a moment to take her hand and ask if she was all right before, much to his disgust, the Merrick women took charge, leading Annie upstairs for a long shower. Afterward, they gathered around her in the guest room to examine her poor feet.

"Not as bad as I'd expected," Avery declared after a thorough examination. "Lots of cuts and abrasions, but nothing that looks deep or dangerous. Considering how far you were forced to run, that's pretty amazing."

"I stopped feeling the pain after a mile or so. I was too scared to think about it, knowing Park intended to kill me."

"The people who did this are monsters," Meg declared angrily.

Her daughter put a hand on hers. "Yes, they are, Mom. But thanks to Annie's courage and Jonah's determination, it's over."

Annie shook her head. "But it isn't over, Liz. It will never be over until Arlen and all the people he employs to harm innocent victims are arrested and their crime spree ended once and for all."

"You've done your part, Annie." Kirby took her hand. "If you hadn't defied that awful man, if you hadn't blown the whistle, they would still be stealing innocent people's hard-earned money."

"That doesn't change things. Until they completely clear me of all suspicion, Agent Johnson made it plain that I'm still a person of interest, especially now that I've told her that a fellow banker was mentioned by Park as a member of Arlen's associates."

The women were shaking their heads.

Avery spoke for all of them. "Now that the authorities saw how desperate Arlen Lender was to have you killed, they have to concede that you were never part of his evil plot."

"Oh, I hope you're right." Despite her best efforts, Annie felt the sting of tears. She eased back against the pillows, and her eyes fluttered, then closed.

At a nod from Meg, the women covered her with a blanket.

"Sleep now, honey," Meg whispered. "And when you wake, we'll all be here."

"Jonah?"

"Pacing downstairs."

Her eyes opened. "My uncle?"

"Downstairs with the men. He said to tell you he's not going anywhere."

With a quiet sigh, Annie drifted into sleep, while the women gathered up her clothes and slipped softly from the room.

"Here's my brave niece." Des was on his feet and hurrying across the room as Annie paused in the doorway.

She shot a quick glance at Jonah before being enveloped in her uncle's arms.

"I'm so glad you're here, Uncle Des, but very surprised. I thought by now you'd have headed home." Under her breath she whispered, "Have they been awful to you?"

"Not a bit." He leaned close. "The Merricks and I have made our peace."

Her eyes widened. "Really? And you're...friends again?"

"We're working on it. But I'm here now and I'm not leaving."

"Aunt Bev...?"

"We talked. She's resting, and told me to stay here as long as I was needed. She's glad you're okay and safe."

"Thank you." She grasped his hand as she made her way to the table, where Billy was busy placing several large platters of beef with all the trimmings.

As she approached, Jonah stood and held out her chair. She gave him a smile before sitting.

He caught her hand and held it firmly in his under the cover of the table.

The family, she noted, was slightly more subdued than normal. "Is there news?"

Jonah nodded. "Agent Johnson isn't very happy with us for interfering. And when we asked her to wait until morning to interview all of us, she had a fit and reminded us that she calls the shots. But I think the fact that the authorities in San Francisco have already made some arrests is easing her temper a bit." He squeezed her hand. "I'm sure she'll want to interview all of us and possibly you again as well. Are you all right with that?"

She smiled. "Jonah, after what happened today, an interview with Agent Johnson is the least of my worries."

After filling their plates, Meg looked around the

table. "I think, on this special night, we need to say a blessing."

They joined hands as Meg said, "We are thankful for the safe return of Annie." She shot a smile at the young woman before continuing. "And we're thankful as well for the return of an old friend who was lost to us and is now found."

While the others intoned, "Amen," Des squeezed his niece's hand and looked around the table with a smile.

And then, with sighs of gratitude and relief, everyone dug into another of Billy's wonderful meals. All except Jonah and Annie, who moved food around their plates and held their silence while shooting sidelong glances at one another.

When they'd finished their meal, Meg said, "Billy, I believe we'll relax on the porch and take our coffee and desserts out there. Maybe the setting sun can bring us some sense of peace."

"Yes, ma'am." He began loading a trolley with plates and cups and saucers, before adding a domed cake plate.

The early evening sun had drifted across the sky and settled at the very pinnacle of the Grand Tetons. Its golden rays shimmered like a benediction, reminding them once again of the gift they'd been given this day.

While the others took their places, Jonah led Annie to a love seat and settled beside her.

In a whisper he asked, "You okay?"

She nodded.

Billy lifted the dome of the cake plate to reveal a

four-layer Black Forest torte drizzled with cherries and whipped cream frosting.

"Fortunately I'd planned this as a surprise for you, Ham, and had it all baked ahead of time. All I had to do was assemble it."

Just as he began passing around the dessert, a police car drove up and Agent Johnson and Chief Crain stepped out and climbed the steps.

While the others groaned, Meg managed to remain upbeat. "You're just in time," she announced.

The agent was about to refuse when Noble Crain said, "You know I've never passed up the chance to sample Billy's cake." He eyed the confection before saying almost reverently, "Black Forest? Isn't that your favorite, Ham?"

"It is," the old man said.

Noble chuckled. "Be still my heart."

The two peace officers settled into wicker chairs and quickly devoured their dessert.

As they were sipping their coffee, another vehicle arrived, bearing the seal of the FBI.

Agent Johnson was quick to explain. "Because this band of criminals targeted banks and investors, the federal authorities requested the aid of a special branch of the FBI. Their agent flew in this afternoon to fill us in on the details, and he asked if he might join us here at your ranch. I hope you don't mind."

The others glanced at one another as a tall man stepped from the car and began to climb the steps.

When his face became more clearly visible, the
evening air was filled with the sound of gasps as they
recognized the newcomer.

Chet turned to Liz, who was staring at the man in
shock. The man who had broken her heart and had left
her at the altar all those years ago.

Her face had gone deathly white.

Mavis Johnson, unaware of the family history, was
smiling as she said, "I'd like to introduce all of you to
Special Agent Luke Miller."

CHAPTER THIRTY-ONE

The Merrick family greeted Luke with mutinous silence.

Chet, seated beside Liz, closed his hand over hers. It was, he noted, cold as ice, despite the heat of the evening. He gently sandwiched her hand between both of his to lend her his warmth.

Although Meg was as stunned and angry by Luke's presence as the others, her good breeding had her saying, "We were just enjoying dessert and coffee. Would you care to join us?"

He shook his head. "No, thank you, Miss Meg. I'll make this as brief as possible. My superior believed that since all of you were drawn into this web of crime, you deserve to be brought up to date by the Bureau."

He leaned against the porch railing and said to Annie, "First, let me assure you that Arlen Lender, whose real name is Allen Leyton, and most of his team have been arrested in San Francisco. A few fish managed to evade the net, but they'll soon be caught, too. You no longer have anything to fear from them."

Jonah held tightly to her hand as the two exchanged solemn looks.

"The few who haven't yet been arrested won't be thinking about taking revenge against you. If anything, they're like rats running from a sinking ship. They want to get as much distance between themselves and their ringleader as possible."

He looked around at the Merrick family, watching and listening in stony silence. "The Bureau kept getting reports of major thefts of large bank investors, and our task force was trying to piece it all together. I doubt that we'd have closed in on them so quickly if it hadn't been for the information gleaned from Ms. Dempsey. At first we believed, as did the bank experts, that she was part of the operation, feeding these thieves inside information. But once your friend Newton Calder got involved in the investigation, he persuaded us to cast a wider net. He proved, beyond a shadow of a doubt, that the woman who'd opened a bank account in Ms. Dempsey's name was a fake. With Newton's help, we located the owner of the car that brought her to the bank, and it belonged to a man named Vaughn Park, another member of Leyton's, aka Arlen Lender's, crime syndicate and that led us to a woman, Jolynn Carter, who was giving Leyton the names of vulnerable investors. Leyton and Ms. Carter were not in our data bank and might have continued this criminal operation for years before we caught up with them." His teeth gleamed in the gathering twilight. "We'd love to have Newton on our team. He's a crack investigator. But he insists that he's retired, and only willing to take on very special cases, and only for good friends. You're lucky to have him on your side."

Jonah and Annie shared secret smiles with Egan.

Ham pinned Luke with a piercing stare. "Why would those criminals go to all the trouble of opening an account in Annie's name and depositing a million dollars? That's a lot of money to waste."

"They didn't see it as a waste of good money, but rather as a way to redirect the bank investigators." Luke smiled. "When you've stolen millions, and intend to get away with maybe a billion, that's a drop in the bucket if it gets an innocent person convicted and in turn gets the authorities to close the books on thefts that threaten the entire banking system."

Luke looked around. "I'm sure you folks have been too busy to watch the news, but I should warn you that the facts of this huge operation have already been made known to the media, and it's the top story around the country. You can expect more than a little interest."

Ham shot him a look of disdain. "It's easy to see that you've been away too long to remember that folks in Devil's Door tend to keep to themselves."

Luke nodded. "Yes, sir. I'm just giving you a heads-up from the Bureau."

Ham shot him another of his famous piercing glares, and the special agent fell silent.

When Luke's cell phone rang, he looked at the ID before saying, "Sorry, it's my superior. I have to take this."

He descended the steps and walked some distance away, keeping his back to them as he talked softly.

Liz grabbed this chance to escape. "I'm sure you'll all excuse me."

She ran down the steps and crossed the distance to the corral, where she'd left her horse, while the others could only watch in helpless silence.

Chet turned to Bo. "Since I'm not needed, I've got some business to take care of."

The others watched the ranch foreman move out of the circle of light in that long-legged stride.

Luke returned to the porch. "I'll be leaving for San Francisco shortly. Are there any questions before I go?"

In the silence that followed, he gave a quick nod. "All right, then. If we have more information, we'll be in touch with your police chief." He glanced toward the corral, where Liz's shadowy figure could be seen leading her horse toward the barn. "If there's nothing else, I'd like to have a word with Liz before I go."

As Luke turned away, Egan started out of his chair with fire in his eyes, until Meg put a hand over his.

He bristled. "I don't want that son of a...that scum talking to our daughter. He's done enough harm."

"Liz is a grown woman, Egan. She'll handle it."

"You know how she was after..." He spread his hands in a gesture of defeat.

Meg said softly, "*Was*. We all know how she used to be. But now you have to trust her to handle it."

Chief Crain, aware of the family history with Luke, got to his feet. "I thank you all for your warm hospitality. I think it's time to drive Agent Johnson back to town."

The agent's eyes grew stormy. "But the interview with the family..."

He shook his head. "Will keep. Especially now that your agency has most of the bad actors rounded up." He put a hand beneath her elbow and their heads were bent in quiet conversation as they made their way to his car.

When the two took their leave, Des Dempsey heaved himself out of his chair. "This has been one of the worst days of my life, and then it turned into one of the best." He bent to kiss Annie. "My niece is safe and her reputation cleared." He crossed to Bo and offered his hand. "And a friendship long damaged has been restored."

Bo got to his feet and the two men shook hands warmly before stepping apart. Then, thinking better of it, they came together again in a great bear hug.

Bo looked Des in the eye. "When Bev is feeling up to it, I hope the two of you will come by for a good, long visit."

Des nodded. "It's a date, Bo." He pressed a kiss to Meg's cheek and shook hands with Egan and then Ham before waving to the others and walking to his car.

*   *   *

"Liz."

Hearing Luke's voice coming from the doorway of the barn, Liz continued leading her horse until she came to an empty stall. Needing to be busy, she turned the animal loose and filled a trough with food and water before stepping out of the stall.

She leaned against the cool wood of the stall door and lifted her head, forcing herself to face the man who had broken her young heart. "Did you forget something, Luke?"

"I haven't forgotten a thing." His voice was deep and rough with feeling. "Not one single thing. Do you know how long I've wanted to talk to you? To explain about that whole awful mess?"

"Are you suggesting that there could possibly be anything left to say after leaving me at the church without a word of explanation?"

"I can hear the anger and hurt in your voice, Liz, and I don't blame you for it. What we did . . . what I did . . . was unforgivable. But I've always nurtured the hope that someday you'd find it in your heart to do just that."

When she remained silent, he said, "You deserve the truth. The whole, ugly truth. Remember when you asked CC to be your maid of honor, she was angry and let you know just how angry when she refused?"

"She told me she disapproved of the wedding, since she never liked you."

"That's what she told me, too. But when she found out that you were going through with the wedding without her, she asked me to meet her at her family's ranch."

Liz arched a brow. "She never told me that."

"Yeah. Well..." He paused. "She was out in the barn, drinking her daddy's whiskey, and had worked up a pretty good head of steam. She was spitting mad. By the time I got there, she was already drunk and she handed me the bottle. She told me that she'd always had a secret crush on me and hated the fact that I never gave her the time of day. I wasn't much of a drinker in those days, but I drank with her to calm my nerves, knowing how much she resented what you and I had. I guess I thought we'd both get drunk, and she'd let off steam, and then I'd talk her into taking part in her best friend's wedding."

"So she drank and you drank. And..."

"And one thing led to another and anger turned to another kind of passion and..."

As the truth dawned, Liz stared at him in openmouthed astonishment. "Are you serious? You and CC...? On the night before our wedding?"

"It gets worse. Afterward, she was going on and on about the fact that we'd been too drunk to use protection, and what if she was pregnant, and maybe we should just run away together and..." He kicked at the straw on the floor. "I panicked. I was imagining you and me coming home from our honeymoon and getting a call from her doctor, and how much you'd hate me." His shoulders slumped. "CC and I drove all the way to

Jackson Hole and found a preacher who didn't know us. When I sobered up and realized what a horrible thing I'd done, and all the people I'd hurt...you, your folks, my folks, CC's folks, hell, I couldn't face anybody. So I convinced myself I'd just power through and live with the mess I'd made."

"How did that work for you, Luke?"

He avoided her eyes. "I've spent my life trying to atone. I guess that's why I gave up ranching and took all those classes to join law enforcement, finally ending up with the FBI. I figured if I stopped enough dangerous criminals, and saved enough innocent people, maybe I'd be forgiven." He looked over at her. "When I was working on this case and realized the key to the crime, Annie Dempsey, was staying with your family, I started hoping, with my divorce final, that maybe you could find it in your heart to forgive me and give me another chance." He swallowed. "I've never stopped loving you, Liz, and wondering what my life would have been like if only I hadn't messed up so badly."

When Liz's horse nudged her shoulder, she swiveled her head and ran her hand along the animal's muzzle, using the moment to turn inward and search for her calm center.

Taking a breath, she faced him. "It's funny. For the longest time after you left me, I went on loving you, and blaming everyone but you. It was my fault for not loving you enough. It was CC's fault for leading you astray. It was your family's fault for insisting that you take a portion of their ranch for us to make a home, instead of letting us choose our own." She paused and took another breath. "I'm glad you came back, Luke."

His eyes lit with hope. "You are?"

"For the longest time I'd harbored this stupid dream that someday my golden boy would return and declare his love, and we would live happily ever after."

He reached for her hand. "We can, Liz. It's not too late."

She pulled her hand free and took a step back. "That was a silly, schoolgirl dream. Then I grew up. Luke, I'm grateful you came back because now I see you for what you are. You're not that golden boy I once loved. But then, you never were. You were weak and careless. And seeing you again, I realize that I've wasted so many years and so many tears. And all I feel now is...numb."

His mouth tightened. "I don't blame you for hating me. I hate myself, too."

"That's just it." She shook her head. "I don't hate you. And I don't love you. I just feel...nothing for you. But there is someone. Someone I've loved for years, and I've resisted letting him know how I feel. Maybe this was what I've been waiting for. Or maybe I just needed all this time to grow up and realize what a special man he is."

She gave him a quick hug. "I wish you a good life." She stepped back.

He reacted as though she'd slapped him. "That's it? That's all you have to say?"

"Goodbye, Luke."

She watched him turn away, head down, hands clenched at his sides.

When he was gone, she heard a rustling sound behind her and turned.

Chet stepped out of one of the stalls. He was holding his big hat in his hands, turning it around and around as he studied her. "Sorry, Liz. I didn't mean to eavesdrop, but I was here, and there was no good way to leave without embarrassing you."

"I'm glad you're here, Chet." She took a step closer. "I can't believe a visit from Luke would be the reason for this sudden feeling of freedom."

"You feel free?"

She put a hand on his. "Free to tell you what I've never been able to say before. I love you, Chet. I've loved you for the longest time, but I was afraid if I put it into words, it would end up with you leaving me, too."

He lifted a big palm to her cheek and stared down into her eyes with a tenderness that melted her heart. "I'm never going to leave you, Liz. Not in a million years. You're the only woman I've ever loved, and the only place I want to be is right here. With you."

"Oh, Chet."

He gathered her into his arms and the two of them poured all their feelings into a kiss that said, more than any words, all the things they'd kept locked in their hearts for a lifetime.

*   *   *

Seeing Luke drive away, and the lights going out in the barn, Meg and Egan caught hands and went off to their room, with Ham following close behind.

Gradually the others made their way into the house, until Jonah and Annie were alone in the gathering darkness.

Jonah turned to her. "Think you can sleep?"

"Only if you're there to hold me."

He framed her face with his hands. "I was hoping you'd say that." He leaned close to kiss her. With a sigh, he took the kiss deeper, before stepping back to take her hand. "Come on. Let's get upstairs."

She drew him back for another kiss. Against his mouth she whispered, "I was so afraid I'd never get to do this again. I thought, when I faced Park with that gun, that it was my last moment on earth."

"Me too." Instead of leading her inside, he picked her up and carried her through the house, up the stairs, and into her room.

Once there, he set her on her feet and kissed her again, this time letting all the fears, all the passion, all the need pour from him into her.

As they tumbled into bed, he groaned against her mouth, "I don't know how much sleep we'll get. But I know one thing. It's enough just having you here, Annie Dempsey, safe in my arms."

CHAPTER THIRTY-TWO

Annie awoke in Jonah's arms and found him watching her.

"Good morning." She stretched. "What are you doing?"

"Just enjoying the fact that you're here. In my arms. In my bed."

"Excuse me. This is my bed. Well, at least while I'm staying here with your family."

"Want to talk about that?"

"About the bed?"

"About staying here."

She wrapped her arms around his neck and pressed her mouth to his. "Are you ... asking me to stay?"

"I am."

"For how long?"

He grinned. "How long have you got?"

"Only a lifetime."

"That works."

"Well, then, I'll consider it."

"What about your life in the city? Will you wake up one morning and wish you were back there?"

"I'll always have a place in my heart for San Francisco. But I've already fallen in love with small-town life."

"And what about my big, loud family? Think you can stand us for a lifetime?"

"Growing up as an only child, I always thought it would be such fun having lots of brothers and sisters. I don't know if you can understand, but this is my idea of paradise."

His smile was quick. "Mine too." He slid out of bed. "Hold that thought. I need to get down to the barn and lend a hand. I've been absent lately, and my brothers have let me know they're keeping score."

"Wait." She slipped out of bed and walked beside him. "Maybe I'll join you."

"In the shower?"

She laughed. "For starters. Then maybe I'll join you in the barn. After all, it's time I learned how to muck stalls and all that other messy work you ranchers do."

"I like the way you think, lady."

Laughing, they showered together and dressed hurriedly before heading downstairs.

In the mudroom, they were pulling on heavy rubber boots when Brand and Casey came rushing in.

"Hey." Jonah looked over with a grin. "Don't tell me you've finished mucking stalls this early."

"We never even made it to the barn."

"What...?"

Casey pointed. "Don't look now, but the circus just came to town. When Brand and I headed to the barn, we had a dozen cameras following us. And microphones stuck in our faces."

Puzzled, Annie and Jonah opened the back door. Seeing the array of television news crews and trucks with out-of-state plates, they started to draw back. Just then, Jonah's agent sprinted up the porch steps and pushed open the back door.

"Hey, Jonah. You're not going to believe who's out here."

"I guess right now I'd believe anything, Max. Why aren't you in New York? What're you doing here?"

"When I heard your name on the news, I chartered a plane."

"You heard my name on the news?"

"Come on. Don't tell me you don't know that J. R. Merrick is all over the news."

"What are you talking about?"

"Best-selling novelist has become the hero of all his novels. It's all they're talking about."

Jonah barely had time to introduce Max to Annie before Bo and Ham slammed into the house looking annoyed and more than a little frustrated.

Ham tossed his hat on a hook. "Somebody had better get rid of all those loonies out there or I'm calling Noble."

"I don't think Chief Crain has the muscle to order them off the property," Bo muttered.

"Well I do." Ham pounded a fist into his other hand. "Tell your New York agent here to send those people packing."

"Do you realize who was trying to interview you?" Max looked from Ham to Bo and back again. "Just Duchess, who happens to have the biggest talk show in the world."

"That female with all those teeth like a shark?" Ham looked at Bo and gave a shake of his head. "I wasn't sure if she wanted to ask us questions or eat us alive."

Max gave a hoot of laughter. "Like I told Jonah a few weeks ago, she's a kingmaker. Just having her mention his name will sell a million more copies of his books. And now, with the whole country talking about how the Merrick family helped break up a huge criminal enterprise, Duchess has the perfect excuse to be here. I'm telling you, you can't buy this kind of publicity." Max headed for the door. "I'll just bring her in."

Jonah caught his agent by the arm and dragged him back. "You're not going out there, Max."

"Are you crazy?"

Seeing the fire in Jonah's eyes, Max sighed and followed him into the kitchen, where Billy was busy setting out a huge breakfast of ham, eggs, biscuits, and hot, deep-fried corn fritters.

Max inhaled deeply and helped himself to a mug of steaming coffee from a tray on the counter. "Leave it to you to live like a king, JR. No wonder you don't want anyone to discover this little piece of paradise."

"Exactly." Jonah glowered at him. "Now, tell me you'll be going out there to send everybody away."

"I will."

That brought a sigh of relief from Jonah, who caught Annie's hand.

"As soon as you give them the interview they came here for."

"That's not happening." Jonah's eyes were narrowed on his agent. "You know how I feel about having my personal space invaded."

"And you know how determined Duchess can be. Once she gets her teeth in a story, she's like a dog with a bone."

Ham shared a laugh with Bo. "And she has the teeth for it."

Max decided to try a little friendly persuasion. "Look, JR, a quick interview. Maybe in your office?"

"My office is a cabin in the woods."

"All the better."

"Which is blocked off as a crime scene at the moment."

"See what I mean?" Max was grinning. "That ought to sell another million copies of your book." He threw an arm around Jonah's shoulders and eased him away from Annie and toward the back door.

"Let's walk to the site of your cabin-slash-office, and you can talk to her along the way and back."

"It's not happening, Max."

Hearing the edge to his voice, his agent nudged him toward the porch. "Give her a few minutes. No more than half an hour. I swear to you, I won't ask for another favor."

His voice faded away when the reporters swarmed around the two men as they stepped outside. With cameras whirling, microphones were thrust into their faces. And in the midst of it all was the woman known throughout the world by a single name, smiling and tossing questions at Jonah to the delight of her fans who made up the largest viewing audience in the world.

The family peered through the window, watching as Max Friend, Jonah's agent, stepped back with a smug smile while the media swarmed around Jonah.

Brand was chuckling. "See that little muscle in my brother's jaw? I'd say that means Mount Jonah is about to erupt."

Casey nodded. "And when he does, look out. Max Friend may become Max Enemy."

Meg clung to Egan's hand and watched the spectacle being played out in front of them. "Poor Jonah. He's fought so long and hard for his privacy."

Ham was shaking his head as he sipped a glass of orange juice. "Mark my words. Now that his readers have found out about this place, they'll start making pilgrimages like they do with those rock stars. He'll have to hire an army of security people to keep them away."

"Or flee into the hills." Bo didn't bother to hide his anger. "How did this get so out of hand?"

With a look of abject sorrow, Annie slipped quietly

from the room and made her way up the stairs, with their voices ringing in her ears.

Jonah and Max stood on the porch, watching as the last of the news crews packed their trucks and began the long trek back to civilization.

Max dropped an arm around Jonah's shoulders. "There now. That wasn't so terrible, was it?"

"Next time, just ask me to slit my wrists and give them a quart of my blood."

"So dramatic." Max chuckled. "But then, writing all that blood and gore is how you earn the big bucks."

"No, Max. I earn the big bucks by discipline and hard work. Anything that interrupts that flow costs me, and that in turn costs you."

Max rolled his eyes. "It was a one-time event. And you won't believe all the mileage you'll get out of this. I'm telling you, JR, your latest book will be the biggest seller of all time."

Jonah shot him a smile. "It better be. Are you staying for lunch?"

"What about that amazing breakfast Billy cooked?"

"That was two hours ago. Before long it'll be lunchtime."

Max checked his phone. "Sorry. My plane's ready. I'm heading out now."

The two men shook hands and Jonah remained on the porch until Max drove away.

As Jonah started toward the kitchen, he could hear the

loud murmur of his family. From the tone of their voices, they were as disturbed by the media circus as he was.

When he stepped into the room, heads came up and a sudden silence descended.

"It's all right." He shot them a wide grin. "They're all gone. Even Max. Now if we can just get that special agent to leave town, maybe we can get back to normal." He sauntered across the room, his gaze scanning them, searching for the one face among them that could restore his sanity. "Where's Annie?"

For a moment nobody said a word. Even Billy, always so animated, seemed to be at a loss.

Finally Meg spoke for them. "Avery found her upstairs. Packing."

"Packing?" He arched a brow. "Why? What's this about?"

Meg was holding tightly to Egan's hand. "She feels responsible for the media intruding on your privacy. She told Avery that she knows how much you hate it and that it's all her fault."

Avery nodded. "I heard her call her uncle to ask if she could stay with him until she can figure out where to go from here."

With an oath, Jonah spun on his heel and stormed out of the kitchen.

As soon as he was gone, the family leaned close, buzzing like bees as they speculated on what would happen next.

Their ordinary lives had become a hotbed of drama.

*   *   *

Seeing the closed door of the guest room, Jonah just stood there, debating on whether to knock or kick it open. What he wanted to do was confront Annie with the absurdity of her plan. What he knew he would have to do was to engage her in a civil discussion.

Civil.

At the moment, he couldn't find a shred of civility in his bones. He was feeling like a barbarian at the gates, ready to plunder and pillage to have his way.

The thought had him frowning as he knocked. Without waiting for a response, he opened the door and stepped inside.

A closed suitcase stood by the door. Annie was across the room, staring at the Tetons in the distance.

At the sound of the door, she turned.

He was leaning on the door, arms crossed over his chest, regarding her with a look that had her poor heart stuttering.

"I can see how angry you are. I'm sorry."

"I'm mad as hell." He remained where he was.

"I know. And it's all my fault." Her hands fluttered, and she gave another glance out the window. "All those cameras and microphones and"—Ham's insulting words flew into her brain—"that toothy shark. I never meant for any of this to happen, Jonah, but I take full responsibility. If I hadn't brought all this to your doorstep, none of it would have touched you or your family."

"Actually, the shark was a surprise. She was nice. And smart as a whip. Of all the questions she threw at me, not one of them was silly or banal. The lady has a brain and knows how to use it."

Her brows shot up. "You…aren't mad?"

"Of course I am. And I'll let Max suffer for a couple of days, just so he doesn't get the notion that he can let this happen again."

Hearing the sound of an engine, she turned and saw her uncle's car pulling up at the back door. "Uncle Des is here." She crossed the room.

Seeing that Jonah hadn't moved, she tried a stiff smile. "I asked him to come and get me. I know it's cowardly of me, but I was hoping to slip away while you were busy with the media."

"You weren't even going to say goodbye?"

She stood before him, forcing herself to meet his piercing gaze. "I'm sorry for all of this. For dragging you and your family into this ugly crime. And then subjecting you to all the publicity. I know it's the one thing you most hate. Looking back, I realize I must have blown into your life like a hurricane."

"That's a good description of you. Hurricane Annie."

"I deserve that." She bent to her suitcase. "And now I'll leave and hope that sooner or later your life can settle down to a normal routine."

"What if I ask you to stay?" He put a hand over hers and the suitcase dropped with a thud.

She lifted her head. "Why?"

He bit back a smile. "Maybe I'm a sucker for stormy weather."

Hearing the hint of humor in his voice, she felt a quick hitch in her heart. "Are you just teasing? Or are you really asking me to stay?"

"I'm not asking that." He waited a beat and realized, too late, that tears were filling her eyes.

"Hey." He caught her by the shoulders and pressed his forehead to hers. "Oh, Annie. What I meant to say is, I'm not asking you, I'm begging you. Please stay, Annie. I couldn't bear this life without you in it."

She pulled a little away to look into his eyes. "After all this, are you sure you mean it?"

"Annie, don't you know yet how much I love you?"

"But the police, and the media..."

"All noise that will fade away. But love..." He tipped up her chin and brushed his mouth over hers, feeling the first of the tremors that always seemed to rock him the minute they kissed. "Love stays. Love like ours can last for a lifetime. Do you love me, Annie?"

"With all my heart."

He gave a long, deep sigh. "That's all we need, babe. I want you here with me. I want to marry you, and spend a lifetime with you here where we can hike whenever we want, and watch the herds of deer and mustangs and..."

She stood on tiptoe to stop his words with a kiss. "It's what I want, too. I want to hike with you, and live with you, and have lots of little cowboys with you..."

"About damned time," came Casey's voice as the door opened and the family spilled inside. "I'm guessing that was a yes."

"Of course it was a yes," Meg said imperiously.

Laughing and squealing their approval, the women pushed between Annie and Jonah to offer hugs and kisses.

Bo grabbed his son in a great bear hug and wished him well.

Egan was slapping his grandson's shoulder while saying, "I hope you and Annie can be as happy as Meggie and I are, Jonah."

"That's my hope, too, Gramps."

Ham stood very still, studying Jonah with a steady look. "I figured a smart man like you would know how to persuade her to stay, boy."

"You approve, Ham?"

"I do. And I agree with your assessment. She's been a hurricane in our lives. A breath of fresh air. Don't you ever forget that, boy."

"No, sir. I won't."

Annie's uncle was hugging her tightly before she drew back in shock. "Uncle Des. You were listening outside the door with the Merricks?"

He flushed. "What can I say? Now that we're friends again, I guess I've just slipped back into the old ways."

She wrapped her arms around his neck and hugged him again. "I'm so glad you'll be able to celebrate with me without feeling uncomfortable."

"Annie, honey, I wouldn't miss a minute of all this."

Jonah shook Des's hand before putting an arm around Annie's waist and leading her across the room. "Are you okay with all my family knowing our business?"

She put her hands on either side of his face and smiled before pouring herself into a long, slow kiss. Against his mouth she murmured, "I guess, as long as you can endure the media circus, I can endure the Merrick circus."

"Thank heaven." He drew her close for another kiss. "Because once you give your word, you're in it for a lifetime, Annie Dempsey, and I'm never letting you go."

EPILOGUE

A few weeks later

It was one of those perfect summer days in Wyoming. A sky so blue it looked like a movie prop, with little white, puffy clouds changing shapes as they drifted toward the distant spires of the Grand Tetons.

The range grass was shoulder high, attracting herds of mustangs that could be seen foraging across the high meadows.

In the kitchen, Billy was having the time of his life, preparing a wedding supper fit for a king.

Beef tenderloin, cooked to perfection, lay resting in foil on the counter. A salad of fresh greens with garden tomatoes was drizzled with a hint of red wine vinegar. Au gratin potatoes were bubbling in the oven. Fresh sourdough rolls were nestled in linen napkin–lined baskets.

Billy put the finishing touches on the Black Forest cake he'd prepared. Tucked into the whipped cream frosting on top were two figures. The groom wore jeans and a plaid shirt and held a book in one hand. His other hand grasped the figure of a bride with a bank ledger tucked under her arm. Both figures wore hiking boots. Behind them grazed a couple of mustangs.

He stood back to admire his work before returning his attention to the champagne, chilling in a bucket.

The men gathered on the back porch, where a long table had been covered in white linen and a dozen or more chairs had been added for the guests.

Des Desmond stood alongside Bo, greeting guests as they stepped from their vehicles.

Jonah's agent, Max Friend, had arrived with a generous new contract, in hopes of impressing his client and making amends for that invasion of the media.

When a police car drove up, Jonah looked over with a frown, until he saw Noble Crain walk around to the passenger side to take his wife's arm. He visibly relaxed.

Seeing him, Casey chuckled. "Don't worry, bro. Brand and I already agreed that if we see any sign of a news truck, or the FBI looking for another interview, we'll strong-arm them away before they have the chance to intrude."

"Thanks." Jonah watched as his grandfather stood talking to Noble and MaryAnn Crain.

Seeing an unfamiliar truck, he said, "Is that the preacher?"

Brand's smile held a hint of a secret. "That's Nonie's truck."

Jonah arched a brow. "Did Annie invite her?"

Brand merely shrugged. "She may have suggested it to Pop, but he was the one who issued the invitation." They watched with interest as Bo opened the door of the truck to assist Nonie. His arm remained around her waist as she looked up to say something, and the two of them shared a secret smile.

Brand nudged his brother. "It's your wedding. You're supposed to be in on all these little details."

Jonah gave a short laugh. "It may be my wedding, but if I had my way, we'd have done what Chet and Aunt Liz did and asked the mayor to make it legal in town, without any fuss."

"I know Aunt Liz is shy, and that suited her and Chet. But most women like fuss," Casey reminded him. "Look at Avery and Kirby. They both wanted to be married here." He gave Jonah a long look. "You having second thoughts about this?"

"Not on your life. I just want the fuss over with so we can spend some time alone."

"Who says you'll be alone?" Casey winked at Brand. "We all know where you're going for that honeymoon. What's to prevent us from showing up at your cabin?"

"My rifle, that's what. Or my fists. Just remember, I'll fight anybody who tries to invade our privacy."

"Wow. Annie's fierce protector." Casey was grinning. "I hope after enough alone time, you come home feeling a little more mellow."

Jonah returned the smile. "Count on it." He turned away. "Here comes Reverend Lawson. I'm going upstairs to fetch my bride."

The women gathered around Annie as she stepped from behind a screen beside her best friend Lori, who'd flown in several days earlier. The two had spent time catching up on all that had happened since they'd been apart.

Annie was wearing a white silk sundress that hugged her body before drifting around her ankles. On her feet were strappy heeled sandals. She wore her hair long and loose just the way Jonah loved it and had tucked a spray of baby's breath in a jeweled clip. It was her only adornment.

"Oh, honey." Aunt Bev, her short hair beginning to grow into soft curls after her last round of chemo, her cheeks flushed with color from the cruise she and Des had taken, caught both Annie's hands and surveyed her with a look of pride. "You're the image of your beautiful mother."

Annie's smile deepened. "Thank you, Aunt Bev. That's the nicest thing you could have said."

"She was as sweet as she was beautiful. And from the day she married your father, she was my best friend. I miss her every day." She patted Annie's hand softly. "I'm so glad you followed the family into banking. And thank you for agreeing to take over the operation of our bank here in Devil's Door. That will ease Des's mind, knowing he can spend more time with me."

"It was generous of Uncle Des to offer me the position of bank president."

"You're the generous one, honey. He's been over-worked for years and so eager to step back from it."

The two women shared hugs.

As they stepped apart, Avery gave Annie a long look. "That dress is perfect. I'm so glad you chose it."

"Thanks to you." Annie turned a little circle, allowing them to see the way the silk swirled around her ankles when she moved.

"And the flowers in your hair." Kirby gave her an admiring glance. "I like it so much better than the veil we looked at."

Annie nodded. "Me too. I want to keep my look as simple as this day."

Liz chuckled. "But not as simple as the wedding Chet and I had."

"It was perfect," Meg said in defense of her daughter.

"It was." Annie nodded. "It was such a happy occasion. And it suited the two of you. Just as, I hope, today suits us." With that, she reached for a cluster of little white bags from a nearby table and handed them around.

As the women opened them, there were murmurs of approval.

"Oh, honey." Aunt Bev held up the jeweled brooch with a pink bow surrounded by precious stones. "This means the world to me. And this symbol tells the world that I'm beating this terrible illness."

She stood still while Annie pinned it to her pale pink dress.

"Oh, Annie." Miss Meg held up her gift. A necklace with two hearts intertwined. "How appropriate, since Egan and I just celebrated another anniversary."

Her daughter, Liz, fastened it around Meg's neck before opening her own bag to discover a heart-shaped picture frame that read *Real love isn't measured by words, but by hearts*. Inside was a photo taken at their recent wedding, showing Liz and Chet looking into each other's eyes with so much love it was dazzling to see.

Avery and Kirby were encouraged by Annie to open their gifts together. Inside, each of them found a silver bracelet etched with the words *Sisters of the heart*. The clasp resembled three pairs of hands clasping.

Lori's bag contained a gold locket with pictures of the two taken when they were in first grade. Engraved on the back were the words *Best friends forever*.

All the women gathered around the bride-to-be, hugging and laughing together.

At a knock on the door, Meg hurried over to open it.

Though Jonah took in the sight of all of them, the only one he really saw was Annie.

Seeing the light in his eyes, the women were smiling as they walked past him, leaving the two alone.

"You look"—he swallowed—"so beautiful you take my breath away. Like that first time I saw you in Nonie's. It was like there was a spotlight on you, and everyone else just faded away."

She stood perfectly still. "It's the same for me. I see you, and nothing else matters."

He stepped closer, his voice low, as though afraid to break the spell. "I love you, Annie."

"I love you, Jonah. I can't wait to spend the rest of my life with you."

He held out a hand. "Then let's get started."

As they walked from the room, he paused by a hall table and handed her a nosegay of white roses.

She lifted them to her face and breathed in their perfume.

At the top of the stairs they paused, smiling at the scene below.

Reverend Lawson stood waiting expectantly.

The family had formed a semicircle around him. Jonah's brothers and their wives were whispering. Uncle Des and Aunt Bev were standing beside Bo and Nonie, who looked so pretty in a pale yellow dress.

Ham stood, ramrod straight, belying his ninety years. Beside him were Egan and Meg, along with Billy.

Lori was surrounded by a group of handsome cow-boys, all of them clearly mesmerized by the sun-kissed California beauty.

Jonah lifted Annie's hand to his lips. "Are you ready to become Mrs. Merrick?"

She leaned close to lay her palm against his cheek. "Oh, Jonah. I've never been so ready for anything in my life. I think you had me with that sexy stare at Nonie's. And then you cemented it when you told me about climbing the Chimney three times, after first breaking your collarbone and then your arm. How can I help but love a guy with so much determination?"

"And I'm crazy about a woman so tenderhearted she helped care for wounded pelicans, but when cornered, knows how to fight."

They were smiling as they descended the stairs. Annie thought again about the danger that had caused her to travel far from the comfort of the only home she'd ever known. She'd felt so alone and afraid when she'd first arrived. It didn't seem possible that here, so far from all that was familiar, she could find so much joy and discover the great love of her life.

And all because of this handsome cowboy who'd brought her face-to-face with mustangs and cougars, and an inner courage she hadn't known she possessed.

Along the way he'd claimed her heart and changed her life forever.

GO BACK TO THE BEGINNING OF THE WRANGLERS OF WYOMING SERIES WITH BRAND AND AVERY'S LOVE STORY IN

MY KIND OF COWBOY

CHAPTER ONE

Merrick Ranch—Wyoming. Spring, present day

Hold on, Brand." Ranch foreman Chet Doyle pulled his mount beside Brand's and said in a whisper, "Look over there."

A band of mustangs melted into the woods and became invisible as two horses and riders crested the hill.

"I see them." Lifting his hat to wipe at the sweat that beaded his forehead, Brand nudged his horse forward.

Ordinarily Brand's vision would have sharpened at the slight movement of fresh green foliage, and he would have paused to watch the herd disappear. Everyone on the Merrick ranch shared his love of the herds of wild horses that roamed these hills. They were the favorite subject of his aunt's photographs, featured in glossy wildlife magazines. The love of mustangs had been the motivating force behind Casey's decision to become a veterinarian, and they were featured prominently in Jonah's first bestselling novel. But it had been a particularly long day with the cattle in the high meadow, now lush with grass, and Brand was distracted by the pain pulsing down his leg. Even the beauty of the countryside, always such a thrill in springtime, failed to lift his spirits.

Usually the sight of the Grand Tetons towering in the distance and the Merrick family ranch spread out below, spanning thousands of acres of spectacular hills and valleys, meadows and highlands, would be enough to have him grinning from ear to ear. Today, his handsome face was etched with pain.

Seeing it, Chet fell silent. The rugged foreman, best friend to Bo and Liz since childhood, had been with the Merrick family long enough to read their various moods. And he'd watched Brand fighting this lingering pain ever since that fall from his mount.

When the ranch buildings came into view, Brand's horse, sensing food, lengthened its strides, adding to Brand's torment.

"I know you want this to end, Domino. So do I. But slow it, boy." He pulled on the reins, and the horse fell back to a plodding walk.

Back at the barn, Brand and Chet unsaddled their mounts and toweled the overheated animals before filling troughs with food and water.

At the house, they paused in the mudroom to roll their sleeves and scrub away the dust of the trail before stepping into the kitchen, where they were greeted by the chorus of voices that had resounded through this house for a lifetime.

"Took you long enough, boy." Across the room,

Hammond Merrick looked up from the tray of long-necks being passed by his granddaughter Liz. "We were getting ready to eat without you."

Liz shot a soothing smile at Chet and her nephew. "Don't you believe a word of it. We knew you were on your way."

"Thanks." Brand managed a smile before helping himself to a beer and tipping it up to take a long pull. "You know you can always get started without us. After a day in the hills, even leftovers would be a feast."

Beside him, Chet nodded his agreement before quenching his thirst.

Brand's grandmother, Meg, touched a hand to her grandson's arm. "Speaking of feasts, Billy made something special." Her smile was radiant. "Your favorite. Pot roast with all the trimmings."

Brand arched a brow. "You usually ask Billy to make that when you're about to hand me some bad news." He gave her a steady look. "What's wrong?"

"Wrong?" Meg glanced at her husband, who was frowning.

"Supper's ready." Billy Caldwell, cook for the Merrick family for twenty years, waited until the family had taken their places around the table before passing platters of roast beef, mashed potatoes, carrots and snap peas, and a salad of greens and tomatoes grown right in the little greenhouse alongside one of the barns. A basket of flaky rolls was placed in the center of the big table, along with cruets of balsamic vinegar and oil.

With a chorus of praise for Billy's hard work, the family spent the next few minutes holding the platters for one another until all their plates were filled.

They paused.

Hammond's deep baritone intoned the words of the familiar blessing. "Bless all of us gathered here, and those no longer with us."

Brand noted the narrowing of his father's eyes, the only sign of the pain he still suffered at the loss of his beloved Leigh. To this day, Bo was compulsive about checking the many fireplaces in their sprawling ranch house and seeing to it that every fire was banked before going to his bed.

Seeing how his father poured himself into his work in order to overcome his feelings of helplessness, Brand grew up doing the same. And when age began to slow down the oldest members of their family, Brand smoothly took up the slack. Whether a sudden spring snowstorm or a late-summer range fire, Brand was always in the thick of the action.

It was just such a storm that had Brand taking a nasty fall from his horse, crashing into a rock, splintering several bones in his right leg. Old Dr. Peterson, at the Devil's Door Clinic, had sent Brand to a specialist in Casper, who used titanium rods and pins to repair the damage, before recommending six weeks of physical therapy. That had added precious time Brand was forced to spend away from the ranch, and after just four weeks, he'd come home.

Over their meal, the men talked of the crops and the weather.

Casey, freshly showered after a long day, buttered a roll. "With a wet spring like the one we're having, I'm figuring we'll have a long, hot summer."

Twenty-three-year-old Jonah, the youngest, was grinning. "I hope you're right. The hotter the better."

Hammond's stern face relaxed into a smile. "I can't remember the last time the range grass was knee-high before June. This promises a good summer and a healthy herd."

"And a lot of smelly, sweaty laundry," Billy muttered, bringing a round of laughter from the others.

During a lull in the conversation, Brand turned to his grandmother. "I take it you're saving whatever bad news you have until dessert, hoping to soften the blow."

Instead of the usual laughter, she took a sip of her tea before saying, "I can't help noticing how, since your accident, you've been favoring your leg."

Under cover of the table, he slid his hand along his right leg, from his thigh to his knee. He frowned. "It's fine."

"It isn't fine."

"Give it time, Gram Meg."

She shook her head. "Time's up, Brand. Dr. Peterson warned you about this when you cut short your therapy in Casper. There was no one in Devil's Door trained to follow up. Now you're limping and gritting your teeth when you think nobody is looking. There's no sense pretending that it will go away all by itself."

As if to hold off the approaching storm, Billy began circling the table, serving slices of carrot cake topped with mounds of vanilla ice cream.

Brand picked up his fork and dug into his dessert. "We're through with this discussion, Gram Meg. My leg will heal."

"Yes, it will. Because I've asked Dr. Peterson to send someone trained in physical therapy to come here to the ranch and work with you."

He lowered his fork. "A physical therapist? Here? And when do you suppose I'll have time for such nonsense? Before I muck stalls at dawn? While I'm repairing the wheel on that tractor after breakfast? After I ride herd on a bunch of ornery cattle until dark?"

"Yes." She folded her hands in her lap, a sure sign that she intended to dig in and not back down. "Before, during, or after. I don't care how you make it work. I know only that you will have to make time in your busy day for regular therapy sessions until your leg is one hundred percent healed."

"In case you haven't noticed, I'm no longer that little eight-year-old you and Pops used to hold down while forcing nasty cough syrup down my throat."

"Really? You're acting just like him."

Brand lifted his chin, biting back the curses that couldn't be uttered in front of his grandmother. "I won't be pestered by some physical therapist asking me to walk on a treadmill or do a series of squats."

"He's already on his way. Dr. Peterson told me that Avery Grant will be here tomorrow. Billy and Liz gave me a hand cleaning out Hammond's old suite of rooms on the third floor. I'm sure our visitor will be comfortable up there for the next six weeks."

"Six weeks?" Brand's voice frosted over. "You're wasting his time and mine. Not to mention a whole lot of money for nothing."

"No matter. It's done."

He tossed aside his napkin and shoved away from the table. His eyes narrowed on his grandmother. "I can't believe you'd do this behind my back."

"You left me no choice, Brand. Once you started avoiding the issue, I realized I'd have to take a stand."

Without a backward glance, he stalked out of the room, his limp so pronounced the entire family could see him fighting to hide his pain.

After hearing his footsteps on the stairs and the slam of his door on the upper level, Bo turned to his mother. "We can all see that his leg's giving him plenty of trouble. But the decision should have been his."

The older woman gave a nod of her head. "I know. I hate hurting him like this. But my years of nursing training told me he'll never heal properly without help."

Old Hammond pointed with his fork. "I agree with Bo. You crossed a line, Margaret Mary."

Bo laid a hand on his mother's arm, hoping to soften

his grandfather's words. "I realize you're the medical expert in the family, and I know you consulted with Dr. Peterson before doing this. If it's any comfort, I agree that Brand needs help. But I also feel it should have been Brand's choice."

Egan rushed to his wife's defense. "Meg's just doing what she knows is right."

At the sudden silence in the room, Meg gave a long, deep sigh. "Being right doesn't make it any easier."

From the head of the table, Hammond declared firmly, "The deed's done, thanks to your meddling, Margaret Mary. Now, either our Brand will learn to work with this therapist or decide to fight him tooth and nail. And I wouldn't blame him one bit if he refused to be bullied into this. In my day, pain was a part of life, especially life on a ranch."

It was on the tip of her tongue to remind her father-in-law that times had changed, but Meg held back, having learned after almost fifty years in the family that her response would fall on deaf ears.

To defuse the situation, Casey turned to his great-grandfather with a grin. "My money's on a knock-down dirty fight between the two. And nobody comes away from a fight with Brand without being bloodied."

Jonah nodded. "I'm with you, bro. I pity this poor stranger who thinks he'll be able to give orders to our grumpy big brother."

The two fist-bumped, while beside them Liz gave a shudder. "As if life around here isn't crazy enough in spring. I can't imagine how having a stranger getting in the way can be anything except trouble. But I have to admit, with Brand in such a rotten mood, it should prove to be an interesting few weeks."

"Easy enough for you to avoid whenever it gets ugly." Meg turned to her daughter. "You can drive off into the hills and snap all those lovely photographs. But I'll be stuck here, mediating between your headstrong nephew and this poor young man sent here to help him."

"You could always go along with me and hide out in the hills. I guarantee one thing. You'll enjoy some spectacular scenery." Liz turned to Chet. "Are the trails dry enough for me to drive on?"

He shrugged. The men in this family weren't the only headstrong ones. This woman, so much like her grand-father, wouldn't care if her truck got stuck for weeks in the wilderness. Whenever she was ready to escape, she did so without asking any of them for their help. "You'll have to keep an eye out for runoff. Some of the trails are too soft to maneuver."

Jonah arched a brow. "You could always go along with her, Chet. Like a bodyguard."

Though the foreman's expression never changed, a slight flush darkened his neck.

"As if he doesn't have enough to do wrangling those herds." Hammond pointed a fork at his granddaughter. "Why, I was exploring those hills when I was only—"

"Half my age. I know, Ham." Liz blew the old man a kiss. "And we're so glad you did. I can't imagine living anywhere else in the world than right here." She turned to her mother. "I think I'll head out in a couple of days. Want to come along?"

Meg merely shrugged. "I guess I'll wait and see how Brand and this therapist get along before deciding whether to stick around or run and hide."

Casey was grinning. "I'm picturing this guy Avery with no neck, bulging biceps, and wearing thick glasses."

Jonah added, "And carrying a megaphone as he belches out orders for Brand, chained to a treadmill."

That had the others chuckling at the image planted in their minds. As they began pushing away from the table, they called their thanks to Billy before going their separate ways.

All but Meg, who poured a second cup of coffee and sat, brow furrowed, deep in thought.

She hoped she hadn't started an all-out war with the hiring of this therapist. Over the years, she'd seen how quickly an ugly incident could get out of control, burning everything in its path, like a range fire.

ABOUT THE AUTHOR

New York Times bestselling author R.C. Ryan has written more than a hundred novels, both contemporary and historical. Quite an accomplishment for someone who, after her fifth child started school, gave herself the gift of an hour a day to follow her dream to become a writer.

In a career spanning more than thirty years, Ms. Ryan has given dozens of radio, television, and print interviews across the country and Canada, and has been quoted in such diverse publications as the *Wall Street Journal* and *Cosmopolitan*. She has also appeared on CNN and *Good Morning America*.

You can learn more about R.C. Ryan—and her alter ego, Ruth Ryan Langan—at:

RyanLangan.com
Twitter @RuthRyanLangan
Facebook.com

Looking for more Western romance?
Take the reins with these cowboys from Forever!

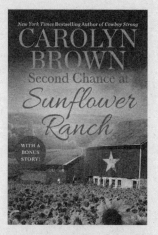

SECOND CHANCE AT SUNFLOWER RANCH
by Carolyn Brown

Jesse Ryan is shocked to return home after twenty years and find the woman he could never forget gave birth to a little girl about nine months after he left—*his* little girl. Addy Hall has her hands full as a single mom. The last thing she needs is Jesse complicating her life even further, especially since she's always had a crush on the handsome cowboy. But the more time she spends with him, the more she wonders what might happen if they finally became the family for which she'd always hoped. Includes the bonus story *Small Town Charm!*

Discover bonus content and more on read-forever.com

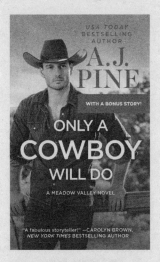

ONLY A COWBOY WILL DO
by A.J. Pine

After a lifetime of helping others, Jenna Owens is finally putting herself first, starting with her vacation at the Meadow Valley Guest Ranch to celebrate her fortieth birthday. Colt Morgan, part-owner of the ranch, is happy to help her have all the fun she deserves, especially her wish for a vacation fling. But will their two weeks of fantasy lead to a shot in the real world, or will their final destination be two broken hearts? Includes a bonus story by Melinda Curtis!

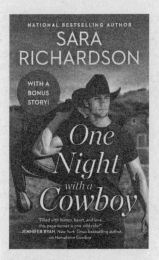

ONE NIGHT WITH A COWBOY
by Sara Richardson

Wes Harding is known as a devil-may-care bull rider—but now, with his sister's pregnancy at risk, Wes promises to put aside his wild ways and take the reins on their ranch's big charity event. Only he didn't count on his co-hostess—and little sister's best friend—being so darn distracting. One kiss with Thea Davis throws his world off-balance. But with her husband gone, Thea's focused only on raising her two rambunctious children. Can Wes convince her that he's the man on whom she can rely? Includes a bonus story by Carly Bloom!

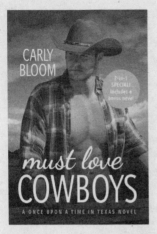

MUST LOVE COWBOYS
by Carly Bloom

Alice Martin doesn't regret putting her career as a librarian above personal relationships—but when cowboy Beau Montgomery comes to her for help, Alice decides to see what she's been missing. She agrees to help Beau improve his reading skills if he'll be her date to an upcoming wedding. But when the town's gossip mill gets going, they're forced into a fake romance to keep their deal a secret. And soon Alice is seeing Beau in a whole new way... Includes the bonus novel *Big Bad Cowboy!*

THE HEART OF A TEXAS COWBOY
(2-in-1 edition) by Katie Lane

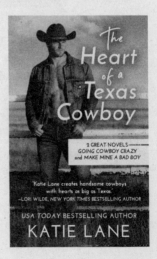

Enjoy these two Western romances heating up the Lone Star State! Slate Calhoun's longtime flame, Hope Scroggs, is back in his life, but the feelings between them are unlike before. By the time he discovers "Hope" is her identical twin, Faith, he's head over spurs in *Going Cowboy Crazy*. Colt Lomax can't forget the night of passion he once shared with local sweetheart Hope Scroggs, a night he wouldn't mind repeating. She tries her darnedest to resist his Texas charm, but something unexpected is about to tie their fates together... and oh, baby, will it ever in *Make Mine a Bad Boy!*